Copyright © 2024 by Joshua Dalzelle

All rights reserved.

No part of this book may be reproduced in any form or by any electronic or mechanical means, including information storage and retrieval systems, without written permission from the author, except for the use of brief quotations in a book review.

BONE SHAKER

TERRAN SCOUT FLEET
-BOOK TWO-

JOSHUA DALZELLE

©2020

First Edition

PROLOGUE

"This is a risky mission to give to a team that, frankly, should be recalled and stood down until it can be rebuilt."

"You're not saying anything I don't know, but orders have come down from on high, and they're not interested in my excuses," Captain Marcus Webb sighed. "Scout Team Obsidian will be put on the trail of our missing ship."

"So now, Central Command is micromanaging NAVSOC?" Michael Welford, director of Naval Intelligence Section, sat across from Webb in the NAVSOC commander's secure office on Taurus Station. The semi-secret base was isolated from the other settlements on Terranovus and was in the process of being dismantled in preparation for the big move to the new planet humanity had just acquired. The new world, named Olympus, was to be a military stronghold while Terranovus would continue to be developed as a colony world, accepting immigrants from Earth as quickly as new cities could be built.

. . .

"Not normally," Webb said. "Right now, Scout Team Obsidian is what everyone at Command thinks of when they talk about NAVSOC after their last successful mission. You know how it goes...the brass hears a team overcame tall odds to complete a high-profile assignment, and then they want to use them over and over so they can tell the civilian oversight they put their best people on the job."

"Thankfully, I have no idea what you're talking about. I was CIA back before there was an NIS," Welford said. "We always operated in the shadows, and most people had no idea what we were really doing, nor did they want to. So, what are you going to do?"

"My hands are tied." Webb shrugged. "I'll have to tell Obsidian they're back on the job tracking down that moron, Edgars. It's my own fault, really. Before I knew what Command was really asking, I slipped up and said Obsidian was my only team not on assignment. I failed to specify that the reason for that was because they were without a proper team leader, a reliable ship, or the necessary equipment. By the time I realized what Admiral Sandor was even talking about, he was already walking back out of my office."

Welford just grunted and took another sip of his drink. The entire mess started when one of the cruiser squadrons they had deployed with a Cridal strike group had been involved in a battle against the ConFed's main fleet. In the capital system, no less. Captain Edgars, the commanding officer of the *Eagle's Talon,* and in overall command of the Terran force, had stupidly involved his ships in an unsanctioned strike against the quadrants only superpower. The move had the potential for putting Earth in the crosshairs once the ConFed figured out who had attacked them and decided whether or not they wanted to retaliate.

The quadrant's political structure quickly devolved as the first salvo of an open rebellion against the ConFed appeared to have been fired. All the UEN ships involved in the incident, except the *Eagle's Talon* herself, had come back to Terran space and reported on the incident afterwards. The squadron was currently quarantined in high orbit over the planet Olympus while Fleet Ops tried to figure out what the hell to do with them. Captain Edgars, along with much of the Cridal strike force, had not returned and were apparently throwing in with the burgeoning insurrection. Sources within the Cooperative's military command had let Webb know through back-channels that their own leadership was in a panic and, apparently, Admiral Kellea Colleran herself had led the attack and hadn't returned.

"I guess I know why you called me to your office now," Welford said, putting the empty glass down beside the bottle of high-end scotch the captain had plied him with. "You want to keep Agent Murphy assigned to your team, right?"

"You have me over a barrel here," Webb admitted. "Murph is your guy, but I have nobody to replace him with currently. If I take another experienced body from Obsidian, it will more or less render them ineffective."

"Wouldn't that be doing you a favor? If I take Agent Murphy back, you'll have no choice but to recall the team."

"You're forgetting two things. First, the reason I haven't brought them back to Terranovus already is that I'm trying to keep Lieutenant Brown out of the wrong hands. Second, we need to find the *Eagle's Talon* and get her back before Edgars uses her in another strike against the ConFed."

. . .

"Ah, yes...I'd nearly forgotten the interest some on Earth might have in your new lieutenant," Welford said. "Very well, I'll authorize Agent Murphy for continued detached duty to the Navy, specifically to 3rd Scout Corps, but you do realize you'll have to give him back eventually, right?"

"You can have him back after they track down our missing cruiser," Webb said. "Consider it payment from NIS for inserting agents into my scout teams without telling me first."

"Fair enough." Welford yawned. "I'll make it happen. Have you talked to *him* yet?"

"Who? Lieutenant Brown?" Webb asked. Welford just pinned him with a pained look that said he didn't believe Webb's innocent act. He knew exactly which *him* the director referred to. The NAVSOC boss sighed, leaning back in his chair. "Yeah, but I didn't have the balls to tell him that I rolled his one and only son into a frontline scout unit."

"The longer you wait, the worse he'll react. Have you thought about the fact that Jason Burke is almost certainly integral to this rebellion? What happens if the two happen to cross paths, and he finds out about Jacob's new job from someone *other* than the friend he trusted to protect the boy?"

"Slight risk of them crossing paths," Webb said. "From what I've been able to put together, Burke's ship was shot all to hell during the battle, and he limped home to put her back together. I'll tell him when the time is right."

. . .

"It's your funeral." Welford shrugged and stood. "Keep me in the loop on the hunt for the *Eagle's Talon*."

"Will do."

1

"This piece of shit is a death trap."

"Can you get it running or not?" Jacob Brown asked. The newly-promoted first lieutenant stood on the tarmac while his pilot, Lieutenant Junior Grade Ryan Sullivan, poked around in an access panel.

"I already got it running," Sullivan—Sully to his teammates—muttered as another spark leapt out to zap him. "It's keeping it running that's the real trick. I'm a decent pilot, but I'm not an engineer...at least not enough of one for what this bastard needs."

Jacob and Sully were the only two members of Scout Team Obsidian standing in the sweltering heat working on the ship. The Eshquarian gunboat had been a state-of-the-art combat ship...thirty years and fifteen or so battles ago. In her prime, she was a platform that rained death down upon her enemies and delivered infantry or supplies with precision and speed. She was even capable of providing orbital superiority in a pinch thanks to an over-powered drive and an impressive array of ship-to-ship and ship-to-surface weaponry. When the model was first introduced, it was touted as being a more reliable alternative to the powerful but temperamental Jepsen D-Series gunships that had filled a similar role in militaries around the quadrant.

In her days since being sold as surplus, however, neglect and outright abuse had turned her into a dilapidated shell of her former self. Most of the major drive components had been replaced multiple times, and not with parts up to the original manufacturer's specs. The weapons were a hodgepodge of pieces grafted on from several other ships and tied into a fire control system that wasn't designed to properly manage them. The powerplant struggled when the weapons and subluminal drive were both pushed hard simultaneously. Structurally, the ship was mostly okay. The hull was beat to hell, but its integrity was surprisingly good, and all the hatches and portholes had good seals.

"What's the main issue?"

"Power MUX controller is a completely different make than the bus interface," Sully said, wiping the sweat off his brow and sinking down to sit on the deck. He'd been working in the access panel that let him get to the box that controlled the power system's multiplexor. Since they had power off the ship, they'd not been able to run the environmental system to keep the inside cool. "Most of the major commands work the same, but there are some syntax differences between the two that, when they come up, lock the system up. When that happens, it does a hard reset, which takes fifteen seconds, give or take, and that's the weird glitch we're seeing. It doesn't happen all the time, but when you try and ask for a lot of current to multiple systems, you're just as likely to lock the fucker up as you are to have the guns and engines both come on."

"Lovely," Jacob deadpanned. "So, the easiest fix seems to be we find a—"

"LT! Message just came in for you!"

"Maybe that's Command sending orders to recall us back to civilization and get us a decent ship," Sully said, groaning as he climbed to his feet to put the power MUX system back together.

"I think you're being wildly optimistic," Jacob said over his shoulder as he walked down the ramp. He jogged back into the workshop space the team was using to try and get the dilapidated gunboat up to the Navy's minimum standards of spaceworthiness. Since they'd been ordered to keep as low a profile as possible, Jacob had not paid the exorbitant price the small air field was going to charge him for a full hangar that could house the Eshquarian ship. Instead, he'd paid the more modest fee for a full workshop, and then just parked the ship on the ramp outside. The shop had been surprisingly well-equipped, and they had been able to set up their own com equipment so they could keep in contact with Terranovus.

"Message is in the buffer," Mettler said, jerking his thumb over his shoulder to where they'd set up their secure com terminal. "It's just addressed to Scout Team Obsidian from NAVSOC. Maybe it's finally some recall orders."

"Maybe," Jacob said, sitting down and logging into the terminal. Sergeant Jeff Mettler was one of Jacob's operators and also Obsidian's medic when needed. The junior NCO sat at a bench, cleaning parts from the ship's main hatch actuators before Sully reassembled and tested the system.

"Lieutenant Brown," the image of Captain Marcus Webb said once Jacob had authenticated himself to the terminal. "Your team's new orders are attached to this message, but I thought the unusual circumstances warranted an explanation from me. Unfortunately, you won't be coming home just yet. There have been some...developments...and we need you to try and track down a missing ship. The UES *Eagle's Talon* has disappeared, and it's assumed at this point her captain has gone rogue, taking the ship and crew to join up with a rebellion that's brewing against the ConFed."

"What the actual fuck?" Jacob murmured as Webb paused, looking off-camera for a moment before nodding and looking back.

"All we need you to do is locate the *Talon* and call it in," Webb went on. "There will be strike teams deployed along the Concordian Cluster to retake the ship once she's found, but we can't send in UEN ships to do the actual search for obvious reasons. Your team is an unknown and currently available, so you drew the short straw. The Eshquarian boat you've stolen should be decent cover for you...lots of surplus Imperial ships in the Cluster. The accompanying data will brief you on the ship, her CO, and the circumstances around her disappearance. I can't stress to you enough how important it is we find this cruiser and bring her home. The quadrant is a powder keg right now, and the ConFed just got punched in the face, hard. Earth cannot afford to be connected to this rebellion, so it would be good if you find the *Talon* before ConFed Intelligence does.

"I know you're supposed to be heading home so that Obsidian can get a new commander and you can finish training, but this is too important, and the brass has asked for you specifically. I'm pulling Scout Team Cobalt off their mission and sending them your way as soon as they make contact again, but that could be some weeks out still. Once I'm able to reposition them, Obsidian will operate under Cobalt's command if you haven't found the *Talon* by then. Good luck, Lieutenant."

The image winked out, and a directory of all the files Webb had sent scrolled across the monitor.

"Screwed again, huh?" Mettler asked, not even looking up.

"It would appear so, Sergeant," Jacob replied, reading through the redacted brief of what was apparently a full-scale naval battle over the planet of Miressa Prime, the capital of the ConFed. It looked like a remnant force of the Eshquarian Imperial Navy had arrived in the Miressa System, intent on exacting some sort of revenge for the ConFed invasion that toppled their empire. They attacked the system's defense force, but then another ConFed battlefleet meshed-in, this one much more capable, and went after the Imperial fleet. Then, against all probability, *another* fleet arrived, this one called Taskforce Starfire in the report, and slammed into the ConFed fleet from its exposed flank.

So much was redacted that it was difficult to follow the action while reading it, but what he could get out of it sent chills up Jacob's spine. This must have been the start of the rebellion against the ConFed Webb had referred to. While they seemed to have a hodgepodge fleet of ships, they managed to take out a ConFed dreadnaught, a ship so rare and expensive it was thought by some to exist in myth only. All of this right over the seat of ConFed power, no less. No wonder Webb was spooked. If a human ship had been involved, and the ConFed found out, all of humanity would be at risk.

"Hey, Mettler, does the name Taskforce Starfire ring any bells for you?"

"Yeah, that does sound familiar," Mettler said slowly. He turned his head and bellowed down the corridor. "Hey, Taylor! What the hell is Taskforce Starfire?"

"It's a Cridal Cooperative taskforce." Corporal Taylor Levin, Obsidian's tech specialist, walked into the main shop area, holding a tablet. "It's actually Admiral Colleran's taskforce, the big dog enforcer the Cridal use when they want to send a message. They're also the unit that has a squadron of our own heavy cruisers deployed with it. Why?"

"It looks like this Admiral Colleran may have gone rogue," Jacob said. "Give me an hour to read through all this shit and I'll brief everyone. Short version for right now is that Starfire may have just kicked off either a civil war or an insurrection, depending on who authorized the attack."

"That's not good news," Mettler deadpanned. "What's our job going to be?"

"One of the heavy cruisers, the *Eagle's Talon*, has disappeared with Taskforce Starfire after the surprise attack in the Miressa System," Jacob said, queueing up the files to read in order. "We're going to go find her and call in the recovery teams to get her back."

"We think one of our own captains has gone that far off the reservation?" Taylor whistled. "This one is going to suck."

"Tell Murph and MG to get their useless asses out to the ship and help Sully get her back together," Jacob said. "We need to be fueled, provisioned, and ready to go by the end of the day tomorrow."

"That's going to be tight, LT. Just putting the fire control system back together will take—"

"Then you'd better stop wasting time talking about it and get started, huh?"

"Just another great Marine Corps day," Taylor grumbled, walking back down the corridor.

"This feels like a whole different ship after letting that crew service the emitter alignment again," Sully commented. "Power came up a lot smoother when we climbed to orbit."

"That's good," Jacob said.

"I didn't say good, I said better," Sully corrected him. "This piece of shit is still a flying deathtrap, but now it's a deathtrap that can get her sorry ass into orbit without the main drive surging and fighting me the whole way."

"How long until we mesh-out?"

"It's another twelve and a half hours to the mesh-out point," Sully said. "The one we want is surprisingly deep in the system, so it'll be a short flight. Normally, they want you jumping into slip-space well the hell away from any populated planets." Jacob and Sully were the only two on the flightdeck, and the pair sat in silence for a time, listening to the ship groan and pop as she pushed as hard as she could for the mesh-out point.

"Since we're up here alone, I feel like we need to—"

"I'm way ahead of you, Lieutenant." Sully held up a hand, pausing to yawn. "Look...I fly the ship and keep her running, and I'm damn good at it, but that doesn't make me an expert at all the skulking about on the planet you guys do. I technically outrank you, but unless I feel you're putting the team at risk above and beyond what is normally expected, I don't plan on interfering with how you run your mission. Just remember, if this goes to shit, I'll be the one who takes the blame, so either don't screw up, or screw up good enough we don't survive to be court martialed."

"I'll do my best," Jacob said, not sure if the pilot was serious about preferring death to a military tribunal.

When Obsidian had successfully completed their last mission to retrieve a vital intelligence asset Command wanted, Jacob had been told to sit tight where they were until the political storm had blown over, then they'd be recalled back to Terranovus. In the course of that mission, their team leader, Commander Ezra Mosler, had been killed by a traitor who just happened to also be their chief engineer, so the assumption was that Obsidian would be stood down until new personnel could be brought in.

Jacob, just freshly promoted to first lieutenant, should only be in command of his Marine ground team, and another Naval officer should be in overall command. Sully was rightfully the CO until they were assigned a new skipper, but the pilot seemed to be willing to divide responsibilities down the middle, at least as long as he thought the jarhead LT wasn't going to recklessly endanger them all.

"Oh, shit!"

"What? *What?!*" Jacob yelled. A moment later, alarms blared, and the smell of ozone and hot electronics wafted from the air vents.

"Hold her steady!" Sully leapt from the pilot's seat and ran off the flightdeck without any further explanation. Before Jacob could gather his wits and object, the pilot was gone, and he was at the controls of a ship he had no idea how to fly.

There were some discouraging *bangs* that reverberated through the hull, and the lights blinked a couple times, but the engine power levels stayed over eighty percent. That's when Jacob looked over to his right and saw that the main reactor output was at one hundred and thirty percent of the safe maximum...and climbing. The small antimatter reactor that powered the small ship had just been serviced and had passed all the safety checks, or so the ground crew claimed. He was no engineer, but Jacob had taken enough course work at the academy to know what happened when an antimatter reactor core breached. Thankfully, it would be a painless death.

"Jake! I'm going to vent the reactor into space while we try to get this runaway resolved," Sully's voice came over the PA. "Bring the engine power down to fifty percent, but do *not* pull the power back below thirty-five while we're venting or they'll go into shutdown."

"Copy!" Jacob grunted, reaching across the center instrument console so he could grab the engine power controls. He dialed them back and checked their course to make sure they were still on their declared flightpath and not about to wander in front of a heavy cargo hauler.

There were a few more *bangs*, two new alarms and warnings on the displays, and then he saw the reactor vents were opened fifteen percent, and the plasma pressure in the manifolds dropped. Once the total power output of the reactor slipped below ninety percent, some of the alarms ceased, but the computer still told him the powerplant was critically damaged.

"Okay, Jake...Taylor and I have fixed the issue with the fuel control module—I think—and we're ready to close the vents and see if it'll throttle back on its own," Sully said, the sounds of people shouting apparent in the background. "Just keep the engines over fifty and let me know if any new powerplant alarms come up."

"Will do!"

He watched as the reactor power dipped until it hit thirty percent, about six percent above where it would lose its ability to be self-sustaining, and then slowly crept back up. The manifold pressures held steady while the power climbed, and once they hit fifty-two percent, Jacob saw that the emergency vents also closed. All but one alarm ceased, and it looked like the reactor was now holding at sixty-one percent.

"Engines back to full power, Lieutenant," Sully said, his voice much calmer now. Jacob pushed the engines back to maximum and held his breath as the demand on the powerplant caused the computer to ramp up the reactor. Once the output hit seventy-six percent, everything seemed to stabilize, and the last alarm light winked out. He sat watching the indicators on the display, transfixed as he tried willing them to stay in the nominal range.

"Disaster averted," Sully said, making Jacob jump as the tall pilot contorted himself back into a seat not really designed for a being of his size.

"What was that all about?"

"Just a little runaway reactor issue, nothing major," Sully said. "The module that controls the amount of hydrogen that goes into the fuel manifold to feed both the matter injectors and the antimatter generator lost its mind, for lack of a better term. This tub has four new modules in the spares compartment, so I'm guessing this has been a recurring problem the old crew has been fighting."

"So, rather than get it fixed properly, they just stock up on spare parts?" Jacob was incredulous. Sully just shrugged.

"You've seen the other field repairs they've done on this piece of shit. Just be glad they stocked up with *new* spare parts and not just a bunch of crap they found at some spaceport swap meet."

"I'm having some real second thoughts about this mission," Jacob said, leaning his head back against the seat and trying to keep his mind off the fact that the same engineer who never properly troubleshot the powerplant issue was the same one who had worked on the slip-drive that was about to mesh them out of real-space.

"Welcome to Scout Fleet." Sully smiled.

2

"Son of a bitch!"

Elton Hollick, formerly *Agent* Elton Hollick of the Naval Intelligence Section, still couldn't get used to the prosthetic right hand he'd been temporarily fitted with while his replacement hand was cloned. His own hand, the one he'd been born with, had been vaporized when some snot-nosed jarhead second lieutenant had hit him with a plasma rifle. Every time the clumsy robotic hand he used now dropped a fork or caused him to stab a toothbrush into his own eye—which had also happened that morning—he was enraged and humiliated about the whole incident all over again.

"If you weren't concentrating so hard on it, the calibration would go a lot faster."

"Shut up," Hollick snarled. "If you hadn't fucked up your previous three operations so spectacularly, I wouldn't have even been in that warehouse when that little shit got a lucky shot off."

"I'm not so sure it was a lucky shot," his breakfast guest said. "I've been hearing some rumors about who that Marine lieutenant actually is...but that's not why I asked to come see you."

"Just get to the fucking point, Margaret," Hollick groaned. "Please, tell me you have something for me to do other than stay here on this Godforsaken planet with my thumb up my ass."

"You're getting back in the game, Elton," Margaret Jansen said, smiling. The expression made her look more like a predatory animal than anything else, a comparison she didn't find insulting in the least. "You've been briefed on the battle in the Miressa System involving the scraps of the Eshquarian fleet and Seeladas Dalton's own taskforce?"

"Of course," Hollick said. "What about it?"

"It turns out that not only did Earth have ships deployed with the Cridal taskforce, but they participated in the battle...took out one of the ConFed's big battleships."

"You're kidding!"

"Not at all," Margaret assured him. "Now, here's where it gets interesting. Captain Edgars, who involved his squadron of cruisers, has apparently decided to throw in with this rebellion. The *Eagle's Talon* hasn't returned to Terran space along with the rest of the ships."

"You seem to think that should mean something to me. I've been out of the loop for a couple years now, remember?"

"The *Talon* is one of the new Victory-class heavy cruisers that Earth is building," Margaret said. "And Edgars was more than just the CO assigned to lead that squadron. He was instrumental in the design and test phase of this class of ship."

"Which means he would have almost certainly had access to the Ark." Realization dawned on Hollick.

"Which means he would have had access to the Ark." Margaret nodded. "This is our next best shot at getting it. We find the *Talon*, we find Edgars, and maybe we can get the location of the Ark out of him and mount a retrieval mission."

"A Victory-class heavy cruiser is no slouch," Hollick warned. "Our remaining Columbia-class ships are no match for her."

"Let me worry about that," Margaret said. "Are you interested in the mission? Or do you want to sit and sulk because you can't get your breakfast into your mouth any better than a toddler?"

"I'm in." Hollick ignored the barb. Margaret was relentless, always verbally jousting and trying to probe for weaknesses she could later exploit. She fancied herself a Machiavellian-type, able to manipulate people into doing things against their best interests, but to a trained intelligence operator like Hollick, she was just annoying. Her ham-fisted attempts to maneuver him were completely transparent, but he played along since he wanted the same thing she did. For now.

"I'll tell the fleet to expect you—"

"I'm taking my team and that's it." Hollick stood and grabbed his jacket. "I'm not playing passenger to one of your incompetent fleet captains...no offense. I'll find the *Talon* on my own, and then I'll call in the cavalry if you're convinced you can put together a taskforce able to tackle a Victory-class heavy cruiser." Margaret's eyes flashed, and she straightened in her chair, but her complaint died on her lips.

"Very well." She smiled again, chilling Hollick's blood. He knew he could only push her so far while she was still able to command the loyalty of the Ull faction that had thrown in with her. As long as they did her bidding, he had to step carefully around her.

"Take your own loyal troops and track the ship down on your own," she went on. "You're certainly more experienced at this sort of operation than my fleet commanders are."

"Undoubtedly," Hollick said. "Don't worry...I'll find her. Just remember, we don't *actually* need the *Talon*, all we need is Captain Edgars."

The gunboat lurched back into real-space with a shudder violent enough to send Jacob's coffee flying out of his hand. It spilled all over the copilot's station.

"Thanks," Sully said drily. "Because this thing doesn't have enough problems without you pouring coffee into the control panels."

"It was more of a splash than a pour," Jacob said, wiping up the mess as best he could with his sleeve. "Why was the mesh-in so rough?"

"The emitters won't stay in alignment," Sully said. "The variance is within tolerance, but on a ship this small, you'll still feel it."

"MG just bit half his tongue off back there," Murph said, walking onto the flightdeck. Staff Sergeant Alonso "Murph" Murphy was the ranking NCO on Jacob's ground team. During their last mission, however, they'd found out he was actually *Agent* Alonso Murphy of the NIS and had been embedded into 3rd Scout Corps to sniff out traitors. For the time being, the agent was still acting as a Marine NCO and stuck in limbo working with Obsidian.

"Good," Jacob said. "If it shuts him up for a few hours then all will not have been in vain."

"I'll let him know how sympathetic you are." Murph stared out the forward porthole at the planet they approached. "So, this is it?"

"Yep. Oorch Prime," Sully said, pronouncing it like *ork*. It's one of the nastier little smuggler shit holes within the Concordian Cluster, but NIS fed us this as a starting point."

Murph snorted. "I'm highly skeptical this newfound rebellion has a presence here. As a rule, they'll want to avoid places that are mostly populated by scumbags who would sell them out for a reduced sentence."

"You can buy intel on worlds like this by paying off someone's bar tab or tossing them a couple of buzz balls," Mettler's voice came from the hatchway. "It won't actually be accurate, and you'll just end up chasing your tail around for weeks." With four large men breathing on the flightdeck, the air was getting hot and stale.

"I feel like there's a hidden meaning in your little anecdote, Mettler," Jacob said.

"I'm just saying...this attack on Miressa is *huge* news all across the quadrant. Everyone knows the Eshquarian Imperial Navy—or what's left of it—spearheaded the attack, and the Cluster is the closest bit of wild space near Eshquaria. Everyone will know they likely ran back here, so every two-bit hustler on every backwater world will be selling information on Imperial warships to all the spooks combing through this region."

Jacob didn't say anything, but Mettler's words stuck in his head as Sully called for an orbital approach vector and punched in the corrected flightpath into the computer.

"That's weird," the pilot murmured.

"What's weird?" Murph asked.

"The computer keeps dumping the new flightpath every time I—Ah! There it goes. All set."

"Holy shit, we're all going to die in this thing," Mettler grumbled.

"Probably," Jacob agreed. "And it likely won't even be due to enemy fire."

"Hey, it was a free ship," Sully snapped. "Since you all seem *so* attached to living through every single slip-space flight and deorbit, go steal a better one."

"Why are you so defensive? It's not like you built it."

"Because, Mettler, I'm the one—with no fucking help, by the way—who has spent the last four months trying to repair every system on it with incomplete tech data and limited parts." Sully turned around to glare at the Marines standing behind him.

"I helped!" Jacob protested.

"Carrying boxes and sleeping in the hold isn't the help I needed. In fact, all of you get the hell out of here...*now!* I don't need an audience to pilot this thing. Go back to the main deck and do whatever it is you disgusting jarheads do when you think nobody is looking."

The Marines, including their lieutenant, quietly filed off the flightdeck, somewhat taken aback by their normally-stoic pilot's outburst. There was some grumbling about naval officers in general, and Sully's parentage specifically, but they still left the pilot to do his job in peace.

"While you're all here and sober, are there any questions on our mission?" Jacob asked. When Angel "MG" Marcos raised his hand, Jacob just rolled his eyes and clarified. "Any questions that aren't more whining about *why us*?" MG's hand went down.

"So, we're just supposed to find this rogue ship? No boarding actions or trying to take on a whole shipboard detachment of Marines loyal to Captain Edgars?" Mettler asked.

"Just spot it, call it in," Jacob said. "We'll try to put a tracker on it, but I doubt we'd be able to get close enough. NAVSOC has scrambled specialized strike teams to take the ship once they have a location."

"Why do you think Edgars did it?" Taylor asked. "Is he a traitor or a revolutionary?"

"Right now, the ConFed has labeled him a terrorist, and we need to find that damn ship before their intelligence service traces her back to Earth," Jacob said. "From what I understand, the Cridal Cooperative has already gotten out in front of things and declared Admiral Colleran a rogue operative and thrown her under the bus. They've publicly claimed she took her taskforce without their authorization or knowledge and are cooperating fully with the ConFed to track her down."

"So, wouldn't that cover Earth? If this Cridal admiral was calling the shots, why would the ConFed want revenge on Earth?" MG asked.

"The Navy isn't taking that chance," Jacob said. "The ConFed isn't known for being light-handed when it comes to doling out punishment, and there's still the matter of one of our more advanced warships now being in the hands of people with unknown intentions."

"Seems pretty cut and dry," Mettler said. "People have finally had enough of the ConFed's shit and decided to do something about it with some real firepower for a change."

"Let's all get one thing crystal clear right now. Earth does not recognize this fledgling rebellion." Jacob's voice was stern, and he meant to cut off that line of reasoning before it could take hold in the minds of his team. "They're not plucky freedom fighters, and we're not the bad guys here for trying to make sure our hardware isn't involved. We have no idea who these people are...we don't know if those Imperial ships were even manned by Eshquarians. What happens if the next time one of our Victory-class cruisers opens up on a civilian target and Edgars kills untold innocents with weapons whose fissile material can be traced to Earth?"

"But—"

"No *buts*, goddamnit!" Jacob slapped the table. "This isn't a poly-sci class at a university. We're not here to debate policy, we're here to do a job and go home…assuming we all don't die in agony from explosive decompression when this scow suffers a critical hull failure."

3

Oorch Prime was exactly what Jacob had expected it to be when he thought of a Tier Three world deep within an undeclared region of space. While all the Tier One and Two worlds had a common aesthetic depending on the dominant culture there, a Tier Three world was a jarring mix of dozens of cultural influences that seemed to be tossed together at random. From the moment they stepped off the ramp after Sully had slammed the gunboat into the tarmac while landing—he *claimed* the aft repulsors had cut out—Jacob could tell they were on a lawless, dangerous world.

"The smell here isn't so bad," he remarked.

"You're just getting acclimated to life out here," Taylor said. "But yeah, this planet is surprisingly clean smelling.

"Let's hurry up," Jacob said.

They moved across the tarmac to where a few kiosks were advertising ground transportation. On Oorch, there were no entry control lines, no customs inspections of the ship, and nobody looking twice at a squad of heavily armed humans strolling casually up to a place that claimed to have *new and clean* vehicles available.

"My friends! What can I do for you?" a squat, powerfully built alien Jacob's neural implant identified as a Satorro asked, his thick arms spread wide in greeting.

"We need a ground car big enough for all of us plus enough cargo space to provision our ship," Jacob said, gesturing vaguely towards the Eshquarian gunboat. He'd been practicing Jenovian Standard, the accepted universal language of the quadrant but, for now, stuck with English. His native language had long ago been added to the universal translation matrix so the Satorro was able to understand him with little trouble.

"You're all such big, strong males! The only vehicle I have that's big enough won't be cheap, I'm afraid to say. How will you be—" Jacob cut him off by slapping down a chit loaded with five hundred credits on it. When the Satorro picked it up and squeezed it to display how much was on it, a wide smile spread across his face.

"I knew you were beings of discerning taste when I saw you walk up! This way, this way!"

The Satorro led them from the kiosk line over to a gravel roundabout, pointing as a large, gray vehicle lumbered around to them. The vehicle was boxy and appeared to be new as its owner's sign had claimed. It cost Jacob another two hundred credits to convince the Satorro to forego the normal forms required to rent the vehicle and just turn it over to them for the day.

"He screwed you over," Murph said once they'd all piled in and told the vehicle's computer where they wanted to go.

"I knew that the moment he didn't counter-offer on my second bribe," Jacob said with a shrug. "It wasn't so much that he'll remember us as anything more than a bunch of dumbass tourists he got over on."

"This guy the NIS gave us...this seems like an odd place to find him," MG spoke up from the back seat.

"Oorch Prime is the last planet with any real infrastructure and some semblance of a government before you enter into the really wild parts of the Cluster," Murph said. "Intel services from dozens of governments keen on keeping an eye on the Eshquarians have set up shop here."

"Anybody else notice that since Murph was outed as *Agent Murphy* he talks like some slimy officer now?" Mettler asked. "*Semblance of a government?* Seriously...who the fuck talks like that?"

"Literate people, for starters," Jacob said over his shoulder. "It doesn't hurt to not be a complete dumbass all the time. You guys should give it a try from time to time."

"I'm getting that put on a T-shirt," Taylor said.

They rode the rest of the way out of town in silence, the whirring of the vehicle's electric drive the only sound as it zipped up the road to the next settlement. Jacob thought it was odd that their target didn't maintain a place in the same town as the largest spaceport. It would make more sense if he had to bug-out, and he'd be closer to all the intel that rode down to the surface with the spacers that operated the ships passing through.

When they approached their destination, Jacob couldn't help but be shocked by what he saw. It looked like the settlement had started as a ramshackle village and everybody who moved there afterwards decided to stick to that motif. Street after street of buildings that looked slapped together with a mix of local construction materials, some bits of old spaceship hulls, and some newer, shiny tech that looked completely out of place.

"If I was trying to find someplace to hide, this would be it," MG said. "Look at this place. I'll bet we're already being watched closely."

"That's a safe bet," Jacob said, leaning down so he could see the aliens on the rooftops staring at their vehicle as it rolled on. "Look sharp, everybody. They may try and stop us to see if we have anything worth taking."

Despite the obvious interest by the locals, they rolled on unmolested to their destination, a three-story structure on the northern edge of town that was distinctive in that it was uniformly assembled from the same material. Upon closer inspection, Jacob thought it had probably been a pre-fab kit someone had brought in and erected quickly. That told him it was likely one of the intelligence services Murph had mentioned, but not one smart enough to put up a listening post that didn't stick out like a sore thumb.

"Taylor and MG stay with the truck," Jacob said when the vehicle came to a complete stop. "Mettler and I will post up on the corners and watch for anyone sneaking around. Murph, you make contact."

They all piled out and deployed quickly. The two staying with the vehicle crouched down near the front so they could use it as a blind and still cover their team. Jacob and Mettler split and went down the alley on either side of the building, making sure there weren't any surprises lurking there, or side exits the people inside could use, before coming back up to the corners and covering Murph. For his part, Murph kept his weapon slung behind him and tried to appear as non-threatening as possible while pressing the button and talking to the hologram of the AI assistant that appeared before him.

"I'm here to see Kellska," Murph said pleasantly. "Please tell him that—"

"Master Kellska is not accepting visitors," the hologram of an alien Jacob couldn't identify interrupted. "Please, respect his wishes and leave."

"Perhaps if you let me properly identify myself, we could—"

"Master Kellska is not accepting visitors," the hologram said again, now flickering wildly. "Ple— Visitors. Visitooors. Viiiisit."

"Ah, damn!" Murph slid his primary weapon around to his shoulder and fired into the locks on the door at close range. By the time Jacob had scrambled from his position to help, the smell of burning plastic wafted through the area.

"Move!" Jacob barked, pushing Murph aside and slamming his boot into the door with as much force as he could muster. His enhanced muscles did their thing, and the remaining lock gave way with a sharp metallic *snap*, and the door fell in as it jumped off its track.

"Entering!" Murph said, sliding past and into the entryway while Jacob and Mettler automatically took up covering positions behind him. MG and Taylor sprinted from the vehicle and posted up inside the ruined doorway, sweeping the area in front of the house in case someone attacked the entry team from the rear.

"Clear right," Mettler said quietly after he swept a small sitting room off the main entrance.

"Main room is clear," Murph said. "Moving upstairs."

Jacob moved ahead and checked that the rear entrance was still locked and secured and was about to follow Murph upstairs when the sergeant came flying back down, not uttering a sound as he slammed into the floor in a heap.

"Contact! Upstairs!" Jacob shouted, running for the steps just as *something* came down, leaping over the rail and landing in the main room with a *thud*. The being was ensconced in some sort of armor that looked unpowered. He could see it had a light, thin build.

Mettler still moved towards him when Jacob raised his plasma carbine, intent on neutralizing the threat when it moved at him in a blur, grabbing the weapon and ripping it from his grasp. The carbine was still slung to his body, so Jacob was yanked from his feet and thrown across the room with enough force to shock him. Apparently, the diminutive figure was a lot stronger than it looked.

"Mettler, hit it!" Jacob called, struggling to get up. Mettler opened fire, bolts of superheated plasma ripping into the walls and furnishings as he tried to track the fast-moving target across the room. Their agile enemy was able to close on the Marine just as Jacob got his feet under him, pulling his tactical knife and cutting the sling away he'd gotten his left arm tangled up in.

Mettler went down with a grunt as an armored forearm took him in the side of the head. Jacob, the blood rushing in his ears as his turbocharged adrenal response kicked in, felt time slow around him as he raised his carbine and snapped off two shots. He had to aim high to not risk hitting his own troop and managed to hit the being square in the back with one of the shots. It staggered forward and turned, pulling a sidearm and squeezing off a shot that, against all odds, hit Jacob's own weapon. The carbine let out a high-pitched alarm and sizzled and smoked as Jacob threw it across the room. The plasma chamber ruptured before it hit the ground, and the effect in an enclosed space was like a concussion grenade going off, knocking both him and his opponent to the ground.

"Stay down, Earth man." The modulated voice sounded as if from a great distance. Jacob pried his eyes open and saw the armored figure stood over him, sidearm aimed at his face. "I'm not here for you." The voice spoke English.

"Who are you?" Jacob demanded.

"Someone who doesn't take orders from one of Marcus Webb's bumbling lackeys," it said, still waving the pistol in his face. "What are you Scout Fleet buffoons doing out here, anyway?"

"I'm not telling you shit. Either you—"

"Stop! Stop, stop, stop," Murph said, struggling to get to his feet. "LT, stand down. She's not a threat...at least not unless you piss her off even more."

"You know who I am?" the figure asked.

"You know who it—*she*—is?" Jacob's asked at the same time.

"Lieutenant Jacob Brown, meet Carolyn Whitney," Murph said. "Also known as the Viper, and she could have killed all of us before we even knew she was here if she wanted to."

4

"The Viper?" Jacob asked. "Wait...Carolyn Whitney? That's an oddly human sounding name."

"Nothing gets by you does it, sport?" Carolyn asked, removing her helmet and winking at him. Somehow, she made the gesture seem like a threat more than a flirt. "It was that damn hologram wasn't it? When we tampered with the message, it went wonky on us."

"How do you know her?" Jacob ignored Carolyn's jab.

"I don't...at least not in person. I know *of* her. And yeah...I knew someone had tampered with the doorman program when it fritzed out in a loop like that," Murph said, limping over to where Mettler struggled to rise. "NIS agents are briefed on all known unaffiliated humans operating outside of Terran space. Omega Force and the Viper are the most notorious, but there are half a dozen others who float around out here. Carolyn here is one of the quadrant's premier assassins and has an ex-Israeli Special Forces partner who, if I'm guessing correctly, is currently holding up MG and Taylor."

"Good guess... but I'm not an assassin," Carolyn said. "Your men weren't harmed. You know, Lieutenant...you look really familiar. Have we ever met?"

"I'd remember," Jacob said. "I've just got one of those faces. So, Carolyn, I'm guessing it's no coincidence you're here the same time we are."

"The timing is, but not the location," she said. "We're looking for the same informant you are, but for different reasons. I'm guessing you're trying to track this new insurrection for Earth's new intel apparatus, whereas I was hired by a private party to do the same." Carolyn appeared to be ignorant of the fact Obsidian was trying to track down a specific ship, not the actual rebellion that had sprung up against the ConFed.

"Speaking of...where's the informant?"

"Dead."

"Dead?" Jacob repeated.

"Did I stutter? Yes, he's dead...and no, I didn't kill him. From what I could tell someone popped him at least a few days before I got here."

Before Jacob could question her further, the rest of his team was led into the room by another human. His people were disarmed and looked appropriately chagrined while the man covering them with a nasty looking plasma carbine just looked bored.

"And who the hell are you?" Jacob demanded.

"That's Carolyn's partner, Abiyah," Murph said. "Formerly of Israel's elite Mista'avrim, and technically considered a deserter, even though the UEAS didn't technically exist when he left Terranovus."

"One of Michael Welford's people?" Abiyah asked Carolyn, ignoring the Marines completely.

"Webb's," she corrected. "Okay, boys...we're going to go our own way, and it would be best if you forget about us."

"Wait, I thought we could—"

"I'm not here to babysit another of Webb's bumbling Scout Fleet teams," Carolyn cut off Murph. "I'm sure as shit not doing your job for you. You've hit the same dead end we did. I wish you luck from here, but I'm not wasting my time leading you by the nose. Don't try to follow us."

"Who the hell was that?" Taylor asked once Carolyn and Abiyah left the home.

"I'll tell you later," Murph said. "LT, we should probably get out of here. Any actionable intel that would have been here is long gone."

"Agreed," Jacob said. "Back to the ship. We'll get off this planet and decide our next move."

The team collected their weapons in silence, a pall of shame hanging over them after the Viper and her partner so easily disarmed and overpowered them. It was a humbling lesson to not be overconfident in numbers or to make assumptions based on the size and shape of the beings they encountered.

"Call ahead and make sure Sully has the ship ready to fly once we get there," Jacob said. "I'm going to take one quick look upstairs, and then we're out of here."

He moved up the stairs quickly and found three additional rooms, two of which appeared to be sleeping quarters, and the last furnished as a sort of sitting room that overlooked the street below. The body of the contact NIS had sent them to meet was lying face down on one of the beds. The early stages of decomp made it hard to identify the species, and there was the expected powerful stench coming from it.

Jacob ignored the corpse and looked over the room, hoping against hope he would notice something that a master assassin like Carolyn Whitney would have missed. There were the expected multispectral holographic imagers dotting the ceilings, part of the home's security system that would upload footage to a remote server or to a recording base somewhere inside, which someone as good as Whitney was supposed to be would certainly have grabbed. But someone like their now-dead contact would have been smarter than just having the normal residential-grade security hardware protecting his property.

Having satisfied himself that the obvious things had been picked clean by the Viper and whoever had killed their hapless contact, Jacob looked for the less obvious. He walked over to the window and, after failing to see how it opened, kicked the composite pane out of the frame with his heavy boot. The cool outside air rushed in while he pulled what looked like a pair of opaque safety goggles from his thigh pocket. He slipped them over his head and selected long-wave infrared on the menu that popped up. It was the setting that would allow him to see the room with the greatest accuracy when it came to minute thermal variations. He looked over at the corpse and saw it was slightly warmer than the room around him as the decomposition process put off a small amount of thermal energy.

Within a few minutes, he found what he'd hoped to see: a hotspot in the wall. The thermal variance that outlined a small rectangle on the inner wall was slight and would have likely been missed if he hadn't let in the cooling air from outside. He put a hand on the wall over the spot on the wall, pulling off the goggles since his hand was so blindingly bright it made making out any detail impossible. He probed around the edge of the synthetic wall material before pulling his combat knife and slowly digging away at the fibrous material. He had barely scratched the surface when his knife dug into something he assumed was some type of sensor.

"Taylor! Get your ass up here," he said over the team channel.

"What's up, LT? Whoa! Is that you?"

"No, dipshit...look to your right." Jacob rolled his eyes.

"Ah," Taylor said after seeing the rotting corpse. "You can understand my confusion after that time you ate—"

"What's this?" Jacob demanded, pointing at the shiny black surface of the device he'd uncovered in the wall.

"Interesting," Taylor muttered, coming closer to inspect. "It looks like an imager. Similar to the type NIS spooks like to hide in walls. It operates a lot like a starship sensor so it can be put behind walls or under floors. How did you find it?"

"Long-wave IR."

"You're lucky. This looks like a rush job, and the sensor wasn't buried too deep. They don't put off a lot of heat while they're operating, but if you detected anything at all that means this one is still active."

"Where's the recorded data stored?" Jacob asked.

"It could be a local source, or it could even be hooked to an active slip-com node and live-broadcasting the feed to another planet," Taylor said just as Murph and MG walked in.

"This our contact?" MG nodded to the body on the floor.

"What's left of him," Jacob said before turning back to Taylor. "Let's assume the source is still here in the house. If this was a system being remotely monitored, they'd have known this guy was worm chow and switched it off, right?"

"Unless this was set up as a trap," Murph pointed out as he looked closely at the device in the wall.

"We've been here almost an hour," Jacob said. "It's not a trap. New objective, find out where this sensor is storing the feed data. Everyone help, Taylor is on point."

The team, taking direction from their tech specialist, ripped into the house as they traced the signal line from the sensor up to the roof of all places. Mettler found an access hatch in one of the closets and shot the lock off with his carbine before MG and Jacob boosted him through the hole. They took turns climbing up, with Jacob going last, his enhanced musculature allowing him to simply leap up and through the gap, landing on the rooftop with a *thud*.

"That still screws with my head watching you do shit like that, LT," MG said, his voice holding equal parts awe and envy.

"Over here!" Taylor waved them to where he was crouched. "It's underneath this environmental unit."

They all got down onto the rough surface of the roof to see what he was talking about. Underneath the environmental unit, which sat up off the roof on metal legs, was a discreet composite box about the size of a cigar box. There were two connectors on one of the short sides, and no other markings or indicators, making it seem like it was probably part of the environmental unit.

"How can you tell?" Jacob asked. "It just looks like a box."

"The cables aren't shielded," Taylor said. "I'm detecting a carrier signal consistent with the type of imager we found in that wall. It's definitely not the type of data signal you'd find on an outdated enviro system like this one. Looks like it's just magnetically hooked to the bottom of this unit."

"Let's pull it and boogie," MG said. "Sully is on the horn now bitching that we're taking too long."

"Pull it," Jacob ordered. Taylor shrugged and popped off the two connectors and, using his knife, pried the box off the bottom of the environmental unit's chassis. When he did, there was an audible *click* and a warbling tone that made everyone freeze.

"And that would be the bomb inside this enviro unit that you just armed," Murph sighed. "If you move the box too far away from the unit...kaboom."

"Taylor, you dumb fuck," MG said.

"You're the one who told me to take it off!"

"Why would you listen to me? I'm a weaponeer, not a tech. It's actually the LT's fault for agreeing with me."

"You morons shut up!" Jacob snapped, his mind racing. "Taylor, I'm going to kneel down next to you and take the box. Once I have it, the rest of you haul ass back down the way we came and get clear of the building. I'll give you sixty seconds."

"Sixty seconds until what, exactly?" Murph asked.

"We need the data on this box," Jacob said. "I can survive a jump off this roof—probably—and I think I can run and clear the edge before the bomb triggers."

"That's some wild assumptions you're making. Why don't we take a moment to think—"

"Your time starts now. *Move!*"

Murph's protests were cut off as four Marines turned and hauled ass for the access hatch in the roof. Jacob watched as they made an orderly withdraw and counted the seconds once he saw the last of his men disappear. His plan was high-risk, but he wasn't suicidal or insane. The bomb had armed once they'd removed it but hadn't detonated. He could assume it was on a proximity trigger, and he would get a bit of a head start before the device would have time to actually detonate depending on how large the radius was. The edge of the roof was only six meters away, and then it was a twelve-meter drop to the street below. No problem...hopefully.

"We're all clear, LT...let 'er rip," Taylor's voice came over the team channel when Jacob was only halfway through his count.

"Standby," he said. After several calming breaths, he shifted his legs around so his left heel was braced against the leg of the environmental unit. The bulky metal box was anchored to the roof, and he wanted to use it to push off rather than risk losing his footing by trying to accelerate too hard on the composite material.

He said one last quick prayer, and then yanked the box to his chest, shoving off on his anchored foot with all his might. The metal leg he braced against buckled, and he pitched forward, reaching out with his left hand to catch himself before he face-planted. Now panicked, he pushed ahead in a wild, uncontrolled leap, clearing the edge just as the warning tone of the box changed and the explosive charge within the environmental unit detonated. The pressure wave pitched him end over end, and he could feel the searing heat as he was flung from the rooftop. He watched, helpless, as the ground rushed up before he could change his body position and get his legs under him to hit in a controlled landing.

Still clutching the box to his chest, Jacob landed in the street on his back. Mercifully, he blacked out upon impact.

5

"He's tough, but that fall fucked him up pretty good."

"You said he'd make a full recovery."

"He will...it's just going to take more than forty-eight hours. What the fuck do you want from me, Murph? He fell two stories onto a hard-packed dirt alley. It's a miracle he's not dead."

"I've been out for two days?" Jacob asked, his tongue feeling heavy and dry.

"What was that, LT?" Mettler asked, shooting a glare at Murph.

"Two days?" Jacob asked, this time his voice stronger.

"More or less. You broke four ribs and dislocated your left shoulder when you hit, but there doesn't appear to be any significant trauma to your spine or head," Mettler said, reading off the tablet he held. When they were in the field, Jeff Mettler served as Obsidian's medic. The medical nanobots they had at their disposal made treatment for most things fairly straight forward, but they couldn't perform miracles. If Jacob had broken bones, they would take time to heal.

"How long until—"

"I wasn't done," Mettler interrupted. "You have a lacerated kidney, bruising of the major muscles that's severe enough I'm worried about clots, and you're bleeding somewhere in your GI tract, and I don't have the equipment to pinpoint it."

"Then how do you know I'm bleeding in— Oh, never mind," Jacob said.

"Yeah...I'll be happy when you can get up to use the head on your own," Mettler said. "To answer your question, you're banged up pretty bad but healing well ahead of what the computer predicted. I figure you'll be up and about within a day, able to move and fight within a week. After a couple more weeks, you won't even know you fell."

"I can live with that," Jacob said. "At least tell me it wasn't for nothing, and we recovered the data on the box."

"The computer is breaking into it now. We're expecting it to be cracked any hour now," Murph said. "In the meantime, we thought it would be smart to leave the Cluster. We're flying at low slip-velocity back towards ConFed space."

"Good, good." Jacob nodded. "That was the right call. Give me an update when the computer breaks into the data recorder. Meanwhile, I think I'll pass out for a while longer."

"Sweet dreams, LT."

"Hey! How they hanging, LT?" Sully asked two days later, when Jacob hobbled up to the flight deck.

"Oddly sore, to be honest," he answered. "Did you know you can bruise your balls by falling onto your back hard enough?"

"I actually did know that."

"Yeah...I just found out. Where are we?"

"About another full day's flight until we reach the ConFed border." Sully pointed to one of the multifunction displays that showed their course, speed, and approximate position in real-space.

"I took the scenic route so we avoided most of the occupation force's patrols in Eshquarian territory. This ship is running clean codes, but everyone is a little jumpy right now after the attack on Miressa. I don't feel like getting hauled aboard a ConFed cruiser to answer questions."

"That wouldn't be optimal," Jacob agreed. "I'll leave you to it. Once we have a better idea where the hell we're going, I'll let you know."

Mettler had cleared him for light duty and had been genuinely shocked at how fast his body had worked with the nanobots to heal most of the damage. The ribs were still tender, there was an overall soreness to his body, and he still pissed blood…but, all things considered, he felt pretty decent. He felt even better when Mettler's stingy ass would fork over a few of the pain pills he had in his kit.

He went slowly back down the stairs from the flightdeck and made his way aft to the galley, where the rest of the team lounged. The computer had cracked the encryption locks on the box he'd risked his life for, and now Taylor worked to extract the data while Murph helped parse it up into something useable. MG, who was more or less useless at that type of meticulous tech work, had mostly been keeping Sully company until the pilot could take no more and banned him from the flightdeck. His actual words were, "Keep that nasty motherfucker away from me." Apparently, MG had been regaling him with detailed stories of various sexual conquests while in the military. Jacob had heard most of them and felt the weaponeer was likely exaggerating the numbers a bit.

"What's the good word, boys?" he asked, shuffling over to the galley and getting a mug of coffee. They'd cleaned out an NIS safe house during their last mission and had walked away with a coffee machine and a couple cases of coffee from a company on a planet called S'Tora. The company had the unlikely name of Rocky Mountain Coffee Co., and the words were in English. Jacob knew there were a few entrepreneurial humans already out in the galaxy making their fortune, but he was impressed that someone had managed to set up an agricultural operation already. He made a mental note to make it out to S'Tora some day and meet the person behind the company. It was probably a great story.

"Taylor is putting together a preliminary review of what was on that data core," Murph said.

"When?"

"He said he'd be ready in an hour or so," MG said. "Do I have to help with this? Sitting around watching hours of security footage isn't really something I'm good for."

"No shit," Jacob deadpanned. "Don't worry, Corporal...your uselessness once again works in your favor. Since you've managed to piss off Sully, you get to go help Sergeant Mettler."

"What's Mettler doing?" MG asked.

"No idea. Hopefully something disgusting," Jacob said. "Get lost."

MG left to go aft towards the infirmary and cargo hold, grumbling the entire time. Murph just shook his head and laughed.

"Part of me hopes I never get sent back to NIS," he said.

"That'd make two of us," Jacob said, sipping his coffee. "Do you get your regular NIS agent pay and your E-6 pay on top of that?"

"My cover had to be absolute," Murph said with a smile. "If I wasn't drawing a paycheck, it'd be pretty easy to begin taking apart my background with a quick call to finance. What I'm not sure about is whether they're going to let me keep it."

"Good news...our contact didn't have many guests so it was easy to parse the data down to what we needed," Taylor said as he walked into the galley. He interfaced his own Navy-issued tablet to the ship's wall display and began opening up video files. "The resolution isn't great since that system used holographic imagers and this tub only has flat displays."

The first video played, and Jacob could see immediately they had a major problem. It was an external view by the front door, and the guests standing outside were unmistakably human, and he knew one of them.

"Elton Hollick," Murph growled. "Looks like he survived you shooting off his hand."

"If you look closely, he has a prosthetic unit on that arm," Taylor said. "It looks like Margret Jansen's One World faction is not only looking for our missing cruiser, they beat us to the punch."

Elton Hollick was a former NIS agent who had been tasked with infiltrating the One World Faction, a radical group led by former Terranovus administrator Margaret Jansen. Their stated mission goal was to more cohesively unite humanity under one banner, something that was already in place with the United Earth Council. She claimed that, until the individual nation states on Earth were dissolved, humanity would never be on parity with the more advanced species of the quadrant. The truth was that Jansen did indeed want to unite Earth...under her rule.

She'd come to Earth once with a battlefleet she'd assembled in secret on Terranovus and was turned back by a rogue mercenary unit called Omega Force and an alien collective called the Cridal Cooperative. When the dust settled, Earth had signed into a partnership treaty with the Cridal, and Jansen, along with her remaining loyalists, fled. Hollick had been sent to report back on her movements, but he'd been turned and now worked for her. Obsidian had run across Hollick before on Jacob's very first mission, and the rookie lieutenant had blasted the veteran agent's arm off with a plasma rifle. He'd managed to escape, and Jacob had hoped he'd died of his injuries, but that turned out to be wishful thinking.

"Kellska...it's been some time," Hollick was saying on the video.

"Not long enough." The alien named Kellska was immediately recognizable as the corpse they'd found in the upstairs bedroom. "What do you want, human?"

"Is that any way to talk to an old friend?" Hollick asked, pushing his way into the home with a pistol in his hand. The view automatically switched over to one of the interior imagers. "We're looking for the fleet that attacked Miressa."

"Oh, you only want the most wanted criminals in all the galaxy," Kellska laughed. "Is that all?"

"I'm looking for a single human cruiser that will be flying with the Cridal rebels," Hollick said. "I've no doubt a low-level gutter dweller like you has no idea where they are right now, but you'll have heard something about where they could be hiding. Are they in the Cluster?"

"No, human...they're not in the one most obvious place someone would look for them," Kellska said. "That's as much as I know, and certainly as much as I'm willing to give you. Now, leave."

"Not very hospitable of you," Hollick said, moving deeper into the home and looking around. "How bad did you screw up to get stuck out here, Kellska?"

"It's none of your concern."

"No, but it's definitely yours. How would you like to get out of here? I can offer you a job with Margaret Jansen's intelligence service," Hollick said, sidling up to the alien and wrapping the prosthetic arm around its shoulder. "Think about it...no more hiding out here in the asshole of the quadrant, looking over your shoulder for your former employer. You would be a welcomed member of the team again, and all you have to do is go ahead and tell me everything you know."

"A change in tactics, I see," Kellska said. "You offer a boon rather than threats of torture. Frustratingly, you're right. I want to leave this place more than anything...even if that means making a deal with the likes of you. What are my guarantees?"

"Just give me what else you know, and we'll all fly off this rock together," Hollick said smoothly. "Back to a planet with a big city again, with all the perks that go with it. One World will offer you a position within our intelligence service as well as protection from your former employer."

"You have cruelly manipulated my desires, human— I mean, Elton Hollick," Kellska said, the indecision plainly visible on his flat face. "Very well...I was being truthful before. This rebel fleet was wise enough to not come back to the Cluster as nearly every intelligence service in the quadrant is looking for them. While I don't know where they may be currently hidden, I do know there was more to the fleet's makeup than just the Eshquarian Imperial Navy remnant as has been widely reported. There was a strike force from the Cridal Cooperative, led by Admiral Kellea Colleran herself, as well as a sizable number of ships from the Blazing Sun syndicate."

"Blazing Sun?" Hollick was visibly startled. "Saditava Mok has thrown in with this insurrection?"

"Not openly," Kellska said. "The fact the ships and personnel belonged to the syndicate isn't widely known. In fact, his own captains likely don't even know, but I have contacts within his personal fleet that gave me the information."

"This goes well beyond the bribing of council members or judges. It doesn't make any sense for one of the quadrant's most notorious gangsters to be playing this game."

"It does if you know that the man who calls himself Saditava Mok used to be a highly placed officer within Imperial Intelligence," Kellska said. "For him, this is likely personal."

"Mok is Eshquarian?" Hollick asked.

"Surgically altered after his departure from the service to change his appearance, but yes," Kellska said. "That's a fact that isn't widely known although it isn't clear if he changed his appearance to fool Blazing Sun's leadership or to hide from the Eshquarians. He secured his place in the syndicate after an overboss named Bondrass was killed under unusual circumstances." Hollick looked at the alien speculatively for a few moments before smiling widely.

"Take him upstairs and kill him," he said to one of the armed men who had accompanied him. "Then toss this place."

"What!? Why? I have told you all I know!"

"And I believe you," Hollick said, his voice full of mock sympathy. "But now, you're a liability. Others will certainly come looking for this same information. I'm sorry, my friend, but I just can't let you stay here alive."

"I thought I was to go with you!"

"Now, why would we want a disgraceful failure like you in our ranks, Kellska?" Hollick laughed. "We both know you were exiled here for cause. Margaret Jansen doesn't suffer fools, and you are most certainly a fool."

Kellska was dragged blubbering out of the room by the two troops

Hollick had brought while the former agent ripped into the house, looking for additional intel. The video split into two views, and now they were also looking into the upstairs bedroom.

"On your knees, alien," one of the troops said, pulling a long blade. Kellska made a show of cowering and going down to his knees...but the troops weren't in position to see him reaching under the low bed. Kellska snapped up with a weapon in his hand, firing into the face of the troop who had been taunting him.

"Fuck!" the other shouted, opening fire just as Kellska turned and shot him in the gut. The force of the blast from the trooper's weapon flung Kellska up onto the bed, where Jacob remembered finding him while the human sunk to the floor, racked by spasms and screaming in agony.

"What is all the— Oh, you stupid sons of bitches," Hollick said when he ran in on the scene.

"Help me!" the wounded trooper moaned. Hollick pulled his sidearm out and aimed it at the wounded man's head.

"Trust me, this is a mercy you want. There's no treatment for the gun he hit you with," he said, pulling the trigger before the trooper could protest. Hollick then went and checked over Kellska's body before pulling out his com unit. "This is Hollick...I need a cleanup crew to the objective's domicile to remove two human bodies and sanitize the house. I want all the security hardware and any personal effects pulled, but leave the alien's body where it is. After you're done, pull back to base and await orders. I'm going ahead alone...you idiots are just slowing me down."

Hollick took another look around the room and walked out without so much as a second glance at his downed men.

"That's more or less it," Taylor said. "There was another vid where four more humans showed up in a ground car with two Ull and cleaned the place up."

"Shit," Jacob muttered. "Not only does One World know about the *Talon*, but they've sent agent shitbag after it, too."

"*Former* agent shitbag," Murph corrected. "He's *persona non grata* to the NIS. Believe it or not, that's a serious thing among spies. Even double agents and traitors are able to cut deals and be brought back in under certain circumstances. Hollick is listed as kill on sight."

"Oh, I intend to do just that," Jacob said. "Let's shelve that for a minute and talk about how the hell One World has caught wind of our missing ship. Another damn traitor?"

"More than likely," Murph sighed. "That's why Webb's got us so far off the grid right now, LT."

"Well, us, Cobalt, and Diamond," Taylor spoke up. "3rd Scout Corps mentioned they were bringing them into the hunt, too."

"And their orders will come through the normal channels, so Hollick will know exactly where they..." Jacob trailed off, tapping his chin speculatively.

"What?" Murph asked.

"I wonder if we could use the other teams' movements to throw Hollick off the trail," Jacob said. "Have orders cut that move them into an area we know the missing fleet isn't to force One World to shadow them in case they're onto something."

"We'd have to be able to get word to Captain Webb without it being intercepted," Murph said. "That's proving to be a bit of an issue lately."

"Let me handle that," Jacob said. "Also, we'll need to—"

Boom!

It felt like the ship had run into a wall. The deck lurched out from underneath them, and Taylor was sent flying out of the galley and down the central corridor. Jacob and Murph had been seated on a bench anchored to the deck, so they slid forward into the bulkhead, the impact sending icy spikes of pain through Jacob's chest.

"LT, you need to get up here," Sully said over the intercom.

"What the hell," Jacob groaned, pushing himself away from Murph and trying to breathe through the pain. "Go make sure Taylor's alive."

"Got it," Murph said, wincing as he climbed up off the seat.

"What the hell happened?" Jacob asked as he stepped onto the cramped flightdeck.

"Slip-drive kicked off," Sully said, pointing at the illuminated instrument panel. "The fields collapsed asymmetrically and jerked the ship."

"Why did the drive cut out?"

"Unclear, but what I can tell you is we've been pissing fuel into space. I isolated the leak to the secondary injection manifold and shut the valves. We're only using the primary side right now anyway thanks to the power MUX issues," Sully said, his hands flying over the switches to clear out the faults.

"While I'm glad the hydrogen wasn't venting into the cabin, how did fuel leak?" Jacob asked, sinking into one of the aft station seats and holding his side.

"The fuel system for this piece of shit is mostly outside the pressurized inner hull, but inside the outer hull plates. There are a couple reasons the engineers thought that was good design, but it makes it impossible for us to repair underway. I'd suggest leaving it."

"You're in charge of the ship." Jacob raised his hands to wave off the responsibility. "What I'm more interested in is if we have enough fuel to make it anywhere, and if the slip-drive is even functional to get us to that place."

"Let's see," Sully said, scrolling through navigational waypoints. "Our best bet is Pinnacle Station. It's a commercial shipping and passenger hub that has all the necessary facilities to repair this heap. We've got enough fuel to make it with some to spare. Reactor is still all in the green, environmental systems are green, too, so I'll begin diagnostics on the slip-drive and figure out what happened."

"Lovely," Jacob said. "I'll go down and make sure MG and Mettler aren't dead. Taylor took a pretty good hit but was moving. Murph is with him now."

"I'll come with you. I need to go down and inspect the drive in person," Sully said, climbing out of the seat. He rubbed his left wrist, where Jacob guessed he had caught himself when the ship lurched back into real-space.

"Let me know if you need any manpower down there," Jacob said. "I don't want to call this in as a mission abort if we can limp her to Pinnacle Station. Once we're there, we'll see about either repairs or swapping ships again."

"Got it."

6

"Everything came back up green. You feeling lucky?"

"Fire it up," Jacob said. Sully turned back to the flight controls and brought the slip-drive back online.

What they'd found was that the fuel leak, even though it had been on the secondary manifold, had caused reactor power to become erratic enough that the computer performed an emergency mesh-in. When it killed the slip-drive abruptly, the port side emitter bank blew out two power nodes, which caused the fields on that side to collapse more quickly than those on the starboard side. That was what caused the hard lurch that had sent them flying. More modern ships—or even just well-maintained ones—were able to absorb and mitigate those small field misalignments. The flying coffin they were in, however, apparently could not.

Thankfully, the power nodes were items Sully had plentifully stocked in the spares kit when they were hastily outfitting the ship for their mission. The repairs were quick: manually lock the shutoff valves on the secondary fuel system to prevent the computer from trying to open them, and then replace the power nodes, all of which took less than an hour.

"Plasma channels open...emitters charging...containment fields stable," Sully muttered to himself as the computer reported the steps of the slip-drive startup on his display. "Pressures are looking good and the emitters are showing ready. This could have been a lot worse."

"How *lot worse* could it have been?" Taylor asked from the hatchway.

"There could have been a blowback from the port emitter array that caused the computer to stall the reactor for safety reasons," Sully said. "Remember...we have no fusion backup on this tub. If the main reactor goes down, we can't restart it. We're adrift and hoping the batteries hold out long enough for NAVSOC to get a recovery ship out here."

"Grim," Jacob said. "So, we're all agreed that Pinnacle Station is our best bet?"

"Agreed," Sully said.

"I'm just a corporal." Taylor shrugged. "I don't give a shit where we go."

"Once we're back in slip-space, I want you working with Lieutenant Sullivan, making a list of repairs needed," Jacob told his tech. "I want things listed by priority, and we'll work top to bottom."

"We were carrying a lot of relative velocity when we meshed-in," Sully said, ignoring them. "Standby...meshing-out in five seconds."

The combat shuttle accelerated and, mercifully, the slip-drive engaged without issue. Jacob pulled up a screen at his station and looked at the distance and time to destination, as well as their fuel consumption rate. It was going to be close, but doable...just as long as they didn't have to drop back into real-space before reaching Pinnacle. Another mesh-out charge would deplete their fuel to the point where they'd be stranded.

"You want to talk about the elephant in the room?" Murph asked, leaning against the doorway to Jacob's cramped quarters. The lieutenant had the only actual stateroom aboard the tiny ship. Sully took the rack just behind the flightdeck, and the others were all down in berthing.

"What elephant?" Jacob asked. All he wanted to do was go to sleep and let his abused body heal a bit more before they hit Pinnacle Station.

"The fact that you have a personal connection with Saditava Mok," Murph said, stepping into the cramped space.

"I was threatened by Mok," Jacob corrected. "Huge difference from *knowing* him. In exchange for us keeping this ship and the money, I owe him an unspecified favor should he call me on a specific com unit. I'm going to assume that doesn't mean I can just buzz him up and ask him to tell me where his super-secret squirrel rebel war fleet is parked. If the *Talon* is with Mok's ships, then it stands to reason he wouldn't be too keen about losing her."

"It's worth a try." Murph shrugged.

"And what if he decides I've annoyed him, and he has me killed?"

"I'll be completely honest with you, LT, I think this ship will kill us all well before Mok gets a chance."

"Well, I'm not going to worsen my odds by pestering the quadrants most notorious crime lord," Jacob said. "If he reaches out during the mission, I'll bring it up then."

"Just try to work it in casually," Murph said.

"Get out. I want to sleep."

"Think about what I said," Murph called over his shoulder as he walked out. "Because, otherwise, we have jack shit on where to begin our next search."

When the hatch slid shut, the lights dimmed automatically, and Jacob was able to, finally, lie back and relax. He thought about what Murph had said and had to admit there was merit in it, but Murph hadn't been there when Mok had confronted Jacob about the theft of the ship and money. It was the scariest thing he'd ever been through, including all the firefights and hand to hand combat with aliens up to that point. Mok had been calm, even polite...but the level of menace and power that radiated off him in waves had left Jacob shaken even hours after the crime boss had left. No, there was no chance in hell he'd be calling Mok to ask for a favor.

The major problem was that if Mok was involved, any call to him about it would make it sound like Jacob was threatening to expose him if his demands weren't met. Chances were good that Mok would no longer be amused by Jacob's antics enough to allow him to remain breathing, and the next port of call they made, some Blazing Sun opportunist would pop him to fill a bounty.

But maybe there was another way.

He rolled off his rack and opened the wall locker, rummaging around on the top shelf until he found what he was looking for. It was a gold disc about the size of a silver dollar. On one side, it was embossed with the symbol of the Blazing Sun syndicate, on the other side was the numeral five written in Jenovian Standard. It was a marker that identified the ship and crew as belonging to the syndicate. There was an ident chip embedded within it that could be scanned by someone with the proper decryption codes to authenticate who they were. The *five* on the one side referred to which of the Twelve Points—the twelve captains in the syndicate right under Mok himself—that the crew belonged to.

Jacob flopped back down on the rack, staring at the ceiling and rolling the coin around in his hand. The beginnings of a plan were forming, but it wasn't without significant risk. He hoped he wasn't operating too far outside of his orders, but Captain Webb had been infuriatingly vague about what methods were available to him to track down the missing cruiser. The NAVSOC chief had simply said, "Do whatever it takes." Not exactly helpful when it came to figuring out what his rules of engagement would be when dealing with a lord of the galactic underworld who commanded a private military large enough to conquer Earth.

He drifted off to sleep, still wrangling with the details of his plan as the ship shook alarmingly through slip-space towards Pinnacle Station.

"Has Obsidian checked in yet?"

"No, Captain."

"This is depressingly familiar," Webb muttered, rubbing his scalp. "That goddamn kid can't follow procedure to save his ass. Where's Diamond?"

"Still en route to the Concordian Cluster. They're...four days out."

"When's the last time we tried to raise Obsidian?" Webb asked his aide, trying to do the math in his head. If Obsidian had already reached the contact, then they should have already gotten the information needed and be on their way out of the Cluster. They also should have checked in as soon as they were outbound.

"Ten hours ago," Bennet said. The Navy lieutenant had served as Webb's aide for as long as he'd been in charge of NAVSOC. "Lieutenant Brown did mention their loaner ship's slip-com system was a bit unreliable."

"A convenient excuse for him to ignore regular check-ins, but I do remember reading that in one of the morning briefs." Webb leaned back and spun his chair to look out his office window over the flightline of Taurus Station, the remote base that was the home of Naval Special Operations Command, or NAVSOC for short. The ramp was littered with far more ships than it normally saw since Taurus Station was being packed up in preparation to move to its new home on the planet Olympus.

Earth wanted Terranovus to be a colony world for civilians, and the powers that be had ordered that the UEAS relocate to their newly acquired planet. The rationale was that Olympus didn't show up on most ConFed navigational charts, and it made more sense for them to base their shipyards and heavy weapons construction there. Webb didn't disagree, he just hated the disruption to his operations.

"Where are we with the Corsair's refit?" he asked. The Corsair was a one-off ship designed and built by humans on Terranovus specifically for Scout Fleet. It had been Obsidian's ship before Commander Ezra Mosler had been murdered by a traitor on his crew who had also sabotaged the ship before fleeing. Lieutenant Brown had been forced to scuttle her and steal another ship to pursue their objective and had, unfortunately, been a bit overzealous while disabling the Corsair. The deranged monkeys on Brown's crew had done so much damage that the ship had to be recovered by 2nd Scout Corps frigate and brought back for a total overhaul. The engineers were still trying to sort out the mess.

"The project lead told me he expected the ship would not be able to fly to Olympus and would need to be lifted to orbit and taken in one of the cargo haulers," Bennet said.

"It would have been better if they'd just set the reactor to overload and destroyed the fucking thing completely," Webb hissed. "But since they left the hull intact, the bean counters in Fleet insist we repair the damn thing and put her back in service. It would have been cheaper to just build a new one from the technical drawings."

"I don't disagree, sir."

"Whatever." Webb spun back around. "What else have you got?"

"This is low on the list with all of the current missions demanding most of your time, but 707 is asking for a meeting with you," Bennet said. 707, whose full designation was Combat Unit 707, was the current leader of a group of battlesynths living on Terranovus as political refugees. The sentient machines kept to themselves, and if 707 was asking for a meeting, it was certain it wasn't something frivolous.

"Go ahead and tell him that I can make myself available at any time for our most honored guests," Webb said. "Use those exact words: most honored guests."

"Most honored guests...got it. I'll send the message to him when I leave."

"If we don't find the *Talon* within the next couple weeks, there's going to be hell to pay. I want options. Just having Diamond and Obsidian flying around trying to track it down isn't much of a plan. By this afternoon, I want a list of all our available assets we could reassign to this, and I want to know what efforts the NIS and Cridal Intelligence are putting in," Webb said. "And right in the middle of such a critical mission, the brass decides *now* would be a good time to move the base."

"Not to mention all the spies we probably flew in with the crews breaking everything down," Bennet said, standing up.

"Thanks for that cheery thought. Ask Director Wellford, as a professional courtesy, if he'd let us know if he has anyone operating on Taurus Station. Be sure to let him know we're about to initiate our own security sweep, and if he tells us the NIS doesn't have any operatives here, we'll assume anyone we find is a One World mole and act accordingly."

"I'll let him know, sir. Is there any reason you don't want to talk to him yourself? I thought you were on friendly terms."

"That's part of the problem," Webb sighed. "My friendship with Michael stems from our time here on Terranovus, back when Margaret Jansen was the planet's administrator. He and I both worked on the Jason Burke problem together and, since we're still here on this planet, the friendship continued. But NIS and NAVSOC should always be distrustful of each other as a checks and balance on two powerful, covert organizations. The two people in charge being too buddy-buddy jeopardizes that, so we'll be going through official channels for things like this."

"Understood, sir. I'll handle it."

"Good. Get started."

Once his trusted aide left and closed the door behind him, Webb spun and looked out across the tarmac again. The Corsair sat on the maintenance ramp, where she'd been towed from the hangar so the building could be used as a staging area for the equipment being lifted up to orbit to the waiting starship that would take it all to Olympus.

There seemed to be no happy middle ground in his job. He either had too many highly trained people sitting around with nothing to do, or he had half a dozen full-blown emergencies and not enough people to cover them all. Having to reactivate Obsidian was the least optimal thing he could have done for such an important tasking as finding the *Eagle's Talon*. He had faith that Jacob Brown would be every bit or better than Ezra Mosler...one day. In the present, however, he was still an overeager junior officer that was a little too confident of his own abilities after a successful mission that he managed with as much luck as skill. Having him go poking around for a group that had the balls to attack the ConFed's homeworld may be setting him and his team up for a bad fall, and in a game with stakes this high, that meant none would likely survive.

He opened up his private slip-com terminal and started to draft new orders that would recall Scout Team Obsidian back to Olympus, where they would stand down until the rest of 3rd Scout Corps caught up. It would still keep Brown out of sight and mind of the people in Fleet Command who had thoughts of using the kid as a stepping stone in their own genetics programs, and it would allow him to take a moment to figure out how he wanted to restructure that team. Murph was technically not even a Marine, and Jacob was a first lieutenant, too junior to be in command of a scout team. He was getting around that technicality by listing the pilot, Sully, as the overall team commander, but Sully wasn't the one calling the shots right now.

His hand hovered over the send icon as he re-read what he'd typed out. Obsidian was still a Scout Team, and Fleet Ops made it clear they viewed Scout Teams as expendable resources. Was he making excuses to recall the team because of his personal connection to Brown and his family? Even if Obsidian was eliminated, they still might manage to forward back useful intel that would help them narrow down the search for the *Talon*.

As if of its own will, his hand lowered and his middle finger caressed the spot on the glass panel that said 'SEND.' Recalling Brown's team was the right thing to do. Many years ago, when he'd been on the front lines as a US Navy SEAL, he'd not considered himself or his team expendable. Now that he was in charge of NAVSOC and controlled dozens of special warfare teams, he'd not changed his mind. It was vital the *Talon* be found and recovered for the safety of all humanity, but putting that burden on Jacob Brown's young shoulders was too much. They'd find another way.

The message containing the revised orders was sent to a messaging service on the planet Ver, which was a dead drop box for when the team was out of contact. Per standard operating procedure, Brown would check in on that box periodically if he couldn't talk to Taurus Station directly. Webb just hoped he bothered to check it like he was supposed to.

7

"Your slip-com array is badly damaged as well."

"How damaged?" Jacob asked skeptically.

"The array is missing," the shop boss said, pointing to where a large section of outer hull platting had come free at some point. Sully had told him they'd lost a few non-critical pieces of cladding during entry, but it looked like the pilot had been overly optimistic about what *non-critical* had meant.

"That section of missing hull is where your slip-com field emitter array would normally sit," the squat, gruff alien technician went on. "Legally, I can't let this ship leave the hangar until you have a working superluminal com system."

"Add it to the list, damnit," Jacob sighed. "And replace the outer shielding that would normally protect it."

"On a ship this old, it'll have to be fabricated, and that will—"

"Cost more. Yes, I'm picking up on the theme here," Jacob snapped. "Just do it."

The tech shrugged, unflappable in the face of the human's growing irritation. He just passed over a beat-up tablet for Jacob to sign off on the repairs and add a payment method. He flipped through the four different accounts provided to him by NAVSOC for operational expenses and chose one to apply all the repairs to. Altogether, it would cost the UEN nearly two-hundred thousand credits to get the ship back from the crews at Pinnacle, but at least it would be spaceworthy and marginally more reliable when it was done. At least, that's what they were telling themselves since it seemed unlikely it could ever become *less* reliable.

"If you insist on flying such an abused and antiquated ship, you should be ready to accept the high cost of maintenance, my friend," the tech said, suddenly boisterous now that money had exchanged hands. All of the crews that worked the lower hangar decks on Pinnacle Station were private contractors that leased the hangars from the station and worked in a sort of loose cooperative, pooling resources where it made sense and cutting each other's throats on everything else.

"Yeah...thanks for the advice, *friend*," Jacob said, turning back to his crew.

"How long?" Sully asked. The pilot had annoyingly insisted Jacob handle the negotiations with the hangar crew.

"Four days," Jacob said. "Give or take. They'll get it done faster if we pay more, of course."

"It's Fleet's money." Mettler shrugged. "Spend it."

"You're not the one who has to settle the tab with NAVSOC once we get back," Jacob said. "We'll get the repairs done, and we won't draw undue attention to ourselves by flashing around more money than our entire ship is even worth."

"Fair point, although, technically, *I'm* the one who will be explaining our expenditures," Sully said. "Either way, you're making the right choice keeping our profile low."

"Thanks," Jacob said. "I want MG to come with me, the rest of you go to the upper decks and find someplace for us to lay low for a few days. Make sure nothing is left on the ship that can identify us."

"Where are we going?" MG asked as the group split up.

"The computer said there was a public com suite two decks

down," Jacob said. "I need to check in with the boss, and you're going to stand there and look tough so I don't need to keep turning around to check my six."

"I can do that."

The pair easily found the com suites, where upon Jacob paid for the use of a Class II slip-com node while MG stood outside the privacy screen, glaring at anyone who walked by. Jacob pulled out his com unit and interfaced it directly with the data jack on the node's terminal. Once it came up and said it was ready, he enabled encryption via his own unit, and then punched in the twelve-character address he knew by rote.

"Code in."

"Obsidian Actual, bravo sierra six one eight kilo kilo," Jacob said to the bored sounding voice on the other end of the connection.

"Copy that, Lieutenant Brown. Standing by for your report."

"Contact was deceased when we reached the domicile. Subsequent investigation discovered that ex-NIS Agent Elton Hollick had been there before us to question the contact, and then killed him. I have no reason to believe that Hollick found anything actionable based on the footage I saw, but it's clear he is after the same thing we are," Jacob said.

"Current status?"

"Still on-mission," Jacob said. "Currently at Pinnacle Station effecting repairs, and then we'll be moving on to the next lead. Once I have access to a secure slip-com node again, I will transmit the full mission report."

"Understood."

The connection went dead without any sort of warning. Jacob shut down the terminal and executed a script on his com unit that would wipe the machine's memory of the address he contacted and the transmission logs of the event. It was a pain in the ass having to use a public system, but it had the added benefit of brevity since he had to call into Taurus Station's main operations center instead of directly to 3rd Scout Corps' command center.

"That was quick," MG said.

"Doesn't take long to say we've spent a lot of time accomplishing nothing," Jacob said. "Let's head up to..." He trailed off as they passed an external porthole just as two massive cargo haulers came about to line up with the upper level docking complex.

"Head up to what?" MG asked.

"Do you remember how many ships they said were involved in the attack on Miressa?"

"Dozens," MG said. "I don't think we ever got an exact number. Why?"

"Recognize the symbol on the aft drive pods on those ships?" Jacob asked. "It's the company logo of Hontuun Movement. They're the largest supplier of fleet logistics for the quadrants civil maritime industry. Any starliner or bulk freighter is kept flying with their fuel and parts."

"Holy shit, LT, what is the point?" MG wasn't what one would call an intellectually curious man. He liked what he liked, so if he wasn't shooting at someone, blowing up their stuff, or trying to steal their women away, he tended to lose interest fairly quickly.

"The point, my musclebound simpleton, is that the logistics involved in operating a sizable fleet—like the one that attacked Miressa—can't be easily hidden from the ConFed when they control all banking transactions," Jacob said. "That fleet is being hidden by a sponsor government."

"I feel like the best thing for us to do at this point is to stop talking about it until you can sit down with Murph and Sully to have a dork-fest about spare parts shipping and fuel," MG yawned. "Since you'll obviously want us out of your hair while you discuss this, it would be a good command decision to give me, Mettler, and Taylor some coin so we can hit up one of the local bars. You know...to collect valuable intel."

"I appreciate the fact you still lie right to my face about what you're doing," Jacob said. "I take it as a sign of respect."

"As it was intended."

"Hiding the ships themselves are no real issue," Jacob said, now in the middle of trying to convince Murph he was on to something. Sully had decided not to stick around and was, instead, going down to make sure the crews had started on the ship like they said they would. The rest of the enlisted men had been true to MG's word and had split to find a bar after a stern warning from Jacob to stay out of trouble and to be unmemorable.

"In low-power modes, they can sit for decades without needing fuel or risk being detected."

"But what's the point of scraping together a battle fleet if you're going to execute one hit-and-run strike and stash the ships somewhere?" Murph said. "Beyond that, you're defeating your own point. You're saying the support systems will give away the fleet, but then you say they can hide almost indefinitely without it."

"The ships, yes. But not the crews. This is where the analysts are wrong, I believe," Jacob said. "The NIS brief theorized that the fleet is either scattered and hidden, or intact and hidden, but definitely in ConFed space, and definitely cut off from their normal supply chains. I don't think that's true."

"You think they found a government to secretly sponsor them," Murph deadpanned, repeating Jacob's original point. "Any of the smaller powers left in the quadrant would have to be suicidal to hide this fleet. If the ConFed found them—*when* the ConFed finds them—whoever was aiding them will have the hammer dropped. I still think they're funneling supplies through Mok's organization."

"An obvious but flawed answer," Jacob said. "Blazing Sun isn't in the business of war. The only reason I'm not dead right now is because I was able to tell Mok that one of his Points was about to make a move on him. That tells you how fragile positions of power are in that organization. I think if Mok were to recklessly risk profits and resources on an ill-fated rebellion attempt, his own people would eliminate him."

"That...makes sense," Murph said grudgingly. As someone who was still technically an NIS agent, he seemed to be committed to taking their analysts' assessments at face value, becoming defensive when Jacob pointed out some of the logical flaws. "So, where do you think they are?"

"No idea," Jacob admitted. "I'm not an investigator or an agent. I'm a glorified ship spotter, if we're being honest. Logically, I would say that it's whoever has the most to gain from a destabilized or weakened ConFed."

"Which would be the Saabror Protectorate."

"Ah! But the ConFed will be well aware of that, too. The Protectorate and the Cridal Cooperative will be the first places they send their intelligence service to look."

"The Cooperative?" Murph frowned.

"Despite Seeladas Dalton's protests, it was an entire Cridal strike group that participated in the attack," Jacob said. "Doesn't look good, and I doubt they're just going to take our dear Premier at her word."

"Shit," Murph muttered, looking over all the notes and material on the table Jacob had been using. "I need to pass this on to my handlers at the NIS." Jacob was unable to control his facial expression at that offhand comment.

"What's your problem?" Murph asked.

"You're still reporting back to the NIS?"

"Of course. Did you think I wasn't?"

"Given that you're not on any mission other than remaining a functional part of Obsidian for the time being, I wasn't aware you were still passing on NAVSOC intelligence to another agency," Jacob said.

"I'm just following standard procedure, Lieutenant," Murph said. "Is this going to be an issue? We still have to work together, but I need to be able to do my job."

"I suppose it's not like I have a choice here short of physically restraining you," Jacob said.

"How about a compromise? I still need to report in, but I'll let you be there and see exactly what I'm telling them," Murph said. "That keeps me within regs on my side, and it lets you know I'm not here spying on Obsidian and trying to undermine our team."

"Deal."

"Have you thought about how we're going to get onto the next lead?" Murph asked as the pair walked out of the mid-level suite they'd rented.

"I actually thought about what you said about reaching out to Mok."

"And you'll do it?" Murph sounded surprised.

"Hell no...I'm not insane," Jacob said. "But I think we have a way to exploit a gap in Mok's security and get ourselves a Blazing Sun smuggling gig."

"How is this any better than my idea?" Murph asked, pinching the bridge of his nose. "You realize our standing mandate for Scout Fleet missions is pretty explicit about engaging in illegal activity, right?"

"I read it," Jacob said defensively. "I'm not a lawyer, but I definitely saw some gray areas in those sections. Trust me, Murph...you'll love this."

"I already don't."

8

Pinnacle Station was, by human standards, unbelievably ancient. It had been expanded and added onto over the course of centuries as each new caretaker configured it to suit their purpose. Nobody was really certain what it had been when its first humble form had been constructed and researchers routinely visited the station to explore the original sections, now buried deep within new construction, to try and ascertain what its purpose had once been and who built it. Since it sat in space, trailing behind an anchoring planet in a heliocentric orbit around its star, it never eroded away or became buried like terrestrial structures did. Save for a few impacts from docking mishaps and a rare meteor strike, the station's older sections looked much like they did when first built.

Since nearly every being in the quadrant evolved on planets with around 1-to-1.75g of gravity, they all tended to think logically that expansion should mean building *up*. The older parts of the mammoth station were the lower levels relative to the artificial gravity generators. These spaces held heavy manufacturing, the main powerplant, and slum residences for those who couldn't afford to live on the upper decks. Like most slums, the lower decks of Pinnacle Station had become a viable host for a robust criminal underground.

The criminals of Pinnacle Station had organized themselves differently than in most places, however, and it was important to know which was which. First, there were the people who operated entirely within the station's ecosphere. They preyed upon the full-time residents, the transient ship crews, and the starliner passengers hanging around waiting to catch a connecting flight. They followed a strict code to keep their activities below the threshold that would cause management to send down security teams to start busting heads. They were, for the most part, harmless. You might lose a few credits or a piece of luggage, but they wouldn't try to kidnap or kill you.

The second group was much more dangerous. They were the criminals who were on Pinnacle as representatives of much larger operations such as Blazing Sun. Their forte was operating complicated smuggling rings out of the station, as well as kidnapping targets of opportunity, providing narcotics for the local crews to sell, and even stealing from ships carrying valuable cargo when they were docked for fuel or repairs. In some extreme cases, they'd been known to steal entire ships themselves when the reward seemed to justify the risk. It was this group Jacob actively sought out as he, Murph and MG descended down into the bowels of Pinnacle Station's lower levels.

"Yeah...still not in love with this plan, LT," Murph said.

"We need an excuse to be in the Saabror Protectorate," Jacob said quietly. "They've locked down their borders, and we're flying a ship with ConFed transponder codes. We have a little bit of built-in criminal cred with the ship we swiped, so let's just see if we can find a job smuggling something across the border."

"Putting aside that you just blindsided us with this theory that we'll find what we need in the Protectorate, you've not put my concerns to rest about what happens if we agree to smuggle something illegal," Murph said.

"Of course, it'll be illegal, dipshit," MG laughed. "Otherwise, they'd just ship it normally."

"You can smuggle legal things, dumbass," Murph shot back. "You ever heard of trying to dodge tariffs and taxes?"

"No. Why would I?"

"I'll handle any potential legal pitfalls we may run into," Jacob said. "Let's just focus on what we came here to do."

"Maybe we'll get lucky and it'll be another load of cash and buzzballs," MG said.

"You're still a member of the United Earth Marine Corps, Corporal," Jacob said as they walked into the lift car. "Whatever narcotics we come across are off-limits."

"It's for our cover, LT! What if someone puts a gun to my head and makes me fire one back to prove I'm who I say I am?"

"What the fuck is wrong with him?" Jacob asked Murph.

"Corporal Marcos technically scored at least in the ninetieth percentile on the aptitude and skills test battery to even qualify for Scout Corps duty," Murph said, staring at MG. "But I'm having a hard time believing that wasn't a fluke."

"Whatever. Boy Scouts." MG yawned.

The lift doors opened, and they were hit with a blast of hot, steamy air that reeked of alien bodies and chemicals. They were down in the engineering levels, and the type of powerplant used in Pinnacle Station—a series of fourteen water-cooled fusion reactors—spit out a lot of steam from the coolant line pressure relief valves. The reactors were nearly two hundred years old and not nearly as powerful as the antimatter reactors used in most starships, but they were simple, reliable machines that didn't explode when something went wrong. There was also the fact that they'd buried the powerplant deep within the station with new construction that would have to be cut away to replace them. When they finally needed to be retired, the station's controlling company would likely have a new system added on to the outside and seal off the old ones, entombing the reactors for the rest of Pinnacle's life.

"What do you want?" The trio turned to look at one of the locals standing in an alcove. The belligerent posture and hands balled into fists made it clear he had no intention of letting them go unchallenged.

"We're looking for someone," Jacob said.

"Who?" the filthy alien demanded, moving to block their path.

"Not you. Now, move," Jacob said, walking towards his tormenter in a way that made it clear he had no intention of altering his course. The alien at first tried to stretch up to its full height and bluster, but rethought its approach when MG flashed a nasty looking flechette pistol he carried under his jacket.

"Perhaps we've both acted hastily in this first meeting," the alien said, now slouching down to make itself seem shorter than Jacob. "There is no need for hostility, and perhaps I can even be of service. Allow me to rephrase my question...whom do you seek and perhaps I can help?" Jacob looked at Murph, who just rolled his eyes and shook his head.

"I apologize for our rudeness, friend," Jacob said. "You look like an honest worker, and I have no doubt you'd never associate with the people we're looking for. It would be best if we parted ways now."

"I see," the alien deflated a bit. "So, you're looking for narcotics or companionship?"

"I'm looking for someone who can speak for the guilds," Jacob said, watching the other's reactions closely. Alien gestures and physiology varied wildly, but there seemed to be a universal constant for biological beings when startled or surprised. Jacob could see the alien twitch, involuntary shudders working through its long limbs.

"Perhaps we should part ways," it said in a rush, already moving away from them.

"Track him," Jacob said. Murph loped ahead, calling out to the alien and holding something in his hand.

"Friend! Wait! I believe you dropped this," Murph said, holding out what looked like a half-eaten protein bar from their ration kits.

"You are mistaken, that is not mine." The alien still pulled away. Murph put a friendly hand on its shoulder.

"Ah, my mistake."

"Slick," MG said as Murph walked back.

"That tracker will have severely limited range down here near all the powerplant machinery, but we should be able to follow him and not be spotted. This way.

The active tracker Murph had slapped onto the alien fired off a burst transmission every five seconds until the battery died. The com units Scout Fleet issued their crews could receive and determine direction and distance for each ping, and then display the data to the operator via their neural implants. Essentially, Murph now had a translucent green arrow in his field of view with a running distance number in meters next to it as well as signal strength from the tracker.

"You think following the first random dude we find is really a strategy, LT?" MG asked.

"He's spooked. Three newcomers show up and threaten him with weapons and openly say they're looking for any guild members...in his mind, we're likely here to settle a score. In a place like this, he'll run to the first person he knows that's in the smuggler's guild and warn them to curry favor with the people who run these lower levels," Jacob said.

"That's actually solid reasoning and tactics," Murph said. "You've been reading all the background material I gave you about the region, haven't you?"

"Nothing else to do while waiting to die from explosive decompression or a slip-drive failure," Jacob said.

Before their slip-com node had failed, apparently from the antenna array being ripped off the hull, Murph had downloaded a full primer from the NIS database on how the criminal elements that worked the region were organized and operated. Jacob had absorbed the material like a sponge, genuinely interested in how all these independent gangs wove together into an underground shadow society that had its own rules and governing body. Saditava Mok was the undisputed kingpin of the region where Pinnacle Station sat, but since it was an interstellar commerce hub, other outfits were allowed representation without reprisal from Blazing Sun.

It was a little convoluted, but Jacob's takeaway had been that

Pinnacle Station's management was well aware of the criminal element operating aboard, but it was far more cost efficient to reach an understanding with them than it was to try and openly fight them. As long as everyone played by the rules, everyone could get along. Jacob had taken this knowledge and assumed the guild leaders would not be hard to find since they weren't openly pursued.

"Can we get audio through the tracker?" he asked.

"Only when we're within forty meters. Once I activate it for audio broadcasting, the battery will die within five minutes," Murph said. "Also, after I trigger it, the unit stops receiving so I can't make it go back to burst tracking mode. It's a one and done type thing."

"Shit," Jacob muttered. "We need to be able to see if it's talking to—"

"We have a tail," MG said. "Two Taukkir. Both looked armed."

"I saw them," Jacob said. "You're sure they're following us?"

"They're not subtle creatures," MG said. "They've been staring right at us and getting more and more agitated. They know I've spotted them."

"Damnit!" Jacob hissed. Taukkir were aggressive and the members of their species on Pinnacle Station were typically part of the first-tier criminals who preyed on locals and transients. The two down here were likely there to jump anyone who looked like they didn't belong and a trio of humans gawking around like a bunch of tourists would certainly qualify.

"We should split up," Murph said. "I'll stay on the target."

"Negative," Jacob said. "Make sure they keep their distance, and we'll hopefully reach one of the guild or cartel players before they make their move."

The words had no sooner left Jacob's mouth than a large, four-fingered hand came out of an opening and clamped down on Murph's neck, dragging him down while three more Taukkir rushed out and slammed Jacob and MG to the ground. Before Jacob could react, a meaty Taukkir hand grabbed his face and slammed his head into the ally deck. Lights out.

"LT...you dead?"

"I wish," Jacob groaned.

"Silence!"

Jacob cracked his eyes open and saw that the rest of his team were restrained and on the deck like he was. There was also a Taukkir standing over them, brandishing MG's pistol, though he seemed unfamiliar with it. They were piled into an alcove that looked like it might have been a disused office.

Jacob, who hadn't even fully recovered from being tossed off a building, had a splitting headache from where he'd been slammed into the deck. His neural implant flashed warnings that he was likely concussed and unhelpfully told him to seek immediate medical attention.

"Where are your pals?" he asked, fighting through the nausea and vertigo.

"I won't tell you to remain silent again," the Taukkir said.

Jacob lay his head back down against the cool deck, taking the moments he had to try and collect himself before their guard's friends reappeared and the real party started. He tried to trigger an alert on his com unit via his neural implant so the rest of his team could swoop in and save the day, but his fuzzy mind couldn't seem to make it happen. In fact, he couldn't even reach out to the com unit at all. The Taukkir had either destroyed it or had it in a shielded box somewhere.

He passed the time by discreetly testing his restraints in hopes the Taukkir had bound them in a way a normal human wouldn't be able to break from, but perhaps he could. He pulled with increasing force against the manacles that secured his wrists behind his back, but they held fast. The effort he'd put into it had sent a fresh wave of nausea sweeping through him, and he closed his eyes again until the worst of it passed. His neural implant, apparently tired of waiting for him to go to the infirmary, informed him it was directing the relatively small number of medical nanobots already in his bloodstream to his head to begin treatment. The little buggers were proven tech Earth had bought on the open market through its Cridal trading partnerships, but UEN Medical had insisted on some restrictions when they began seeing widespread use. His implant was programmed to only send them to repair damage in the brain, heart, or lungs if no other treatment was available. Apparently, they wanted more real-world testing before allowing the machines to roam free throughout the body's most sensitive areas.

As he always did, Jacob could swear he could feel the microscopic machines as they detached from whatever they'd currently been anchored to and entered his bloodstream, moving on the orders of the neural implant towards the swelling in his brain causing him so much trouble. The door to the room they were in banged open just as his implant informed him that he had an insufficient number of nanobots in his system to effect treatment and advised him to remain calm and immobilized until he could reach an infirmary.

"Have they talked?" a new Taukkir demanded.

"This one has, but you injured its head, and it appears disoriented. By their deference to the one called El-tee, we can assume it is the leader," the guard said.

"El-tee," the newcomer grunted. "You are human, correct?"

"That's the rumor," Jacob said, not bothering to open his eyes.

"Some time ago, we saw a human like you. It killed some of my clan. What do you have to say about that?"

"I'd say you're stalling right now until the person really in charge gets here," Jacob said. "We both know you'd not risk angering the cartels by grabbing us against their own safe passage rules down here. And for what? Because *some* human at *some* time beat up on your people? Come on...you'll have to try harder than that."

"Nobody knows you're here." The Taukkir sneered. "The cartels and the guild won't care what we do to you, because they have no idea who you are or why you're looking for them."

"Look, asshole...I'm too injured to listen to you prattle on pointlessly," Jacob sighed. "Just get to the point."

"You've searched them?" the Taukkir asked.

"Yes...and we may have a problem," the guard said quietly. "The leader was carrying this." He held out the gold Blazing Sun marker Jacob had planned to use as a way to muscle into the guilds and get a smuggling job.

"You are part of Blazing Sun?" the Taukkir asked, his voice now carrying an entirely different tone and inflection Jacob couldn't place.

"That's what that means," Jacob said. "Hence the reason we were down here to see a guild representative. They're waiting on us." There were some grunts and cursing outside the doorway as the other Taukkir caught a glimpse of the marker and realized what it meant. Holding a marker meant they worked *directly* for Blazing Sun in some capacity, and the syndicate was not known to tolerate their people being messed with.

"Tell the one who hired us that the situation has become more complicated," the lead Taukkir said. "If he wants these people, he has little time before we cut them loose."

"That's not good enough! If we don't—" the conversation was cut off as the guard stepped back in and closed the door. It was another thirty minutes before the door opened again, and when it did, the person in the doorway was one that they least expected or wanted: Elton Hollick.

"Fuck me," Murph spat out. "Could this day get any worse?"

"Oh, I assure you it can, Agent Murphy." Hollick smiled. "As you're about to find out."

9

"They should have been back by now," Mettler said.

"I'm not getting a position ping off their com units anymore," Taylor said. "That could mean they've moved into an area where the local network has gaps, or maybe a shielded area used by the people they were trying to make contact with."

"It *could* mean that, but it probably doesn't," Sully said. "I think by now it's safe to assume they've hit a snag. All three com units dropping off at the exact same time? Come on."

"You're in charge right now, Lieutenant," Mettler said. "What's our move?"

"I'm a little out of my depth," Sully admitted. "Usually, there's a team commander and a ground team leader so all I need to do is worry about flying the ship. Other than grabbing the biggest guns you have and rushing down to the lower decks, what ideas do you have?"

"Lightly armed, discreet sneak and peek," Mettler said. "Let's just at least be in the area. If we happen to see them and the indicators are that they're fine, we just move on. If they are in trouble, we'll be a lot closer if we move now. Sully, it'll probably be better if you stay here and help coordinate our movements."

"You mean stay out of your way," Sully said, rolling his eyes. "I am fully aware where my skills lie, and this sort of thing isn't it. Keep me in the loop and let me know the moment you have eyes on Lieutenant Brown and if he's under duress."

"Will do," Taylor said. "This is probably all for nothing. Knowing that trio, they've made contact and are out partying it up, having a great time."

Jacob wasn't having a great time.

At a time when he needed his wits and senses sharp, the cumulative injuries he'd suffered lately made him feel like he was watching the scene while underwater. He couldn't think clearly, and his body felt weak, diminished. Elton Hollick just stood in the doorway, smiling widely down at them but making no move to come inside.

"I knew the NIS still had Kellska listed as a Cluster intel asset, so it wasn't a big leap to think that Earth would send someone there to shake him down," Hollick said, leaning against the doorframe. "I thought they'd be a little more discreet and send a couple agents, or even a contractor, so imagine my surprise and delight when one of Marcus Webb's teams came clomping up to the house...and not just *any* team, but the one whose young lieutenant blew my arm off."

"Everything is just coming up aces for you, huh?" Jacob asked.

"I can't complain." Hollick shrugged. "It's just lucky for me that you never bothered checking your ship for trackers when you roared away from that planet. I got everything Kellska knew, but I figured you still had access to that Veran's intel network, so it wouldn't hurt to squeeze you for information and repay the favor for this." He held up his prosthetic hand and waggled the fingers.

"So...what are you doing here, Brown?"

"You mean you have a tracker on my ship and you didn't bother going down to the hangar and checking on it before pinching us? We're not here because we know anything...Webb sent us out to collect Kellska, he was dead, so we're heading home. If we hadn't blown a fuel line and had to stop for repairs, you'd have tracked us all the way back to Terran space."

Hollick just looked at him skeptically. Normally, Jacob's first instinct would be to bluster, threaten, annoy, or just stonewall Hollick until an opportunity for escape appeared or the rest of his team showed up. Right now, he was in such a bad way he was only trying to delay what he saw as inevitable for the sake of Murph and MG. It was likely Hollick would only take one of them as a prisoner, and he wanted to make sure it was him and maybe manage to keep his people alive, though that was a slim hope.

"So, you're just heading home?" Hollick asked, his tone making it clear he didn't believe the story.

"Why not? We were already heading that way when we were asked to divert to pick up an asset. I don't even know what they wanted with him."

"The problem with you, Brown, is that you're so damn convincing at playing an idiot, I can't even tell if it's an act or if you're really so clueless?"

"Thank you."

"That wasn't a compliment, you idiot," Hollick hissed, turning away. "Well...that's enough of trying this the easy way. I only need to take one of you back to Jansen, so who wants to ride with me for weeks of unending torture and who wants to just die right here?"

"I'll—"

"Not you, Brown," Hollick said. "You look like you wouldn't survive the trip back up to the docking arms. Probably not MG either, since he's not the brightest bulb, certainly not someone with any information I need. I guess that leaves you, Murphy."

"Fuck off," Murph spat. "You'll have to kill all of us because I'm not going."

"I'm going to sedate and have you taken up there unconscious,

Murphy," Hollick sighed. "You've been hanging around these guys too long and it's eroding your brain."

"I'll go and cooperate if you leave them alive," Jacob said.

"Do I look like an idiot?"

"Mind if I answer that?" a velvety voice said from the corridor just before one of the Taukkir doubled over and dropped, holding its midsection. Hollick's head snapped over, and he snarled in rage.

"Whitney! What the hell are you—" that was as far as he got before the Viper pulled a long blade from the gut of the Taukkir she stabbed and shoved the bulky alien at Hollick. The former NIS agent was cagey, and he spun away from the assassin and pulled what could only be a grenade out from his side pocket. It was a move that seemed to stun everyone, even Carolyn Whitney.

"Seems a little bit overkill, doesn't it, stud?"

"Get back, you bitch!" Hollick shouted, spit flying from his mouth. He was already out of sight from where Jacob laid, but he could tell the ex-agent was deathly afraid of Whitney. Like most aggressive men when they were afraid of something, Hollick reacted with even more aggression in the hopes of bluffing the Viper into backing down.

"Now, see...that just wasn't very nice, Elton," Whitney said, her voice like steel cords rasping together. The few times Jacob had met the woman, she always seemed to be laughing at some joke only she got, but now, all the humor had bled out of her voice. "If I were you, I'd put the grenade away and leave. I'm not here for you. Don't make this personal."

"Don't you threaten *me!*" Hollick snapped, his voice coming from further away.

"Put the grenade away, you imbecile," Whitney said. "You know if you use it, you'll set off every security alarm for three decks. Just walk away, pissant."

"We'll run into each other again, Whitney...count on it."

"What a drama queen," Whitney said, walking fully into the room. "Sooo...how's it going?"

"Been better," Jacob said. "You?"

"Can't complain. I suppose you'll want me to get you out of those restraints and help you out of here before the rest of the Taukkir come back, so let's make this quick. Why are you poking around Pinnacle Station, Lieutenant Brown?"

"We stopped to repair our ship," Jacob said. "I was telling Hollick the truth about that. While we were here, we decided to poke around down here and see if the guilds knew anything about a missing fleet."

"So now, Scout Fleet is doing investigative work?" she asked, the laughter back in her voice. "I thought you guys mostly just sat around in space and took notes about arrivals and departures."

"Mission creep," Jacob deadpanned. "We're trying to stay on the trail while its hot until Terranovus sends someone qualified."

"If you want me to free you, you'll have to do better than that."

"Look, Whitney, those Taukkir won't be gone for long," Jacob said. "How about a truce and an agreement to share info in exchange for getting us the hell out of here?"

"Since you seem to know less than me, that seems one-sided. Got anything better?" Jacob just stared at her helplessly, unable to kick-start his brain into gear enough to come up with a better reason for her to cut them loose.

"No? Well...good luck, sport. Oh, and maybe this will help." She pulled the Blazing Sun marker out of a pocket on her tactical vest and flipped to at Jacob. It hit him in the forehead and bounced off onto the deck.

"Thanks."

"Don't mention it. See ya, boys!"

"She's seriously going to leave us tied to the floor?" MG asked.

"She was stalling for time," Murph said. "She's going after Hollick but needed to let him get far enough away that he felt comfortable. Abiyah is probably out there somewhere, ready to intercept him. Right now, we're competitors looking for the same information. She was never going to help us."

"Which leaves us still screwed," Jacob said.

"I still like her," MG said, earning death stares from both his companions.

"This way," Mettler said, trusting that the information Sully had sent to his com unit was accurate. The lower engineering decks of Pinnacle Station were a labyrinth of pipes, cables, and nearly identical alloy bulkheads that went on and on. They'd gotten a short ping from MG's com unit over the public network, which allowed Taylor to get a general area, but it was still a daunting task considering all the places covered by that single public Nexus node.

"If we'd had more than just that single status ping, I might have been able to get a more precise location," Taylor lamented. "As it is, we're going to be— What the shit?"

"Taukkir," Mettler said. They'd had to stop at one of the junctions as a trio of the bulky aliens sprinted by them. "And they're in a big damn hurry to get somewhere."

"You think?" Taylor asked.

"Interesting," Mettler said. "Let's follow and see what's up." He drew his sidearm, a comparatively low-tech pistol that used gunpowder and bullets that wouldn't set off the station alarms if he fired it. Obsidian kept a few cases full of old-style Earth weapons since they seemed to be overlooked in a galaxy full of energy weapons and magnetic projectile drivers.

Taukkir were strong, but not particularly fast, so the humans were able to jog and keep up with them, trying to stay back enough so as not to be noticed. The aliens broke off the main corridor and made four turns back in what looked like a long-disused office complex before halting in front of an open door, where another Taukkir gestured wildly to a dead one on the ground.

"We had nothing to do with it! Why would I kill your buddy, and then come back in here and chain myself to the deck?"

"That's the LT," Mettler whispered. "They must have got themselves caught. Typical."

"Probably MG's fault...dude's an idiot," Taylor said softly.

"That's five of them and two of us," Mettler said. "Do we give them a warning or take out as many as we can before they get organized?"

"I like your enthusiasm, but I think it's still illegal to just murder someone here," Taylor said. "We'll have to talk to them first."

"Fine," Mettler sighed, holding his pistol down against his thigh. "Hey! You! What's going on here?" Given what he knew about Taukkir and their excitability, Mettler had been expecting them to act surprised and jumpy. Instead, they just calmly turned and regarded him.

"Who are you with? These humans, or the Hollick-human?"

"*Hollick?*" Taylor hissed. "What the hell is going on here?" Mettler waved him off, thinking fast about how best to answer.

"We're with the humans you've captured," Mettler said. "How can we go about getting them released?"

"You won't be," a voice said from behind the two Marines. "We'll be taking them, and you, with us."

"And who the hell are you?" Mettler demanded.

"We represent the Concordian Guild, and you will be coming with us to answer some questions."

"Oh, for fuck's sake." Taylor threw his hands up in disgust. "Is there anyone else that's going to join this party?"

10

"This is your marker?"

"It is," Murph said. Taylor and Mettler had been hustled into the room the others had been held in and the interrogation began. Apparently, the guild rep had changed his mind about moving them. Jacob was in no shape to handle being questioned and had Murph take over for him while he lay on the floor with his eyes closed.

The alien took out a hand held device and placed the marker in the slot without any further questions. Murph's stomach dropped as he realized the marker wasn't just a fancy coin to flash but had an active data core that could be accessed. The guild leadership likely had the right decryption codes, and it was equally likely the information on the marker would expose their con. He sat silently while the alien looked through the information on the small golden disk.

"Which of you is Jacob Brown?"

"That'd be him." Murph pointed to Jacob. "He took a pretty good beating and isn't feeling too perky right now."

"I see you used to run cash loads for one of the Points...the one who was just recently killed. You freelancing or have you affiliated yourself with another Point?"

In the Blazing Sun syndicate, there was Saditava Mok at the top, and below him were twelve captains—Points—responsible for executing his orders. Each Point was responsible for a different aspect of the overall operation, but all reported back to Mok. The ship they'd stolen had been running money for a Point that had intended to try and overthrow Mok. Jacob had informed the crime boss of the plot, resulting in Jacob being allowed to continue breathing. The Point that had been intent on betrayal hadn't been so fortunate.

"Our captain has an understanding with Mok himself, if you can believe that, but we're operating independently at the moment," Murph said carefully.

"This doesn't say anything about working for Mok, but it does have a blanket protection clause attached to it," the alien tossed the marker back to Murph. "Not many people get that, not even some of Blazing Sun's leadership. We will honor it."

Murph wasn't entirely sure what was happening, but he saw the guild rep order his people to stow their weapons and release them, so he just went with it. He'd assumed the marker had information stored on it like a memory core, but from what he'd just seen, it seemed to be more like an encryption key that allowed access to information stored on a Blazing Sun server somewhere on the Nexus. It made more sense as it allowed the syndicate to edit information immediately rather than have markers with bad information floating around out there. Mok must have edited their marker to add Jacob as the owner/operator of the combat shuttle they jacked. Talk about dumb luck.

"If you'd like, we can have the Taukkir gang brought in and you can do with them as you see fit," the rep said. "I will point out that once they realized who you were, they did come and get us."

"I don't see any need to involve them further," Jacob said, sitting up and rubbing the back of his head. "Just a misunderstanding, and we're not trying to make any turbulence in your area here. Let's just leave well enough alone since nobody was permanently injured or killed."

"A wise and generous decision, Captain. The security manager here on Pinnacle has an understanding with us, but that doesn't extend to allowing bodies to start piling up for disposal even down here. Now, I suppose the only question I have is, what were you doing down here inquiring after us to begin with?"

"Just looking for some gainful employment. We stopped here for repairs, but right now our hold is empty, and we don't have anything else lined up."

"Preference of cargo?"

"No narcotics, no slaves," Jacob said. "We've had bad luck in that area before."

"If not slaves, how about passengers?" the alien asked.

"Passengers?"

"I'll explain further in a more appropriate setting," the alien said. "Please, take some time to get rested and seek medical attention. When you're ready to discuss work, just come back down to this level and my people will find and escort you to me."

Before Jacob could reply, the alien had turned and walked out of the room, his people falling in behind him. The Marines just looked at each other in confusion.

"Let's get you to the infirmary, LT," Mettler said after scanning Jacob's neural implant to take stock of his injuries. "The damage isn't that bad. You probably feel bad enough, though, that you don't believe that."

"Sounds about right," Jacob said.

The pitiful group slunk back to the lifts, their first foray into the underbelly of Pinnacle Station a resounding failure. Jacob looked forward to being treated in one of the top-tier medical units in the upper decks, and his men wanted to go back to their suite and lick their wounds. Out of everybody, Jacob's injuries were by far the worst, and it didn't help he'd already been hurt before they even came down to the lower decks.

By the time they made it back to where their suite was, it felt like they'd been transported to another world, and their misadventures down below were just a dream. They drew some startled looks as they shuffled to their unit, but nobody called for security or tried to stop them. When the door to their suite opened with a soft sigh, the Marines all seemed to make the same noise...right up until they looked inside.

"Hello, boys." The Viper lounged on one of the couches while her partner, Abiyah, sat at the small bar.

"This day has to fucking end sometime," Mettler said. "It just can't keep going on and on."

"Obsidian has checked in, sir. No indication they got your abort orders."

"Of course," Webb sighed. "What other good tidings have you brought me?"

"We've identified two NIS agents and our first One World faction spy in the relocation crews, sir," Bennet said, then hesitated.

"What?" Webb snapped.

"Part of Lieutenant Brown's report said that Elton Hollick had been at the drop before them, looking for the same information," his aide said, flinching as Webb's face morphed through various expressions of pure rage.

"Why am I just hearing about this?"

"It hadn't been filtered through the analysts yet to verify it was legit," Bennet said, unflappable as always in the face of his boss's barely contained temper. "They'd sent your office a heads up that they'd checked in and to expect the report once it had been processed."

"Stupid mother—"

"There's something else," Bennet headed off another tirade. "You'll like this even less."

"I highly doubt that."

"We've had independent verification that the Viper is working in the area, possibly on the same problem as Obsidian." The news stopped Webb dead in his tracks. He'd met Carolyn Whitney back on the mission when he'd been sent to kill Jason Burke, Jacob's father. In fact, her partner, Abiyah, had been on Webb's kill team.

"Who verified it?" he asked.

"Filtered down through the shared intel reports with NIS," Bennet said. "She was spotted in the Concordian Cluster, and an observational asset indicated she departed the area about the time Brown's report says they were doing the same. The asset is through the Zadra Network, but it's listed as a Class I informant."

"So, the intel is clean," Webb murmured. "If she's chasing the same thing, we have to assume an outside source hired her. The Viper won't work NIS or Naval contracts."

"Orders?"

"We need to get in touch with Brown and warn him. Obsidian cannot handle Whitney. She'd tear through them like tissue paper and kill them all without remorse if they get in her way," Webb said.

"No mean trick with all the spies around here," Bennet said.

"I think we need to relocate for the time being," Webb said after a few minutes. "Alert the *Kentucky* to prepare for our arrival. Just us, you and me. We'll sneak up there and use her com suite to make sure nobody gets a good listen at what we're doing."

"Aye, sir." Bennet spun and left the office, closing the door softly behind him.

"Chased out of my own damn office again," Webb griped, turning back to the windows.

The UES *Kentucky* was one of two NAVSOC command and control ships Webb had available. She was a frigate-class vessel dressed up to look like an average, nondescript bulk freighter of the kind that littered the quadrant, but she had an incredibly sophisticated avionics and weapons package that made her able to sniff out intel, run operations from a remote location, or shoot her way out of trouble, if necessary. Webb had used the ship once before to escape the confines of Taurus Station when it became clear his base had too many security leaks. The fact that was still a problem galled him, but he had no time to deal with it at the moment.

A harsh banging at his door made him almost jump out of his skin, his thoughts flitting away as he turned, ready to defend himself if need be. What walked in was, hopefully, friendly.

"Captain Marcus Webb," the bass voice rumbled from the towering figure. "Greetings."

"707," Webb said to the battlesynth that had stormed his office. "Is this a social call?"

"Of course not," 707 said. Webb just sighed. It was easy to think they were all the same since they were machines that looked almost identical, but their personalities varied as much as humans' did. That being said, he missed Lucky's sense of humor and warmth. 707—who refused to take any sort of name other than his designation—was ramrod straight and did nothing that wasn't in furtherance of his goals or mission.

"We alerted you that we would be coming."

"Oh, shit...that's right." Webb snapped his fingers. "We've had a lot going on with the move and the— You know what? It's not important. Is this something that can be done quickly? I have to catch a shuttle up to the *Kentucky* to handle my field ops remotely for the time being."

"I will accompany you," 707 said, just stating it as if there were no issues with a non-affiliated alien superweapon waltzing onto one of the most secret vessels in the entire United Earth Navy.

"I, uh...I suppose we could work that out," Webb said. "You're still technically working with us as an advisor, right?"

"I have not been notified of a change in status," 707 said. "Unless you have revoked it, I still hold the assimilated rank of colonel when advising human military forces."

"Then let's go," Webb said, standing up. "You can give me some advice on the ride up. Is it just you?"

"I have two others standing outside your door." Webb suppressed a shudder at the sheer amount of firepower loitering around his command center. If they had a mind, three battlesynths could kill everyone in the building before anyone could be alerted to mount a defense that had a chance of stopping them.

"Plenty of room on the shuttle."

"We will be bringing our own ship. It is small."

"Okay, then...plenty of room in the hangar bay. Let's go."

"Whitney," Jacob moaned. "We have to stop meeting like this. I feel like you're stalking me...if you want a date, just ask."

"Not bad," the Viper said, smoothly rising to her feet. "Snappy, decent timing. Much more fun than most of the stuffy Navy types I meet out here since Earth started groping about blindly in the quadrant. But just so you know, I *am* stalking you."

"Since I'm still breathing, I'm guessing Mok didn't hire you to kill me?" Jacob asked hopefully.

"Mok has his own crews for that and, for the last damn time, I'm not an assassin," she said. "Your benevolent crime lord also lacks the artistry or subtlety to hire someone like me. He likes to make a statement, sending a sledge hammer to do the work of a scalpel."

"Whitney, I'm literally almost dead on my feet," Jacob said. "What's the deal here?"

"I missed Hollick," she said. "Abiyah was staged up in the best place to ambush him as he fled back to his ship, but he slipped through somehow. His ship is already gone."

"You're after Hollick? Who hired you?"

"I'm not after him, but he's my best bet to get the information I need since he seems to be a step ahead of you. I wanted to get him back on my ship where I could...encourage...his cooperation away from the prying eyes of Pinnacle Security," she said. "After that, I'd probably sell him back to Michael Welford."

"So, what are you after?" Jacob slid down onto the couch with Mettler's help.

"I'll call a medic team from one of the infirmaries," Mettler said, walking over to the panel by the entryway.

"I'm hunting the same thing you most likely are: the composite fleet that punched the ConFed in the nose with that attack on Miressa," Whitney continued. "I thought I had an inside line since I heard of a certain merc crew I'm on okay terms with had been involved, but they're not answering my calls through any of the usual channels."

"Merc crew," Jacob repeated numbly. "One that happens to have another human in it?" Whitney looked surprised for a moment.

"Ah," she said. "I suppose Welford and Webb would make sure their forward observers were aware of Omega Force. Yes…the crew has a human captain, and rumor has it they took out a ConFed dreadnaught during the battle, so it stands to reason they'd be hiding along with the other ships."

Jacob's head swam, and not entirely from the brain trauma. Omega Force, his father's crew, had been involved with this insurrection against the ConFed. Did Webb know this? His feelings about his father had recently shifted from a flat, blind hatred to something more…complicated. He was surprised at his own hesitancy when it came to reporting to NAVSOC that the old man might have been involved in something that could put Earth in danger. Would they send a kill team after him…again?

"So, you're looking for the *Eagle's Talon*, as well?" Jacob asked.

"Captain Edgar's ship," Abiyah provided when Whitney just looked confused. "Part of the escort force from the UEN."

"Oh." She shook her head. "My employer is looking for a different ship, but the two will likely be together still."

"You're after the *Defiant*," Murph said. "Seeladas Dalton hired you to find her missing strike force, likely asked you to either capture or kill Admiral Kellea Colleran."

"You're a sharp one." Whitney winked. "I can only confirm my target…and yes, it is a kill or capture contract. My employer was quite annoyed that her most trusted military officer took off with a whole strike force after trying to kick off an intergalactic civil war. The Cridal Cooperative is in no position to fend off the ConFed, so they'll probably offer Admiral Colleran on a platter to Miressa to smooth things over."

"I know a little about this interconnected dynamic," Murph said. "If you hurt Kellea Colleran, Burke *will* kill you."

"I can handle Jason Burke," Whitney scoffed. Jacob had been watching her eyes as she said it and could see it was all bluster. She was genuinely afraid of his father. What could he have done to put that sort of fear into a legendary assassin loaded with cybernetic upgrades to the point she was barely human anymore?

"Can you handle Crusher and Lucky, as well?" Murph pressed. "His whole crew will come down on you. I know you're some badass killer from the boundary worlds, but this—"

"Why do you even care?" Whitney snapped.

"I don't," Murph said. "At least not about you personally. But your trying to take out the admiral could create complications for us trying to complete our own mission."

"And?"

"I suppose there's no point in appealing to your humanity?" Jacob asked. "If we don't recover the *Talon*, Earth could be in the crosshairs."

"You suppose right, Lieutenant," Whitney said. "I was taken from Earth in the 1940s. You think I relate to anyone on that planet anymore?"

"How about you?" Jacob asked Abiyah. "You ready to risk the lives of everyone on your homeworld to fill some contract?"

"We're done here," Whitney said before her partner could answer. "I came here because I thought we might trade some useful intel with each other, but I can see now that you idiots have nothing. If Webb had any brains, he'd recall you before you really screw something up out here."

"What the hell was that all about?" Taylor asked once the pair had left the suite.

"She was fishing," Jacob said. "They don't have any leads, and she hoped we might have gotten something from NIS to point her in the right direction. She's also probably bugged this suite so keep in mind they're likely listening right now."

"Agreed," Murph said. "She seemed genuinely agitated, but she's so far removed from humanity and part machine now to the point I'm not sure she even has real emotions. That flirty act she uses is something she uses like a weapon."

The conversation died off as Mettler came back into the main room trailed by two med techs from Pinnacle Services, a private company that handled all the hospitality and public services for the upper decks of the station. They came over and scanned Jacob's neural implant so it could tell them his species and pertinent medical information. Humans were now officially in the Master Species Database, so the staff on Pinnacle could effectively treat him, although most of what they did was pump him full of medical nanobots and slave them to his neural implant. With the wide availability of the miraculous little machines, this was the standard treatment for nearly every species and most afflictions.

Once Mettler paid the med techs and hustled them out of the suite, the energy seemed to be sucked out of the group. Jacob's eyes drooped as the meds kicked in, and the rest of his team, not able to freely discuss the mission, stared off into space. Jacob felt a bit lost, and it wasn't just because of the meds casting a fog over his brain. This mission had seemed fairly straight forward: go get a likely location from their contact, lay eyes on the *Eagle's Talon*, call in the cavalry, then go home. He needed to talk to someone back on Taurus Station, but Webb had him so paranoid about spies and traitors that calling the 3rd Scout Corps Operations Center was iffy. Fleet OPS was out of the question. Even NAVSOC HQ had lots of eyes around that could intercept any message he tried to get to Webb.

"We'll talk to Big Boss tomorrow when we can get a secure slipcom node," Murph said, using their nickname for Captain Webb. Little Boss was the name of Commander John Toma, 3rd Scout Corps' commanding officer.

"Agreed," Jacob slurred. "Everyone, get some rack time. We'll try to get out of here as early as possible. Taylor, did you talk to the crew lead working on the ship about that thing?"

"Huh? Oh! Yeah. He said he found three and removed them," Taylor said. "The ship should be ready soon."

"Good. We need to get out of here ASAP." Jacob struggled to his feet. "Lots of unfriendly people about. Crash out, boys. One person on watch, three-hour shifts, fight amongst yourselves on who goes first."

They were still arguing by the time he reached the master bedroom and flopped onto the soft mattress.

11

"We good?"

"This settles the account, sir," the crew boss said. "And I thank you for the generous bonus for me and my crew...I promise you won't be disappointed with our work."

"I'm sure I won't," Jacob said, handing over yet another credit chit. "And this is to help you and your people forget you ever saw us." When the boss squeezed the chit to activate the display and see how many credits had been loaded onto it, his eyes widened.

"Consider yourself forgotten, good sir. Your hangar fees are paid for the next six rotations so you and your crew can depart at your leisure."

"My thanks," Jacob said. The rest of the crew climbed all over the dilapidated Eshquarian combat shuttle, inspecting all the work that had been done. They'd paid to get the major problems worked out, but the ship was far from what Sully would consider mission capable, or even completely safe. More than money, the problem was time. To properly refurbish the shuttle to even the bare minimum of UEN safety specs, it'd have to be almost completely dismantled and rebuilt with fresh components. NAVSOC was given a lot of leeway in this area, and Jacob was able to ignore most of what would get a Naval vessel decommissioned and focus on all of the safety of flight issues.

"They didn't bother blending these patches into the rest of the hull, but everything looks solid," Sully said when he walked up. "All of the system work they did appears to be up to snuff, too. Taylor and I just ran a full onboard diagnostic, and short of firing up the slip-drive inside the hangar, it looks like most of the major issues have been addressed. She's also been fully serviced and provisioned like you requested."

"So, we're all dressed up with nowhere to go," Jacob said.

"Huh?"

"The ships ready, we're ready, but we don't have a destination or a target," Jacob said. "Hopefully, our pending meeting with the guild master will kick up something. Is there power on the ship? I'd like to use the com room aboard her rather than one of the disgusting public booths."

"She's on dock power." Sully pointed to the thick, multi-conductor cable that snaked across the deck and plugged into the ship near the port engine nacelle. "Slip-com node is already powered up from the testing we did."

"Thanks."

Jacob walked around the ship once, checking all the work he could see from the hangar deck. The shuttle was surprisingly large on the outside given how cramped it felt on the inside. He saw a new section of hull patching that covered where the new slip-com array would sit. The newer slip-com systems had field generators, which were miniaturized and built into the node, but this ship still had the older array that needed space away from the interference of all the other running avionic systems.

Inside the cargo bay, his Marines inventoried all the gear to make sure the repair crew hadn't helped themselves to anything. The armory was locked up tight and still secure, but the rest of their gear was in transit crates strapped down in the hold with cargo nets. If they were missing anything, it'd be better to find out before they left.

"LT," Mettler nodded to him. "You're looking better."

"Well, that's good because I still feel like shit," Jacob said. "Once you're done in here, go ahead and get set up for a trip back down to the lower levels. I'm going to check in, and then we'll be ready to head down and try to salvage this mess."

Jacob left them to their work and slipped into the cramped com room, a secure little alcove with only room to stand and face the terminals. He slid the hatch closed, the anti-snooping countermeasures activating automatically once he flipped the switch to lock it. The first address he entered into the terminal once the node booted up and stabilized was for a dead-drop message box he and Webb had set up as a way to bypass the normal channels. He didn't expect anything to be there, so he was surprised when he saw two new messages, one from Webb, the other from his aide, Lieutenant Bennet.

He read through Bennet's first and all it said was that Captain Webb was relocating his operations temporarily to the *Kentucky*, his preferred C&C ship, and that Big Boss wanted to be briefed personally on what in the hell they'd been up to. The next message, from Webb, was actually a set of orders canceling his current mission and recalling him to Taurus Station. He frowned as he read the new orders, confused as to what might have changed.

Part of him was secretly relieved they were being recalled back to Terranovus, where someone else would be put in command of Obsidian. The other part of him was disgusted by his relief at being able to shirk his duty. He read through the message again, and there was little ambiguity to it; come home, regroup, reorganize, and live to fight another day. Reading between the lines and knowing Captain Webb somewhat on a personal level, he also took the message to mean he may have lost his commanding officer's confidence. Letting Obsidian stumble around blindly in the wilds while a civil war between ancient intergalactic superpowers was brewing could be just as dangerous as Edgars keeping the *Eagle's Talon* attached to a rogue Cridal strike force.

After taking a moment to collect his thoughts, he reached for the encrypted tablet Taylor had put in the alcove. After logging in, he searched for the address for the *Kentucky*'s com section and punched it into the node terminal, waiting as two ends negotiated a connection so the encryption routines could do the same. It was almost ninety seconds later before the bored face of a specialist first class resolved on the screen.

"Code in," she said.

"Obsidian Actual, bravo sierra six one eight kilo."

"Current status."

"Dixie Romeo," Jacob said, using the code phrase to let the operator know he wasn't under duress and the call wasn't an emergency.

"Standby," she said, and the screen went black. When it flicked back on, it wasn't the bored com tech staring back at him.

"Brown! Where the hell have you been?!"

"Sir!" Jacob barked, startled. He jumped and stood at attention, banging his head on the curved ceiling of the cramped alcove. "We've not had a functional slip-com node since halfway to our first waypoint. We've just gotten the ship spaceworthy again, and this was my first chance to contact you directly."

"Where are you?" Captain Webb asked.

"Pinnacle Station, sir."

"Why? What happened to the ship?"

"Secondary fuel manifold blew a fitting and jettisoned most of our fuel. Pinnacle was the closest place we could safely reach to effect repairs," Jacob said. "While here, Murph and I had a plan on how to use our ship's former ownership as inroads to tracking down the *Talon*. I've only just now read your orders calling us off the hunt."

"You are such a pain in the ass, Brown," Webb sighed. "I'd love to make you suffer for it, but most of the time it's legitimately not your fault."

"Thank you, sir."

"Shut the hell up."

"Yes, sir."

Webb looked off-screen for a moment, seeming to be typing on a terminal at his desk, completely ignoring Jacob. This went on for the next five minutes or so. Jacob simply stood there and said nothing. If the military had given him one useful skill in life, it was the ability to wait around for no reason at all without knowing how long he might be there.

"Are you standing at attention?" Webb finally asked.

"Uh, yes, sir."

"Good. Stay like that." Webb plinked away on his terminal, again ignoring Jacob for the better part of ten minutes before turning back to the camera.

"Tell me your idea on how you're going to find the *Talon*, and then I'll let you know if I'm still scrubbing your mission or not."

Jacob filled him in on his theory that the fleet might run to the Saabror Protectorate to hide since ConFed Intelligence couldn't easily operate there. Webb remained a statue as he explained how he was going to use his Blazing Sun marker to try and get a smuggling load into the Protectorate, and then, once past their border fleet, go snoop around a few places their database indicated might be interesting.

"What you lack in brains you make up for in grit and ambition, I'll give you Obsidian boys that much," Webb said after Jacob had wrapped up his brief. "So, what was your plan if Saabror Security caught you actually smuggling something into their territory?"

"We didn't really have a *plan* per se—"

"Do you idiots even know how big the Protectorate is? You were just going to fly about randomly and ask the locals if they'd seen a big shiny UEN ship?"

"That wasn't *exactly* what we were going to do. This plan is still evolving—"

"Let me help you out," Webb said. "Your idea about the Protectorate is a good one, but you don't have the resources to pull it off. More importantly, we already know they're not there. The Zadra Network has come through, and we've received positive confirmation on one of the Cridal frigates when it flew too close to Colton Hub on their way out of ConFed space. We can reasonably assume the *Talon* will still be with Kellea Colleran's formation.

"The smuggling angle is interesting but dangerous. We give Scout

Fleet a *lot* of rope to hang themselves with, so be very careful about using legitimately illegal enterprise as cover. UEAS Command has been known to come down on NAVSOC crews for infractions even when it was in the service of the greater good."

"I understand, sir."

"No, I don't think you do. Listen to me harder than you've ever listened to anything in your life, Lieutenant. *Be. Very. Careful,*" Webb annunciated each word as he leaned into the camera. "Am I clear?"

"Crystal, sir. Does this mean we're back on mission?"

"I'm sending the data dump now," Webb said. "I'm already moving forces out in the direction of the Cridal ship sighting so they'll be ready to move when you lay eyes on the *Talon*. I'm putting an insane amount of trust in your judgement and ability to operate beyond the bounds of your experience and training, so don't screw me over, Lieutenant. If you feel like you're in over your head, pull the plug and bring it home...no recriminations."

"Aye, sir."

"I'm going to keep Diamond out near the Cluster as a contingency in case the frigate sighting was a ruse or the ship wasn't part of the larger fleet," Webb said. "Good luck."

"Yes, sir. Obsidian, out."

He had an odd relationship with Captain Webb thanks to the connection the NAVSOC commander had with Jason Burke. Normally, some pissant lieutenant wouldn't be calling a captain for something as mundane as a mission report, but Webb had taken special interest in him given who his father was, and the fact Obsidian had taken a beating from the time he'd been assigned to the team. He took Webb's overly-military way of speaking to him as a sign of affection from a man who wasn't comfortable with telling a subordinate he gave a damn if he lived or died.

After shutting down the node, Jacob leaned back against the bulkhead, blowing out a huge breath that was part exasperation, part relief. He was still on mission...yay! Also, he was still on mission... goddamnit! When he secured all the equipment and left the alcove, his mood worsened when he saw who stood at the base of the ramp.

"Whitney?!" he yelled in exasperation. "What the hell do you want *this* time?"

"Lieutenant Brown," the Viper said, looking mildly embarrassed for being there. "I have had a change of heart. Perhaps we might work together since our goals happen to align right now."

"In other words, Hollick escaped, and now you're back to not having a clue where to find your target," Jacob said. "Or—and this is equally plausible—you do have a location but need us to serve as a distraction and/or cannon fodder. Right?"

"You're correct in the first part, not even close with the second," Whitney said. "I'm not sure what you've heard about me, Lieutenant, but I work with care and precision. The only people who need be afraid are my targets. I don't put people in harm's way, and I don't abide collateral damage."

"What's your proposal?"

"Just an information swap," Whitney said. "No need to fly together. In fact, it'd be better if we didn't."

"But if you don't know anything, what do I get out of this?" Jacob asked.

"I never said I didn't know *anything*, I just said I needed a location."

The pair stared each other down for another few seconds while Jacob chewed through the problem in his mind. Sharing classified intel with the notorious assassin—or whatever she was pretending to be—was out of the question, but perhaps he could nudge her in the right direction if she was able to give him something useful in return. The data dump that Captain Webb had promised hadn't arrived yet, so he had precious little to offer in any case.

"I might have a general area that would help you start your search," he said finally. "What do you have in exchange?"

"For that bit of intel, I could possibly give you the exact composition of the insurrectionist fleet," she countered. "With that, you'll be able to tailor your approach when trying to recover your ship." Jacob pretended to think about it, but she had him. Knowing exactly the classes and numbers of the ships their QRF would be facing once he gave them the *Talon*'s location was crucial information. It would allow the Navy to prep the force, and then refine it once he confirmed the information himself.

"One of the ships was spotted near Colton Hub when it flew too close to the station," Jacob said, putting on a show of giving it reluctantly.

"The Hub," Whitney murmured. "Interesting."

"How so?" Jacob asked.

"It's not important," she said, tossing him a datacard. "It's all on there."

"You were just carrying this around?"

"Let's just say I had faith in your good judgement," she said, winking. Jacob could only laugh at how easily she'd played him.

"I'm sure I'll see you out there."

"In that boneshaker you're flying? You'll either get there much later than I will or, more likely, not at all."

"Boneshaker?" Mettler laughed. "My great-grandfather used to say that."

"That's probably because your great-grandpappy and I are probably about the same age," Whitney said. "While he was fighting in the Second World War, I was busy being abducted by aliens and sold in a slave market."

"Sounds like a hell of a story," Mettler said.

"Not really. That's pretty much it," Whitney said.

"What's it mean?" Jacob asked.

"It's what they used to call junk cars that were beaten up and likely to leave you broken and bloody on the side of the road," Whitney said. "Seems to describe your ship."

"It describes this whole damn mission so far," Jacob grumbled.

"We good, Lieutenant?" Whitney asked, seeming anxious to be on her way.

"We're good. Safe travels."

"You too." She eyed the shuttle up and down one more time. "You'll need it."

"I feel like we'll be seeing her again," Murph said after she left.

"Oh yeah," Jacob agreed. "Probably sooner than later. Come on... let's get this job done and get out of here."

"We expected you sooner, but it's not as if we had a set appointment. This way."

"I thought it would be best to get our ship in order before coming down here and talking to you about work," Jacob said, trailing behind the same guild master who had interceded on their behalf with the Taukkir.

"Sensible," the alien said, sounding bored.

Jacob had come down with Murph and MG again, wanting to show confidence by not increasing his detail size while still allowing Taylor and Mettler to position themselves close by in case things turned to shit...again. They were led back down through the maze of corridors, past ear-splittingly loud engineering sections, through what appeared to be an illegal squatters' development in what used to be a service bay before reaching a well-guarded entrance.

The three were patted down, relieved of their weapons and com units, and told they'd get them back on the way out. Jacob just nodded and triggered one last burst transmission from his own com unit before handing it to the sentry. It would hit the local Nexus and let the other two know the last area they'd been. Given the level of security the guild masters had in place around their lair on Pinnacle, it would be more likely Mettler and Taylor would just be calling into NAVSOC to let them know where the others had disappeared to if they didn't come back in the allotted time.

"Nice hideout," Murph remarked.

"Pinnacle Security knows exactly where we're at, of course," their guide said. "This is all just added security against the locals and any rivals who arrive and feel like setting up shop. Speaking of which, what is it you think we can do for you?"

"Just looking for a paying load," Jacob said. "We're heading out towards Colton Hub to escape some unpleasantness in the Concordian Cluster and thought it'd be nicer to be paid to fly there instead of dead-heading all the way out."

"I had thought you were going into Saabror territory? This certainly changes what I might have available," the alien said. "What sort of cargo are you willing to carry?"

"We'll be passing through the heart of ConFed territory in an Eshquarian ship," Jacob said. "Even as old as she is, there's still a better than normal chance we get stopped and boarded when we hit a provisioning waypoint. Ideally, we'd be carrying something easily hidden in the smuggler's pods and not something we have to strap to the deck in the hold."

"That certainly limits your usefulness. Most of what we transfer through here is quite large, more fit for an actual cargo ship and not your small shuttle."

"So, there's nothing available?" Jacob asked. He could tell by the alien's extended explanation he was being set up for something.

"I didn't say that, I'm just trying to determine your comfort level," the alien said. "Your marker status helps us bypass lengthy security checks, of course. Normally, Pinnacle Security won't bother trying to run a sting down here, but ConFed Intelligence and Eshquarian Import Control have both run operations trying to clear us out of here. As you can see...we've outlasted one of them already."

Definitely being set up for something.

"And I'm sure you're well aware, my marker will give me safe passage through any Blazing Sun-held territory, right?" Jacob asked.

"It certainly helps," the alien admitted. "Nobody would dare mess with the load on one of Mok's ships except a brazen few."

"Let's speed this up. You obviously have something in mind. Just tell me what it is, and I'll let you know if I feel like taking the risk."

"It's a data core," the alien said after a long, uncomfortable moment. "As it turns out, it needs to go to Colton Hub, and you just happen to be going that way."

"What's the size? Is it packed in a way it can be stored outside the pressurized zones?" Jacob asked, businesslike. He knew a real smuggler wouldn't ask, or even want to know, whose data core it was or what was on it. Asking questions like that was a surefire way to peg him as something other than what he claimed.

"The hardened case it's in is about this big—" the alien used his hands to mime a box about forty centimeters across, "but it can't be stored on the outer hull, if that's what you have in mind. The case is passive...no internal heat source, but it is impervious to radiation and can't be detected by normal scans."

"That works just as well," Jacob said. "What's this job pay?"

"Sixty thousand credits. Half now, half on completion."

"Sixty *thousand* credits for a courier run?" Jacob could hardly believe it. "This makes me think this item has people pursuing it who might want to take it from me."

"This is a take it or leave it deal," the alien said. "A runner with a marker coming here looking for work is unbelievably convenient but hardly critical. I can find half a dozen other crews who would kill for the chance to earn that kind of money for a delivery run."

"Calm down, we'll take the job," Jacob said. "We're going to be leaving shortly. Can you have it to the hangar soon?"

"I'll be giving it to you now. Be aware that once you touch this case, you are entering into a binding agreement that you will do everything in your power to deliver it to the agreed upon point. Your lives mean nothing to the people moving this. If some of you must die to protect the case, that's what you will do."

"Binding agreement with whom?" Jacob asked. "I'm already under agreement with Blazing Sun...I thought this was their cargo."

"It's going to them, but it's not from them. It's also not important you know who it's from other than the fact they have the means and the will to hunt you down and destroy you should you try anything foolish," the alien said.

"Fair enough," Jacob said. "Let's get this show on the road." The alien cocked its head at that for a moment before turning and waving to one of the guards to bring the case forward.

"Indeed," the alien said, pulling out a slim device and handing it to Jacob. "This is the information that will get you to your contact on Colton Hub. It is inaccessible until it detects it's within the Hub itself, then it will provide you the information you need. Any attempt to tamper with it or cheat the security measures and we'll know."

Without another word, he turned and walked off as the case-bearer came up to them. The whole meeting had been bizarre. They hadn't been given any names from the people they'd met within the guild on Pinnacle, told instead it was better if they couldn't remember who they'd spoken to. Then, the guild's secret bunker in the bowels of Pinnacle had been oddly empty with only the people who absolutely had to be there to give Jacob the case being in the room.

"Brown, you there?" Sully's voice came in over Jacob's earpiece once he reclaimed his com unit from the door sentry.

"I got you, Sully," Jacob said, waiting as his team finished collecting their weapons. "What's going on?"

"You might want to get back here on the double," the pilot said. "A ConFed task force just arrived and are heading right for Pinnacle. They're broadcasting their intent to board and search any ships of interest. The rats are currently fleeing, and unless we want to get caught up in a blockade, we need to get going."

"On our way!" Jacob said, breaking into a run. "All units, scram, scram, scram! Back to the ship as fast as you can run."

"What's happening?" Murph shouted.

"No idea, but I have a feeling it might have to do with this." Jacob waved the hard case he'd been given as he ran.

12

"Any change?"

"No, sir."

    Lieutenant Commander Morse paced the small bridge of the *Zephyr*. Morse was the commanding officer of Scout Team Diamond, and for the last six months, his crew had been yanked from one side of the quadrant to the other by 3rd Scout Corps. The scuttlebutt from Taurus Station was that Diamond was getting jerked around because Obsidian kept shitting the bed. The other team's CO, Commander Mosler, had been one of the best in Scout Fleet...but he'd been killed in action, and now Obsidian was being led by some rookie jarhead lieutenant. Morse didn't pretend to understand the inner workings at HQ, but he couldn't understand why Commander Toma didn't just recall Obsidian and stand them down. They seemed to be doing more harm than good right now, if the rumors were to be believed. Of course, it might have something to do with NAVSOC's big boss, Webb, seeming to take such a special interest in Obsidian. Commander Toma probably figured it was a battle not worth fighting and let his boss meddle as he saw fit.

"I've never been put into a holding pattern *after* being given clearance to de-orbit," Morse griped. "What the hell is going on?"

"Port Control still isn't giving me a clear answer on when we'll be able to land, sir," the pilot said. "You want me to ask for an orbital insertion vector and take us back up?"

"No, no." Morse waved him off. "We're already down here, let's just wait to see what happens."

The *Zephyr* banked gently into another turn that would take them back away from the starport they were trying to land at. They'd been stuck in a holding pattern for the better part of three hours, something Morse had never seen happen, especially on such a third-rate world. What made it all the more intolerable was that they were coming in as the cleanup crew, talking to secondary contacts within the Concordian Cluster after he'd already heard from a friend that NAVSOC knew the rogue fleet wasn't in the area.

Morse sat back in his seat, forcing himself to stop fidgeting and making his pilot and Marine captain nervous. Something felt off, but he couldn't put his finger on it. On the situation display, he could see that there were only two other ships in the holding pattern and that some vessels coming down from orbit were being given direct landing vectors. The government of Madir-3 wasn't wholly corrupt like a lot of other vassal worlds, but they were just willing enough to take bribes that Morse was starting to think about cracking into his expense account.

"Sir, the two other ships are climbing up and away from the pattern," the pilot said, frowning. "Climbing away hard."

"Did they get tired of—" a brilliant flash outside lit up the bridge, and a deafening thunderclap shook Morse off his feet.

"Incoming fire!" the pilot shouted, slamming the throttles against the stops and pitching the ship hard to port.

"From where?!" Morse said, forcing his brain back into gear.

"Those shots came from orbit!" Captain Delco said from his station. "Three shots!"

"At us?! Delco, call this in and—"

"Sir, we potentially have an issue," Lieutenant Bennet whispered to Webb. Things on the *Kentucky* were relatively quiet, and the NAVSOC chief had volunteered to take a bridge watch while the ship loitered in orbit over Terranovus.

"Yes?"

"We've had some incoming reports of various Scout Fleet ships and units coming under fire...not all of them have checked back in," Bennet said.

"How many attacks?"

"Four, sir. Two in the Concordian Cluster, one on a 2nd Scout Corps trawler near the Saabror border, and the *Northstar*." Bennet looked around the quiet bridge, seemingly not comfortable talking about it in the open.

"The two in the Cluster...Diamond?"

"Their distress call was cut short, and now they're not responding, sir."

"Fuck," Webb hissed. "The *Northstar*?"

"Damaged, but Captain Saraceno managed to fight back and win. He said he's collecting the wreckage for analysis."

The *Northstar* was 2nd Scout Corps' premier ship, a purpose-built machine that looked like a battered old bulk freighter but could punch back like a newer destroyer. Her CO, Captain John Saraceno, had racked up an impressive list of successful missions and had become one of Webb's go-to tools for anything from discreet observations to direct action interdictions.

"Tell Captain Saraceno to get his ship back to port," Webb said, rubbing his head. "Get our NIS liaison up here. We'll need their help to see who survived and who did this. Send a message to Obsidian, warning them that it looks like someone is targeting deployed NAVSOC units."

"Sir?"

"It isn't obvious to you? Catch up, man. Someone has leaked operational data to our enemies, and they're using it to poke out our eyes. Without Scout Fleet out there, we have no direct intel. Get to work."

"Aye, sir."

Once his aide was gone, Webb reached over to the touch-panel on his right and called up the *Kentucky*'s CO, Commander Duncan.

"*Sir?*"

"Send someone up to relieve me, Duncan," Webb said. "We've had something big come up. Better prep her for departure, too. I want to be able to break orbit at a moment's notice."

"*Aye, sir, I'm on it. I'm sending Lieutenant Commander Teague to relieve you now.*"

Now that he had nothing to do but wait for relief and for Bennet to get the NIS agent out of the rack, the icy hand of true fear wrapped its fingers around Webb's heart. The units that had been attacked represented nearly a quarter of deployed Scout Fleet units, but they hadn't been assigned to the same mission. This meant these were either random attacks against astronomical probability, or an enemy had access to real-time intel on his deployed units and had chosen now to act. The near-simultaneous nature of the attack told him the smart money was on the latter, but he needed to keep an open mind and let the evidence dictate his response.

"Damnit!" He snarled, smashing a fist into the armrest of his seat, making most of the bridge crew jump. This couldn't have come at a worse time—something that further bolstered his theory these were not random attacks—and he had no choice but to leave his remaining units on-mission. If they didn't kick up the location of the *Eagle's Talon* soon, he'd be answering some very uncomfortable questions from the politicians back on Earth. The regular fleet was also getting impatient and wanted to do things their way, flooding regions with ships in a grid search that Webb knew would be the absolute worst thing they could do in this situation. He needed to deliver results, and soon.

When a bleary-eyed Commander Teague came onto the bridge, Webb gave him a brief turnover, and then stormed off towards the office reserved for his use. By the time he'd closed the hatch and logged into the terminal on the desk, he had three waiting messages from the NIS liaison aboard the *Kentucky*, stating she'd be up to his office ASAP. He thought about breaking protocol and reaching out to Director Welford himself, but decided against it. All the normal chains of communication were suspect at this point, but the head of NAVSOC having secretive, off-the-record conversations with the NIS Director tended to make the wrong people perk up and take notice of what he was doing.

He quickly pulled up all of Scout Fleet's current mission files and reviewed them, making notes as he waited for the NIS agent and his aide to get to the office. Before getting too deep into the details, however, he took the time to send a coded message to Obsidian's new slip-com node, letting Brown know he might be targeted. Even though he had told Bennet to do that very same thing, he still felt compelled to reach out to the team to offer encouragement and guidance. He ordered them to stay sharp but press on. After tapping the stylus against his lips for a moment, a tic he'd developed while thinking, he pulled out his com unit and hit the first name on the screen.

"I'm on my way back up now, sir," Bennet said.

"Go down to the cargo hold and ask 707 to come up, as well," Webb said. "Make sure you word it as a polite request and not a demand or an order."

"You want one of the battlesynths up near the bridge? In your office?"

"Did I stutter?" Webb snapped.

"Aye, sir...retrieving one battlesynth," Bennet said and killed the channel.

Lot 700, a group of battlesynth political refugees living on Terranovus, was an enigma. They lived quietly in their compound far out in the desert, nearly a thousand miles east of Taurus Station, completely isolated and self-sufficient. The battlesynths seemed content to just be left to their own devices but, every once in a while, they'd send an emissary out to talk to Webb, and they always seemed to have access to information they shouldn't. Webb and the late Ezra Mosler had tried to pry a little around the edges and see where they were getting all the good intel from, but 707 had clamped a lid down on it and asked them politely to stay out of his affairs.

Half the people in the UEN, who knew what a battlesynth actually was, were terrified anytime one of them came stomping onto a Terran ship. He knew Commander Duncan wasn't thrilled about having three of them sitting in his cargo hold, but he didn't put up too much of a fight over it. He'd agreed to bring them along because 707 had asked him for a favor, but now he thought he saw a way to try and pry that lid up again and take a peek at Lot 700's intel source.

It was all about having the right kind of leverage.

"Reactor is at full power. Engines are lagging a bit, but we're okay."

"Looks like the ConFed fleet isn't bothering to pursue everybody fleeing the lower hangars," Jacob said, rotating the holographic tactical display so he could see where the group was deploying. "They're moving to make sure the bigger ships in the docking complex can't get clear and escape."

"Looks like your theory that they're here for that data core is off, LT," Taylor said. The corporal leaned in through the open hatch, his arms stretched over his head and hanging onto an exposed conduit.

"It just means they have no idea who has it right now, not that I'm wrong," Jacob insisted. "Look! Assault barges are breaking off the main fleet and heading to the lower decks. They're going to— Ah, shit."

"What?" Sully asked.

"The only reason they'd be landing an assault force on the lower decks is because they're going to round up the criminal element and do a search," Jacob said. "They're going to hit hard and fast, and they don't trust Pinnacle Security to do it, so they're after something specific."

"And if they grab that guild master who gave you the core..." Taylor left the thought hanging in the air.

"Oh," Sully said. "Yeah...shit."

Jacob leaned back in the seat, staring intently at the display as if he could will the ConFed ships to ignore his little shuttle as it zipped along in a flotilla of other, similar ships away from the station. Sully had debated back and forth about staying with the group or veering off and heading for a mesh-out point alone, but in the end, decided that keeping in the group and not standing out was the smarter move. Jacob trusted the pilot to make those decisions since he wasn't exactly an expert in space combat tactics.

He took his mind off the details of flying the ship and thought hard about the situation they were in. If a ConFed cruiser intercepted and captured them, the UEN and United Earth Council would disavow any knowledge of them or their mission. Those were the risks Scout Fleet crews faced during even the most mundane mission. If it all went to shit, there would be no diplomatic efforts to recover them. It was something he rarely thought of unless they were in a situation like this, where capture seemed like better than even odds.

Jacob's gut feeling told him the guild master on Pinnacle wouldn't give them up even if the ConFed shock troops got a hold of him and squeezed. They'd been waiting for a suitable crew to ferry the data core, and Jacob's purloined Blazing Sun marker had vetted them as such a crew. It indicated the data core was highly valuable to some very important people...people the guild master wouldn't betray. Of course, it was also equally likely the alien they'd dealt with personally had escaped himself, and he had nothing to worry about, but with the way his luck had been going on this mission, he didn't count on it.

"Corporal Levin, would you please go back in the engineering bay and standby on the manual engine control reset," Sully said, frowning.

"What's wrong now?" Jacob asked.

"Engines are surging, and we're dropping off," the pilot said, calm as ever. "I can't maintain this acceleration. This loose formation is going to pull away from us."

"On my way— *Shit!*"

A meaty *thunk* let Jacob know his tech specialist had hit his head on a low-hanging condenser pipe, the same as he and Sully had done a few times as they'd left the flightdeck. Jacob laughed but never took his eyes off the tactical hologram. As Sully had warned, the other ships pulled away, still under their full acceleration while his shuttle started to fall off. The other ships weren't roaring away, but the DeltaV was high enough that, soon, they'd be caught out in the open, alone.

"How is this even possible?!"

"Relax, Lieutenant," Sully said. "This is just part of the issue with mismatched components, not another failure. Once I have Taylor reset the controller, we'll get full power back."

"How long?"

"I've chopped power to zero, so another five minutes until the emitters bleed down enough to do the reset."

The time seemed to tick by while the other ships pulled further away. So far, all the ConFed ships were still maneuvering to form a blockade to trap the larger freighters at their docks, but he'd still be more comfortable once they were well away. A soft *chime* from his panel made him look back to the hologram. A new contact had appeared on the *other* side of the system, coming at them from the direction they flew.

"Who are you?" he asked himself as the computer chugged through the incoming sensor data to resolve the contact. They had a database of known ship-types it could match to if the newcomer didn't fire up its ident beacon.

"What's it doing?" Sully asked, reaching over and hitting the intercom switch. "Hit the reset now, Corporal."

"Just drifting down," Jacob said. "Adjusting course and coming to bear on the formation ahead of us, but it could also be lining up to intercept Pinnacle."

The computer found a type match a moment later. Sully let out a slow whistle.

"You don't see those very often," he said. "I think we're going to try something a little drastic here. Standby."

Jacob watched as the now-identified ConFed assault carrier flew deeper into the system, still not broadcasting an ident beacon or issuing any demands. The assault carrier was exactly the type of ship you would bring in if you wanted to run down a bunch of small cargo ships and shuttles you suspected of smuggling something you wanted. This class of assault carrier had a compliment of two hundred and seventeen fighters, eighty-two assault boats that could land troops anywhere, and forty-six gunships that could hammer targets on the surface of a planet or duke it out with another ship in space.

Sully waited until the controller reset was complete, and then smoothly pushed the power all the way to maximum, swinging around onto a course perpendicular to the one they'd been on. The little ship shuddered and surged ahead on her new course. Jacob could see they were splitting the difference between the taskforce at Pinnacle Station and the assault carrier that had just arrived. On the long-range sensors, he could see that two other groups of fleeing ships had also been corralled by ConFed ships, but they were too far away for him to tell what type.

"What's your master plan?" Jacob asked.

"Going to accelerate to mesh-out velocity, and then we'll engage the slip-drive and get the hell out of here," Sully said. "I'm taking us out towards Colton Hub, but not on a direct vector that could be tracked by the ConFed."

"Wonder why nobody else has thought of that," Jacob wondered aloud. Mesh-out points had nothing to do with anything other than the arbitrary spot in the system that local governments had agreed on for ships to depart the system. It helped control the traffic flow, but from a technical standpoint, a ship could mesh-out anywhere assuming they weren't near any planetary bodies with significant gravitational pull.

"They will," Sully said. "A ship out by itself in this sort of situation makes it a sitting duck and draws attention. Once they realize the carrier is actually there to intercept them, they'll scatter. It'll be too late by then, of course."

"So, we're the smart ones this time."

"No...we're probably still screwed. The ConFed Fleet is very good at this sort of thing. We'll be lucky to make it out of— Ah, there we go." Sully pointed to the tactical display where another ship had just appeared. This one was a lowly frigate, but it was also only a million klicks off their port side and turning to intercept.

"Shit," Jacob muttered, watching the big capital ship commit to them. "We gonna make it?"

"It'll be close," Sully said. "Slip-drive is primed, we just need more relative velocity for mesh-out."

Jacob sat silent and let Sully work. He could make out what the instruments were telling him, and it looked like they would just make it before the frigate could get them in weapons range. Of course, that assumed their engines wouldn't hiccup again and cut their acceleration. While he watched the numbers converge, an alert splashed across the panels on his side, and he saw immediately what they were warning him about.

"Frigate has just fired! Three plasma cannon shots inbound!"

"Can't juke, no time," Sully grunted, sweat beading up along his hairline. He reached up and grabbed the lever on the overhead console that controlled the slip-drive engagement and stared hard at their relative velocity numbers, seeming to will the last bit of power from the worn-out engines that he could.

"Impact in six seconds!"

"Now!" Sully shouted, shoving the handle forward. There was a shrill whine from deeper in the ship, and all the portholes instantly blacked out, protecting the occupants from the brilliant slip-space energies flowing around the ship outside.

"Well, that was exciting," Jacob deadpanned, his body crashing after the adrenaline charge he'd gotten from almost being caught by the ConFed. He looked over and saw that Sully leaned back in his seat, looking like he felt much the same way.

"Why did they fire on us?" Sully asked. "I figured they'd broadcast demands we heave to and wait to be recovered."

"They weren't warning shots," Jacob said, gesturing to where the tactical hologram would normally be projected. "The computer had calculated the intercept points, and it looked like they meant to hit us. It was a long range shot, so maybe they assumed we'd see it and slam on the brakes."

"They're not that sloppy." Sully shook his head. "The ConFed may be a corrupt cesspool, but their fleet is top notch. If they opened fire, they intended to splash us. Their sensors probably saw our type and velocity and correctly surmised we were close to mesh-out and rolled the dice."

"A frigate pops into real-space just close enough to try and grab us and tries to shoot us down without any warning or demands," Jacob said. "Perhaps I gave our guild friend too much credit, and he talked as soon as they got him."

"Good job not getting us dead, Sully," Taylor said as he swung on the conduit line back onto the flightdeck. "Everything seems okay back there for now."

"It's a seven-day flight out to Colton Hub," Sully said, yawning. "I'm going to hit the rack, and then I'll go down and check everything over again with fresh eyes."

"I'll take first watch," Jacob said. "Taylor, tell Murph he's relieving me, and then you're up after him."

"What about MG and Mettler?"

"Mettler can relieve you, but I don't want MG up here unsupervised," Jacob said.

"And his stupidity gets rewarded yet again," Taylor muttered as he turned and walked back down the center corridor.

Jacob reached into his thigh pocket and pulled out a pack of issue stim tabs, popping a couple to keep him alert through his five-hour watch shift. He climbed out of the copilot seat and went to the auxiliary station at the rear of the cramped flightdeck, activating the terminal and accessing the ship's new slip-com node. There was a new message in Obsidian's dead drop box that originated from the UES *Kentucky*. It was from Captain Webb, explaining that Scout Fleet teams and ships were being hit all across the quadrant. His eyes widened in shock as he learned Scout Team Diamond had been completely wiped out, and the *Northstar* had taken a beating but managed to escape.

He leaned back and closed his eyes, saying a quiet prayer for Lieutenant Commander Morse and his team. Per Webb's message, it was likely that whoever was taking out Scout Fleet units had no idea how to find Obsidian. Their ship, the Corsair, had been dragged back to Terranovus, and there were very few people who knew the details of how they acquired the ship they were currently in. UEN regulations were pretty explicit about things like pirating and theft, so the reports filed with NAVSOC were a little vague on things like the fact they had killed the original crew and flew off with a known smuggler's ship.

After answering Webb's message with a coded acknowledgement that would tell his CO he'd received and understood his orders, Jacob pulled up as much information as the ship's limited database had on Colton Hub. He didn't want to risk accessing the NIS database with his ship's slip-com node since it could possibly be used to track them. He'd only been working in Scout Fleet a short time, and he was already extremely paranoid, seeing One World traitors behind every odd happenstance or message. Having Hollick pop up at two different locations hadn't done much to help.

In the remaining hours of his watch, he put together a plan for when they reached the Hub. He made a reminder to check the personal journal of the ship's previous owner for any more background information on the infamous facility, and even kicked around the idea of reaching out to Whitney to see what she knew or, more accurately, would be willing to share. By the time a bleary eyed and grouchy Murph walked onto the flightdeck, Jacob felt like he had the barebones of a pretty solid plan.

13

Colton Hub was nothing like Pinnacle Station, save for the fact that each was an independent, self-sustaining artificial habitat in space that had their own cultures, politics, and rules.

While Pinnacle was a respectable place that cooperated with local governments and was widely considered a crucial resource for interstellar trade and commerce, Colton Hub was seen as a scourge. No government claimed the Hub, nor did any want to bother wasting the resources to tame it. Some few had tried and, after burning through money and troops at equal rates, had slunk off and left it to its own devices.

The station had started life as a refueling platform for long-haul freighters back before starships had the legs to make it across the quadrant without replenishing. Unlike most platforms, Colton Hub wasn't anchored in a star system, it sat in deep space, which made it tricky to navigate to. Since everything in space moved relative to everything else, Colton Hub was never in the same spot when you came back. The station updated its position relative to the galactic center every fourteen hours and eleven minutes on a publicly accessible Nexus node. That would put you in the general area, but the updates were deliberately fudged so that nobody could mesh-in right on top of them. It gave the dirt bags that inhabited the station time to evacuate should a ConFed taskforce pop into real-space intent on dropping the hammer.

"That...does not look safe to be aboard," Murph said, looking at Colton Hub through the shuttle's high-resolution optics. "Is it on fire and venting?"

"It's both...and that's normal," Jacob said. "The habitat vents atmosphere from a hundred or so holes at any given time. The crews repair the holes, new ones pop up. The fires happen now and again when one of the exhaust vents from the reactors ignites trash that lands near the ports."

"This happens often?" Taylor asked skeptically.

"The hub is the only thing within three hundred lightyears that has any significant mass," Jacob said. "Anything that gets tossed out of a ship in the area will eventually be pulled back down to the station."

"How the hell do you know all that?" Sully asked.

"It was in the ship's database. The previous owners had some pretty detailed information on Colton Hub, actually," Jacob said. "The captain even had some detailed maps of an area they call the Catacombs, where you really don't want to go unless you absolutely have to. He used it to hide from time to time since nobody wanted to go down there to dig him out."

"Incoming transmission from the station," Sully said, flicking a switch to put it on the overhead speakers.

"*Incoming Eshquarian light-ship, we have you on approach. Your transponder codes have been recorded, please provide your ship's registry name, cargo, and intent.*"

"We are the light cargo shuttle, *Boneshaker*," Sully said into his mic, giving the name the team had christened the ship with after leaving Pinnacle. "No inbound cargo, intent is to find a load heading back towards the Concordian Cluster." After all the mechanical failures and near misses, the crew had decided that maybe the curse of flying an unnamed ship had some teeth to it.

The station didn't immediately respond, and as the time dragged on, the more Jacob feared their ship had been recognized. The previous crew frequented Colton Hub, and even though they'd swapped out all the coded transponders, the visual profile of the ship might be spotted by a sharp-eyed sensor operator familiar with the previous crew.

"*Boneshaker, your landing is approved. Please proceed to public hangar bay thirty-four, landing pad twelve.*" The channel went dead, and the navigation panel lit up with course corrections from the station's automated system, directing them to the correct hangar. Like Pinnacle, Colton Hub was built on a scale that boggled the mind, so large that when they were still a full kilometer from the hangar bay outer doors, the construct was all they could see out the forward portholes.

Sully expertly shut down the drive and slid the ship through the atmospheric barrier and into the hangar, deploying the landing gear and swinging them gracefully around onto landing pad twelve. He positioned the ship so that the bow was pointed out towards open space, a precaution in case they had to flee for their lives once again.

"Hey, your gizmo from that smuggler just lit up!" Mettler shouted up to the flightdeck from where he and MG sat in the galley.

"The data card that's supposed to tell us our new contact," Jacob said. "I guess it detected the signal from the station it looked for."

They left Sully to secure the ship from flight mode and settle up their account with the deck boss as far as landing fees and fuel costs and went aft to the galley. The alien script on the card glowed in a brilliant blue, and the edge of one side glowed yellow, indicating it was now ready to be accessed. Jacob took it and placed it on a lit yellow pad by the terminal that sat in one corner of the galley. The terminal gave a quick double-chirp to let him know it was reading the card.

"This seems surprisingly straight forward," he said as the instructions scrolled across the screen. The galley terminal was an isolated, stand-alone computer, so any nasty little surprises someone might have put on the data card wouldn't be able to jump onto the ship's network and ruin their day. "We need to take this card down to a computer terminal on Zult Deck—I think that's right under the main promenade—and access it from there. That specific terminal will give us the current location of this Dekav Qozulun we're supposed to meet, as well as a physical description."

"And that terminal will also make sure Dekav knows what we look like, as well as where we are the moment we access it," Murph said. "Smart. We can assume that terminal will also be watched."

"Safe bet," Jacob said. "Let me check in with the *Kentucky*, and then we'll get this party started. I'm taking MG with me, Murph and Mettler will trail behind and watch for any observers, and Taylor will stay with the ship to route coms and help Sully."

―――――

"I'm sending you help," Webb said without any preamble or greeting when the slip-com channel stabilized. Jacob had been startled when the captain answered the call personally. "To be more accurate, I screwed up and mentioned you were in a bit of trouble, and help is now coming to you whether you want it to or not."

"I don't understand, sir."

"That could be the title of your autobiography, Lieutenant," Webb sighed. "You'll figure it out when they get there. The reason I'm giving you warning is that I don't want you moving from Colton Hub *until* they get there. Also—and this is *very* goddamn important—keep as much control over them as you can. We cannot afford an incident with these guys."

"I think I know who's coming, sir," Jacob said, exhaling in relief. At first, he'd thought Webb had told his father about his predicament and that Jason Burke was going to come swooping in to *save* the day again. The last comment by his CO told him it wasn't Omega Force on its way...but someone who could be equally destructive. "Which ones are coming?"

"Three of them. The only one I know for sure is their leader since the others never introduced themselves," Webb said. "Just keep in mind they're there to assist, but you're in command of the ground team. That means you get the blame if they go off script and wipe out an entire deck. Webb out."

The terminal blanked out before Jacob could even tell him what they'd found out about their new contact or what their plan was to retrieve the information Fleet Ops wanted. He realized Webb either knew there were severe leaks in his organization and didn't want the information broadcast through the *Kentucky*'s com system, or Obsidian was so far off-mission that he wanted plausible deniability when the court martials started. There was also the slim chance that Webb was beginning to trust him and allow him to work within the loose command structure the rest of Scout Fleet did, calling his own shots and being largely left alone to get results.

"Ready?" Murph asked when Jacob stepped out of the cramped com room.

"Ready."

After briefing the team about their incoming assistance, the ground team geared up, anxious to get started. MG and Jacob walked down the ramp and into the sweltering, fetid air of the hangar bay. It was a medium-sized public hangar, with only nine other ships currently in it, but room for eighteen more. Sully had already been outside, talking to the ground crews and making arrangements for fuel as well as hooking up external power to the ship. He gave them a casual wave as they rounded the corner of the port engine nacelle and headed for the exit into the station.

The hangar exit dumped them into a wide, crowded corridor lined on either side with carts and booths on the way to one of the six main promenades on Colton Hub, where the bulk of commerce took place. Despite its reputation, there was still a decent amount of legitimate business that took place there, and these were the areas it happened. All of the illegal stuff was still kept out of sight, save for the flagrant narcotic use by the station's citizens, right out in the open in front of an indifferent security force.

"Second stairwell," Jacob said. All of them had a map of the local area, as well as their mission objectives loaded into their neural implants. MG just nodded and moved towards the opening to the stairs while Jacob scanned ahead for any threats. Despite all the laughter and normalcy of people going about their business, there was an undercurrent of danger and tension Jacob couldn't shake. He felt like a mouse in a maze while people watched who had little interest if he lived or died, only that he gave them what they wanted.

Zult Deck was directly below the Promenade Deck and was the first peek for the Obsidian crew at the seedy nature of Colton Hub. Most of the spaces on the deck were meant to support commerce taking place above so there was the expected storage and administrative nooks dotting the passageways. There were also some sights that made Jacob bristle, and he had to remind himself, forcefully, that he wasn't here to save the galaxy, he was here to do a job for his homeworld.

In one of the alcoves, there were aliens being kept in individual cages while someone in charge gave instructions on where each was going. The pair made jokes while trying to guess which were being sold into slavery and which were being offered on the menu later. Jacob looked over and shook his head at MG when he noticed the big weaponeer had much the same reaction he did once he realized what he was seeing.

Some of the other sights included drug dens, narcotic distribution on a scale that went well beyond recreational, and black-market weapons sales where powered carts loaded down with military-grade munitions were tagged for delivery to various ships. Jacob just shook his head and kept walking. The public Nexus access was up ahead, and it only had a few beings milling about, talking over the slip-com system or digging through pages of information.

The specific terminal kiosk they'd been instructed to use was, thankfully, open, and Jacob was able to quickly pay for a couple hours of use and put the data card onto the machine's pad so it could be read. The minutes dragged on with no indication anything was happening, and he was afraid that either the card had been damaged or the contact had been spooked somehow.

"Ah! There you are." The voice emanating from the terminal spoke in unaccented Jenovian Standard, and there was no accompanying image so Jacob could see who spoke to him.

"Here we are," Jacob said. "We gonna make this deal or what?"

"How many are you bringing?"

"Just me and my partner here," Jacob said.

"And you have what I was promised?"

"I have an item I've ferried from Pinnacle Station to Colton Hub... beyond that, I have no idea what it is or if it's what you want. That's between you and the guild master who gave it to me for transport."

"Pragmatic stance for a smuggler," the voice said. "Very well... come to the place displayed on your screen, and I will pay the rest of your fee for the cargo."

"See you soon," Jacob said, switching off the terminal after the location was loaded into his neural implant.

"I like how you said that ominously...like you're just itching to go in there and fuck him up," MG said. Jacob ignored the jab and checked his loadout one more time.

"We need to go back up," he said. "Two levels above the Promenade Deck."

"Elevators are over there," MG said. Jacob thought it over and saw no particular risk with the station lifts as opposed to laboring up all those stairs.

"Take point," Jacob said before keying in on the short-range team radio. "Form up. We're taking a lift to our next destination, and I don't want us all spread out."

If it wasn't for the fact that they were all human, the two groups looked completely disassociated from each other. The pairs were dressed in such a way they naturally looked like two distinct groups. Murph and Mettler didn't speak to Jacob or MG as they walked into the large cargo lift car since they couldn't be sure how thorough their buyer's surveillance was.

"It's close. This way," Jacob nodded to his left as he and MG exited the car. They would walk slowly while the other two went up one more level, and then took the stairs back down to fall in behind them again. If anyone noticed, it would almost look like Murph and Mettler were tailing the other two with the intent of jacking them.

When they reached the section of offices where their contact was, something seemed...off. The lead team proceeded with caution, MG pulling a sidearm and keeping it by his side while Jacob had his hand inside his long jacket, gripping his own weapon. The door they needed was partially open when they reached it. Jacob nodded to MG, and the pair pulled out their main weapons: short-barreled plasma carbines that didn't have a ton of power, but were great for close quarters combat.

"Go!" Jacob said, shoving the door open and letting MG rush inside even as he cut the corner to cover his partner's back. The smell in the office was pretty bad, and Jacob had suspicions what that meant.

"Clear!" MG called from the back room. "Smelly, but clear."

"Anything interesting?"

"A desk, some weird looking chair, a picture of a planet with a red sky... Oh! And another dead alien on the floor."

"Funny," Jacob said, lowering his weapon. "That's it. I'm pulling the plug on this mission. NAVSOC is going to have to send—"

BOOM!

Jacob was thrown off his feet by the explosion, and MG was stunned, losing his balance, and toppling over. Jacob tried to turn his head and see what happened, but when he did, he looked down the business end of someone's heavy blast pistol, a weapon that would evaporate his head if the owner flicked the firing stud.

"Can you hear me?" a voice that sounded like it was at the end of a tunnel called.

"Who are you?" Jacob demanded, stalling until MG could get to his feet. His partner had been a room over and behind a desk when he'd gone down so, with any luck, he'd shake off what Jacob assumed had been a stun grenade much sooner than he'd be able to.

"You can call me Tulden, Jacob Brown. I'm with ConFed Intelligence...and I've been waiting for you."

14

"Terrific."

"Lose the weapons," Tulden said. Jacob did as he was told, tossing aside his primary weapon and both sidearms.

"ConFed Intelligence, huh? How long have you been tracking us?"

"Tracking you? Don't flatter yourself, human. I was waiting here for weeks to see who would deliver the data core to this drop point. So...where is it?" Tulden asked. He had a relaxed competency about him, holding his weapon ready and positioning himself to cover the doors and Jacob at the same time.

"You don't think I'd have been stupid enough to bring it *with* me, do you?" Jacob asked, now losing hope that MG was in any shape to try and get the drop on the agent. "This isn't my first smuggling gig, chief. That core isn't even on this—"

"You're not a smuggler, Jacob Brown," Tulden said wearily. "You're a member of Earth's clandestine military force that works separately from the Cridal Cooperative. Oh...you probably want to warn the two members of your team you had trailing you to hold off. There's an anti-personnel mine in the corridor I'd hate for them to trip."

"Bravo Team, hold position," Jacob keyed his mic. "Back off and find cover, do not approach the objective."

"*Copy,*" Mettler's voice came back immediately.

"Smart," Tulden said. "No point in wasting men on a doomed rescue charge."

"I appreciate the warning about the mine," Jacob said, deciding that antagonizing the agent would be both fruitless and foolish. "So... now what?"

"You're new to all this, aren't you?" Tulden asked, lowering his weapon slightly but not putting it away. "You seem competent enough as a soldier, but you're not quite as sensitive to the details you should be if you had experience in clandestine operations."

"New enough." Jacob shrugged. He sensed he was treading on dangerous ground. ConFed Intelligence wasn't something to be trifled with, and a wrong move or answer on his part could have bigger consequences than just his brains blown out. "How did you know someone would be coming here with the data core?"

"Got a tip-off," Tulden said. "They had some backchannel contacts through my organization, and I was alerted that a human crew posing as smugglers had obtained the core, slipped the blockade at Pinnacle, and was heading for Colton Hub. It was one of your people, actually...a human." Jacob blinked in surprise at that.

"The fact you're telling me that doesn't make me super confident you're going to let us live," he said. "So, why should I even pretend to consider turning over the core?"

"Let's speak plainly," Tulden said. "I know the reputation ConFed agents have, but I'm not particularly fond of killing just for the sake of killing. In this case, I think we have an opportunity to be mutually beneficial. We both get what we want, we both walk away still breathing. Interested?"

"I'm listening," Jacob said.

"You likely have no idea what's on that data core, but I do...and I need it back. What I *think* you're after is the location of the rogue fleet that attacked Miressa Prime, and you likely heard it was spotted in this area. Let me take another guess and say you want to know where that fleet is because there are still human ships with it and you don't want any reprisal from the ConFed for their actions. Am I close?"

"I'd prefer not to confirm or deny anything at this point," Jacob said. "But I'm still listening."

"Of course," Tulden laughed. "So, instead of poking around in the dark, you give me the core, and I tell you the last known location of the fleet?"

"If you knew where they were, then the ConFed fleet would have already been here in force," Jacob scoffed. "I'm not *that* new to this."

"The small fleet that attacked the capital is immaterial," Tulden said. "We're trying to find out who supports them, who is backing them. Logistics wins wars, Lieutenant Brown. More than ships and soldiers, being able to outspend your enemy and keep pumping materiel into a fight is what wears them down, breaks them. We find their backers, we stop a civil war before it even starts without wasting our own ships."

"You're an intel spook and a professor of military doctrine?" Jacob said, slipping into old habits with the sarcasm. "I'll go so far as to confirm we're looking for the rebel fleet that attacked the capital system, but for reasons I won't divulge to a foreign operative. The thing that's bothering me is that this is all a little unorthodox. A single agent lying in wait, ambushing us, and then immediately trying to cut a deal? What's your angle here?"

"Let's just say that, if I can accomplish my mission where others have failed miserably, I would be in a very good position within my division," Tulden said. Jacob had to suppress a laugh…bureaucratic back-stabbing was, apparently, a universal trait, and Tulden just outed himself as a glory hog. He wanted the big prize all to himself so he could move himself ahead in the game.

Jacob was at one of those crossroads Commander Mosler had warned him about before his untimely death. There was no manual, no operational instruction, and no specific orders to fall back on to tell him what the right choice was here. If he screwed it up, however, the Navy and the Marine Corps would throw him to the wolves. He'd likely see prison if this went badly.

Taking stock of what he had, he had to concede that the data core wasn't useful to him despite its importance to others. He couldn't access it, had no idea what might be on it, and didn't even know specifically who it was supposed to go to. The ConFed agent already knew about human ships in the rebel fleet, had already known they were coming, and he apparently got the information from one of their own. On the surface, this seemed like a reasonably safe risk despite the fact he didn't trust Tulden any further than he could throw him. The agent coughed up just the information he needed too quickly, and at a time where he held all the advantages. He didn't even try to squeeze Jacob for the core, just came out offering a deal.

"Any chance you could tell me what's on that core that's so important you're offering me such a sweet deal for it?" Jacob asked.

"No chance at all," Tulden said. "If you're in, you need to decide quickly because, if you're not—" he waved the weapon he held meaningfully, "I'll need to get to work on getting that core the hard way."

"Just to be clear, I give you the core, you give me the fleet location," Jacob said. "I'd also like to toss in the human's name who gave us up, as well as assurances from you that human involvement in this insurrection will be erased or severely downplayed." Tulden seemed to think it over for a few moments.

"Not unreasonable," he said finally. "The fact that there were a couple human ships in the Cridal strike force is already common knowledge, but I can spin that to your advantage. I also can't give you the name of the person who sold you out because they never gave it to us. What I can do is go back through the dispatch I received and give you the slip-com node address they sent it from."

"That's better than nothing, I suppose," Jacob said. "How do you want to do the trade?"

"I'll be at your ship in three hours," Tulden said. "Is that sufficient time for you to retrieve the core and have it there?"

"Barely, but I'll make it work," Jacob said, keeping up the ruse that the core was masterfully hidden somewhere clever when the truth was, he had just left it sitting on the ship.

"No tricks," Tulden warned. "I'm no fool, and you won't be able to take me by surprise."

"Got it," Jacob said. Tulden turned and left without another word, walking through the door and turning left, taking him away from where Murph and Mettler were posted.

"Bravo Team, Alpha Two is down. Close on my position but move slow and scan for any explosive devices." He assumed Tulden had deactivated the mines when he left, but he hadn't said anything about it before disappearing.

Murph and Mettler appeared in the doorway a moment later, both looking confused. Jacob just pointed over to where MG was just stirring, waving them away when they tried to help him up. The pair picked the weaponeer up after righting the desk, sitting him down on it so Mettler could examine him.

"He got his bell rung," the medic said after a moment. "Likely mild concussion, nothing serious."

"Feels serious," MG slurred.

"It would be for someone with a normal brain," Mettler said. "But you'll be fine."

"Douche."

"What happened, LT?" Murph asked.

"Ambushed. ConFed Intelligence was waiting on us—and they knew it was us coming—and we just walked right into the trap," Jacob said, groaning as he climbed to his feet. He'd not had time to fully heal from his previous misadventures before the stun grenade scrambled his insides again. "I really need to get a new hobby besides having my internal organs damaged by blunt force trauma."

"ConFed Intelligence was here? As in, an agent was here? And you're still alive?" Murph asked.

"We cut a deal," Jacob said. "He knows roughly where the fleet is, but ConFed Intel is chasing the money backers before hitting them. They want that data core back really bad, and he's willing to give us the location and downplay Earth's involvement if we hand it over. He seems to be a bit of a pragmatist and isn't keen on torturing all of us if he doesn't have to."

"Interesting," Murph said, the skepticism dripping off his words.

"I was about to pull the plug on this mission when we found another dead alien contact." Jacob waved towards the back office. "But then this clown shows up and starts making offers. I get the feeling that if I didn't accept, he wasn't about to just let us walk away with no hard feelings."

"Yeah," Murph said, rubbing his scalp. "Shit...you're right. If you turned him down, we'd be grabbed before we made it to the ship and have a professional interrogation crew getting the information from us."

The team collected their gear and headed back for the lifts. Jacob took point, and Murph watched their rear as Mettler helped MG along. The medic drew the short straw since he was about the same height as the injured man, and they could move faster with MG leaning on him instead of reaching up for Murph or Jacob.

Even with his head still fuzzy from the concussion blast, Jacob's thoughts were racing as he tried to cover all the angles and plan for any contingency. Unfortunately, a short-handed Obsidian on a ship he barely trusted to stay together didn't have too many options available to them. It's likely that Tulden knew that and felt comfortable offering them a deal so readily since they couldn't really pose much of a threat to him or his operation. Jacob just wondered how much firepower the agent had on the station. More highly trained operatives like him, or perhaps a full platoon of shock troops just waiting for the chance to tear someone apart.

When they reached the ship, nothing seemed out of place, but the ramp was lowered when Jacob had explicitly ordered them to keep her locked up. The hairs on the back of his neck stood up, and a fresh surge of adrenaline chased the cobwebs away as his over-stressed mind snapped back into focus.

"Look sharp," he said, unslinging his weapon and walking up the ramp with Murph. Mettler sat MG down on one of their transit crates and joined his crew, weapon ready. The trio began clearing the ship from stern to bow, finding nothing odd except for one thing: Sully was asleep in the cramped compartment just aft of the flightdeck, but Taylor was missing.

"He was taking watch," Sully said, yawning as he sat up in his rack. "I didn't hear the alert for the ramp dropping over the intercom, so it was either disabled or I slept right through it. Did he go off looking for you guys?"

"We're not overdue," Jacob said. "And I'd hope he would know better than to just wander off and leave the ship hanging open."

"He would," Mettler said firmly. "Taylor is a solid Marine. Something is wrong or he would be here."

"Fuck, Murph...check our cargo!" Jacob snapped. "All that bullshit with Tulden may have been to delay us." Murph ran down the corridor to the engineering spaces where the data core was stashed.

"What's a Tulden?" Sully asked.

"I'll explain later," Jacob said. "Mettler, we're sweeping the outside of the ship, and then we're searching the local area for Taylor. Maybe we'll get lucky and this is just a—"

"Cargo is secure. I moved it to another location for now until we can find a better place to stash it. I'm worried that its original spot might be compromised. I also found out how the ramp was dropped without anyone knowing," Murph said, out of breath as he came back. "Access panel was opened, and a tap was placed on one of the data lines...I can't tell who made the tap, but it was advanced enough to worm in and command the ramp open and the alarms off while being hooked to a non-essential bus."

"That takes a decent amount of knowledge," Jacob said. "I'm still leaning towards Tulden and his ConFed buddies."

"Agreed," Murph said. "And he'll be here in a couple hours."

"Well, let's make sure we're ready to greet him," Jacob said. "MG, you good to go?"

"If it means fucking up whoever grabbed Taylor, then yeah...I'm ready to kick some ass, LT."

15

Marcus Webb didn't like where the evidence he'd collected was pointing.

He'd been up for nearly three days straight, personally going through the raw data to try and figure out what happened to his Scout Fleet crews. It had been an effort borne of desperation as he frantically searched for proof that the obvious wasn't true. But the deeper he dug, the more he had to admit it to himself, someone high-placed within NAVSOC was feeding live intel to the enemy. It had resulted in the deaths of over two dozen highly trained operators and a trawler crew of eighty-six spacers.

The timing of the events left little doubt. The teams had been given recent move orders, all under tight security and through back channels, and all of them had been hit within days of relocating. The loss of Team Diamond was an especially brutal blow. With Ezra Mosler dead and Obsidian at half-manning, Diamond and Cobalt were the only full-combat ready 3rd Scout Corps teams he'd had available. The other five teams were all waiting on replacement personnel or hadn't even been fully activated in the first place.

After admitting to himself that someone within his inner circle was a traitor, he was now trying to zero in on who had opportunity. Now, he only hoped it was just one person who had betrayed their homeworld and not a network of people within NAVSOC. The former could be dealt with by a single execution, the latter meant not only would he be unable to chop the head off the snake, but his own life would probably be in danger once they knew he was on to them.

"Bennet!" he roared, not bothering with the intercom.

"Sir?" his aide asked once the hatch slid open.

"Tell Commander Duncan to get departure clearance from Terranovus," Webb said, standing up.

"Where are we heading, sir?"

"We'll file a flight plan for Olympus," Webb said. "We might detour along the way, but I want to be out of short-haul com range of Terranovus as soon as possible, and inform Taurus Station that *all* Scout Fleet operations will be run out of this ship. We have enough handlers, don't we?"

"We should, sir," Bennet said, consulting his tablet. "There are nine qualified black ops handlers aboard at any given time, and we're down to three units still left in the field."

"Good...then get your ass moving. Tell Duncan he has a move order and to start breaking orbit as soon as we have clearance."

"Aye, sir."

If he couldn't root out the traitors in time to help Obsidian, he could at least bypass them. By running the operations directly out of the *Kentucky*, he cut out at least three layers of bureaucracy and potential security leaks from Taurus Station's administrative and secure communications sections.

Even if he found them, he was just patching a leak in a crumbling dam. The real problem was Margaret Jansen and her goddamned One World faction. She'd managed to get a beachhead in among the UEN's officer corps and had been successfully recruiting well after the Cridal had chased her and her Ull allies away from Earth. What was really depressing was that they'd even declassified and made public what she'd been up to on Terranovus; building a secret battle fleet, conspiring with alien powers against Earth, and attempting to assassinate a sitting US president and, somehow, all that only managed to increase her recruiting. When he thought about it too much, he could swear he felt a stroke coming on.

He walked over to the wall display and pulled up the star chart he wanted, checking the established routes and trying to decide where he could best position the *Kentucky* to help Lieutenant Brown without being too close. The last time Brown had checked in, they'd just arrived on Colton Hub, a place with such a nasty reputation that it almost defied belief. Obsidian was also the first Scout Fleet team to ever visit the infamous deep space outpost. Webb was nervous about sending the kid into a snake pit like that, but he was more nervous about what would happen if the ConFed discovered the *Eagle's Talon* in a rogue fleet that had attacked their capital. The ConFed would, without a doubt, retaliate against the Cridal Cooperative as a whole, but they'd probably burn Earth to a cinder just as an object lesson.

"Come on, Jake...don't let me down, kid."

"That's him...just walking across the deck without a care in the world."

"He'll have backup placed around the hangar," Murph insisted. "Let him get inside the ship."

The ConFed agent approached the ship cautiously but confidently. He would discreetly check each concealment spot when he passed it, but he didn't slow or break stride. The lack of timidity, and the fact he didn't seem too bothered about checking behind him, just directly to the sides, told Jacob his backup must be near the entrance to the hangar bay.

"Show time," Jacob said, walking to the end of the cargo bay deck and standing there with his hands on his hips, making sure to look as bored and non-aggressive as he could.

"Lieutenant Brown," Tulden said in greeting, stopping five meters from the edge of the ramp. "Is everything in order?"

"More or less," Jacob said. "You have what we want?"

"It's here," Tulden said evasively. "The core?"

"In there," Jacob jerked a thumb over his shoulder. "I'm not doing this out in the open where one of your guys can take a shot at me as soon as it appears."

"I thought we'd gained some level of trust between us," Tulden said.

"You're kidding, right?" Jacob laughed. "I appreciate you letting me keep my brains inside my head, but you're still a ConFed Intel agent, and your reputation precedes you. But yes...we are still operating under the accords we agreed to previously."

"Can I come aboard?"

"Be my guest," Jacob said, turning his back on the agent and walking into the dimly lit hold. Tulden followed, appearing a little less confident and trying to see into the hold before committing to fully entering. Jacob ignored him and strolled to the hatch that led to the ship's interior as if he hadn't a care in the world.

Tulden, apparently satisfied Jacob wasn't setting him up, stepped over the threshold into the ship, placing his right foot down on the trigger pad for an anti-personnel stun mine. Hundreds of darts launched out of the two mines, one on each side of the entryway, and stuck in Tulden's exposed skin. Before he could react, the small darts unleashed their high-voltage payload. The darts were all networked and communicating so that the amount of jolt delivered was just enough to incapacitate, not barbeque.

"Close the ramp," Jacob said. Murph got up from behind one of the stacks of transit crates and ran to the control panel while Mettler and MG brought a heavy chair over they could strap Tulden to.

"I wish Taylor was here...I'm getting readings on a lot of wetware, LT, but nothing that my med scanner can positively identify," Mettler said. "I can't tell you for sure if closing the rear ramp will cut off the signal."

"Let's assume it won't," Jacob said. "Doesn't matter. Wake him up." Mettler read Tulden's neural implant to determine species-specific dosage for the stimulant cocktail that would shake him out of the shock the mines had given him.

"Brown...you've just made an unbelievably stupid mistake," Tulden said. The agent's eyes cleared and focused on him alarmingly fast, and Jacob figured he must be loaded with all sorts of gadgets from ConFed Intel that would help him out in situations like this.

"Those are the only kinds of mistakes I make, asshole," Jacob said.

"What is an asshole?" Tulden cocked his head as he puzzled the term out.

"Doesn't matter. Where's our crewman?"

"So, I can infer you're missing someone on your crew, and you think I had something to do with it?" Tulden asked. "Why would I bother? That's a lot of work for no payoff. I already have you and your ship. We had an agreement in place to trade the core for information. Why would I jeopardize that to play games by abducting a single member of your crew?"

"Hey! I'm asking the questions here. You think that— What?" Jacob shrugged off Murph's insistent tapping on his shoulder.

"A word, LT?" Jacob turned and followed Murph back to the corner of the cargo bay.

"Why did you interrupt? I think I was doing pretty good," Jacob whispered as Mettler and MG stayed with the prisoner.

"No, you were a sloppy mess," Murph said. "Maybe let me do the interrogations next time since I'm actually trained to extract information, not just annoy and confuse the subject. Either way, I don't think he's lying."

"Yeah?"

"Yeah," Murph said. "He's right...as any sort of counterintelligence tactic, this makes no sense. I think we should see if maybe he can help us find Taylor. Time is not on our side...the longer he's missing, the less likely we'll find him alive. If we find him at all."

"Damnit," Jacob hissed. "You think he might know something?"

"He wouldn't have walked in here alone if he had any idea one of ours had been taken," Murph said. "But his resources and local knowledge far exceed our own, and we still have something he wants."

"New deal," Jacob said loudly, walking back over to the chair. "We offer you our profoundest apologies for zapping you, still agree to hand over the core, but you give us a hand seeing where our misplaced crewman is."

"You are the oddest being I've ever encountered," Tulden said, peering intently at Jacob. "You seem to completely change course without knowing all the facts or giving your decisions any real forethought. I genuinely can't tell if you're a tactical genius or a complete imbecile."

"So, you in or out?"

"You invited me here, attacked me, imprisoned me, and now you want to modify our deal so you get *more* in return for the data core?" Tulden asked.

"Pretty much, yeah."

"Fine," the agent said, slumping back in his seat. "I'll try to track him down. Give me the Nexus Access Address for his com unit and we'll start there."

"MG, free our new friend, please," Murph said.

"If you do something like this again, Lieutenant Brown, I promise I will have you and your crew killed. Painfully," Tulden said. "I prefer to get what I need without undue violence, but my patience has limits, and you've just reached them."

"Understood," Jacob said, trying to sound genuinely contrite and failing completely. "Get us our guy, or tell us where he is, and we'll hand over the core without delay." Tulden just stared at him for a long moment.

"Very well. Please, open the ship back up. I'll come back when I know something. This could take a little bit of time so don't expect miracles."

"I'll take what I can get," Jacob said.

"What should we be doing right now?" Murph asked once Tulden had disappeared.

"We're no good to Taylor in the condition we're in," Jacob said. "I know you're all going to fight me on this, but I need you rested up more than I need you loose in the station chasing your tails. I'm taking first watch, and I want everyone else in their rack."

"LT—"

"This isn't a negotiation, Corporal," Jacob snapped at MG. "You're injured and dead on your feet right now. I want you resting and healing so that when we get a location for Taylor, you're ready. Got it?"

"Aye, sir," MG snarled. The weaponeer stomped off towards berthing, muttering angrily the whole way.

"Like a big, musclebound, borderline-alcoholic toddler," Mettler said.

"Nothing borderline about it," Murph said. "I'll relieve you in four hours."

The sleek, windowless ship that touched down gently in one of the small hangars meant only for official station personnel was like nothing the deck master had ever seen before. It had broadcast the proper authentication codes to land without challenge, but it looked nothing like the boxy VIP shuttles preferred by the cartel bosses or the nondescript ships used by their personal envoys.

The silver ship was also small. Almost the size of a short-range fighter, but it had three slip-drive nacelles in a tri-star configuration, a rarity as most ships used the more stable twin-nacelle configuration. The deck master thought that perhaps it was an unmanned courier ship, which would explain the less stable, but more powerful slip-drive layout. When the hatch opened in the side of the hull, however, he wasn't at all prepared for what stepped out.

Nightmares. He'd only heard of them in legend and almost believed they didn't really exist: Battlesynths.

"C-can I help you?"

"You may. Our ship will require fuel and a drive coolant flush. One of us will remain and supervise your people. Once you are finished, you are not to approach the ship again. Understood?"

"Y-yes, of course. Fuel and coolant. Right away."

"My thanks," the metal monstrosity said. Two of them strode off across the hangar deck while the third remained with the ship, staring at him. Fighting down the urge to simply run away, he signaled one of his underlings over and relayed the requests, dumping the whole thing in his lap.

The deck master had heard rumors when he'd first had the misfortune of coming to Colton Hub about a single battlesynth that had killed a bunch of people in the lower decks, crazy stories about how it ripped them apart with its hands...and that was just one of them. If the trio he'd just met were intent on violence, he'd rather wait it out in his office, and he'd damn sure not do anything to draw their attention to him.

"How did they get clearance to land in—"

"I don't care how they got it," he hissed at his subordinate. "All I care about is that you and your crew will do anything and everything to make sure they're pleased with our service. Treat them *better* than if Saditava Mok himself had just landed."

"You're in charge." The young yejic shrugged, waving over his crew to start service on the odd ship.

Jacob sat through his second watch within the last twelve hours. After Murph and Mettler took their turns staring at the external security feeds, he'd decided to let the injured MG sleep through his shift since he couldn't get to sleep himself, anyway. He was sick with worry about Taylor, and even though he logically knew there was nothing he could do without usable intel, just sitting on the ship while his teammate and friend was out there was gnawing at his already frayed nerves.

Tulden still hadn't contacted them with any leads, and that worried Jacob all the more. It meant that Taylor likely hadn't just wandered off for his own reasons but was grabbed by someone who knew what they were doing and would know how to shield his device signatures from the Nexus.

"What the hell?" he muttered, taking manual control of one of the aft imagers as something odd caught his eye. It looked like two beings in fire-resistant suits at first, but once the imager focused in on the pair, he could see what they were and knew what they were there for.

"Captain Webb wasn't messing around with sending backup."

He climbed out of the seat with a groan and walked back to the cargo bay to greet his guests. By the time the ship's ramp hit the hangar deck with a metal-on-metal *bang*, the two battlesynths were already standing there.

"707," he greeted the one standing to the right.

"Lieutenant Brown," Combat Unit 707 replied. "This is my network intrusion and counterespionage specialist, Combat Unit 784. Combat Unit 701 is watching over our ship. We are here to assist you in completing your mission."

"I'd be lying if I said I didn't need the help," Jacob said, nodding politely to 784. "You guys still going by your designation numbers or..." he left the question hanging.

"That is acceptable," 707 said. "There has been some...discussion... about adopting names as a way to fit in with our hosts on Terranovus, but we have yet to reach an agreement."

"What's your opinion?"

"I am one of the undecided holdouts."

"Well...come on aboard, and I'll brief you on just how bad this shit show has gotten," Jacob said.

Over the next ninety minutes, he laid out how poorly their search for the *Eagle's Talon* had gone, how One World seemed mixed up in it, and that they were now shutting down everything until they learned where their missing teammate was. 707 took the entire brief in his usual stoic manner, which was useless for Jacob when trying to figure out what the hulking machine thought about what they'd done so far. For some reason, the battlesynth's approval of him meant something, and he really couldn't figure out why.

"I agree that all effort must be made in recovering Corporal Levin," 707 said finally. "Captain Webb agreed to give me your location when the other Scout Fleet units were being eliminated in the field. My original intent was simply to protect you and, by proxy, your team. However, I feel like we can be of better use helping you meet your objectives so you can return to base safely."

"Can't argue either way," Jacob said. "We should probably—"

"Someone approaches the ship," 784 said, his voice making Jacob jump. 707 had the deep baritone one would naturally expect from such a being, but 784's voice was pitched up almost half an octave and had an odd accent. It just reinforced to him that these were sentient individuals, not autonomous kill-bots that were all just copies of each other.

"That's Tulden," Jacob said, peering around 784 to look at the monitors. "He's ConFed Intel with a lot of connections here on the station, so he probably already knows you're here. No point in having you hide."

"We did not try to disguise our presence," 707 said. "If this Tulden is an agent of any worth, he will know we are here."

"We got a hit on your crewmate's com unit," Tulden said as the ramp dropped, not bothering to greet him. "It was a short ping. It's possible whoever is holding him let their shielding slip for a moment."

"It is more likely this was deliberate, and this is a trap," 707 rumbled.

"Agreed," Tulden said, eyeing the two battlesynths. "You've been keeping secrets from me, Lieutenant."

"And will continue to do so," Jacob said. "They're with me and operating independently from Khepri. That's all I can say about them." Khepri was the homeworld of the pru, the species that created the synth race. Khepri was also one of the Pillar Worlds, a signatory of the original ConFed charter and ally of Miressa. The political implications of a few of Khepri's battlesynths roaming around with Terran military could be sticky.

"They're free beings," Tulden said, sounding disinterested. "Synth mercenaries aren't unheard of."

"We are not—"

"Supposed to be talking," Jacob cut off 707's indignant outburst. "I'm paying you to fight, not interrupt."

"As you wish," 707 said, his voice flat. Jacob shuddered inwardly at what might have happened if the battlesynth hadn't caught onto the ruse and decided it'd had enough of his mouth.

"I'll give you the location, but you're on your own recovering your crewmate," Tulden said. "I'm not getting involved in what's likely an internal Terran squabble."

"I won't need you," Jacob said. "The location?" Tulden tossed him a data card that 784 snatched out of the air, reaching in front of Jacob's face before he could even get his hand up.

"There's the location and a couple other helpful things on there," Tulden said. "I'll be in touch." Jacob watched the agent walk away, disappearing into the thin crowd near the main entrance.

"What do you guys think?"

"While it may be a trap, we will still need to investigate," 707 said. "Would you like us to do it and report back?"

"No! We're going. Taylor is our man...but I'd appreciate any help you can give me."

"You will have it," 784 said, seeming to approve of Jacob's insistence of fighting his own battles.

16

"You okay, MG?"

"Locked, cocked, ready to rock, LT." MG smiled. "Let's go get our boy."

"Okay, nothing fancy...let's just take it to them. Battlesynths will be on point, Murph and Mettler will watch our six," Jacob said. "Let's move."

Planning a military operation within a space station that, at least on the surface, was a civilian shipping hub was a challenge. Colton Hub might have a wild west vibe to it, but a fully armed assault team with two battlesynths piling out of a ship and storming up the main corridors would get them some unwanted attention from the various private security firms that kept the peace.

In order to keep their rescue op discreet, Jacob had been forced to rent storage space well away from the main market areas. They'd then loaded up one of their grav-sleds with all the gear they thought they'd need, packed away in black plastic transit cases, and set up a hasty operations center, complete with medical equipment for Mettler to treat Taylor, if necessary. It was over two kilometers away from the ship, which Jacob didn't like, but it offered them a semi-fortified position to fall back to in case things went completely haywire.

"I detect no hidden anti-personnel devices," 784 said as they approached the area where the com unit had been detected.

"Advance," Jacob ordered, his weapon up and ready. The area they searched wasn't like the partitioned rooms near the market areas or the living quarters. They weaved through a labyrinth of pipes and conduit. Tulden had marked the area as part of the fresh water reclamation system on the map he'd given them. The noises from the pipes groaning and banging, as well as the whine of boost pumps kicking on and off, muffled their approach, but it also made it easier for someone to set up an ambush.

"Standby, we will clear the area," 707 said when they reached the exact point where the com unit had been detected. When the battlesynth commander rounded the corner, Jacob could see it pause, standing up a little straighter and looking quickly his direction.

"Is it him?" Jason asked, a lump in his throat.

"Not...entirely," 707 said, standing aside.

A human hand, severed at the wrist in such a ragged manner it looked like it had been torn off, lay on the floor next to a deactivated com unit. There was little doubt whose hand it was.

"Mettler, come take care of this," he said, bending down and picking up the com unit. A shadow fell over him, and he looked over to see 784 looming over him, holding out his hand expectantly. Jacob just shrugged and handed the device over.

The battlesynth retreated some distance before trying to turn on the device, obviously concerned it was booby-trapped in some way. After a minute's inspection, he came back and handed it to Jacob. "They have left instructions."

Let's trade. I want the core, you want the rest of Corporal Levin back. No tricks or games, Brown. Bring the core to Zimic Deck, section 45-3. Come alone or the next piece you get might be one Levin can't live without.

Jacob wordlessly handed the unit over to Murph and turned to watch Mettler doing his best to stabilize the appendage with the limited gear he had. The look on his face told Jacob he didn't have a lot of hope it would work.

"This is all the way on the other side of the fucking station!" Murph fumed. "This was just to screw with us or to delay us. The next one *will* be a trap."

"Tell Tulden to meet us down here," Jacob said. "I'm having some suspicions about who's pulling the strings here."

"Yeah?"

"Yeah," Jacob said. "That message…it was written by a human."

"Fuck me…it's in English," Murph muttered. "I've been out here so long that all the languages start to just blur together because of the implant."

"Make the call."

"Lieutenant Brown," Tulden greeted him when he walked into the area. The agent still showed that same lack of fear when approaching them and had readily agreed to come down to where they were. Jacob wasn't sure how he felt about the agent being so openly accommodating.

"Where is Elton Hollick?"

"Excuse me?"

"Elton Hollick…the man who told you we were coming when you were watching that door where you ambushed us. Where is he?"

"I don't know, exactly," Tulden admitted, recovering quickly from his surprise. "A man by that name contacted a colleague of mine, who put me in touch with him directly. He told me a human crew posing as smugglers had the data core I pursued and would bring it to Colton Hub. He was even so kind as to give me the name of the contact and location of the drop."

"And he just did this out of the goodness of his heart?" Jacob asked.

"Of course not," Tulden scoffed. "We made a deal. He's the one who informed me there were Earth ships within the rogue fleet that attacked Miressa Prime. He wanted a specific ship...a cruiser called the *Eagle's Talon*. In exchange for the data core and the fleet's exact location, I was to provide him with the ship once the ConFed battle-fleet moved to eliminate it."

"Wait! *That's* where you got the fleet location from? Hollick?" Jacob raised his hand to interrupt. "You never mentioned that."

"I'm an operative, Lieutenant," Tulden said. "I never volunteer information when I don't have to. After he and I came to an agreement, I made some inquiries with my contacts in the fleet and found out they're not quite as ready to move as we'd assumed."

"So, what is all this about?!" Jacob shouted, waving at the bloody stain on the deck. "This asshole is carving up my crew!"

"When I didn't simply kill you all and search your ship, I assume Hollick thought I had double-crossed him and was now working with you," Tulden said. His voice was almost clinical as he surveyed the macabre scene. "I suppose that's technically true, but I'm getting the feeling this is personal. He wants you to suffer."

"It's personal," Jacob confirmed. "You're saying you don't know where he is?"

"He's quite skilled. I'm embarrassed to say I've not been able to track him down as of yet, but we're still working on it."

"If I don't get my guy back, the core is as good as gone," Jacob said.

"Ah," Tulden said. "So now, I should be motivated to help you locate your antagonist. I have to say, Lieutenant, that getting mixed up in an internal human squabble isn't something I'm interested in."

"Just flush him out or get him to come at us," Jacob said. "You don't have to go to him, but we need a location where he might be keeping my teammate." Tulden just stared at him for a moment, his face expressionless.

"Let me see what I can do," he finally said. "There are a few favors owed to me by the larger security firm aboard this station. They might have better luck tracking Hollick's hiding spot down." Jacob gave him the location of the rented storage space they used as a base of operations.

"You have two hours."

"If I can do it at all I'll have it done in one," Tulden said, recording the location on his own device

"It was not wise to trust him," 707 said once Tulden retreated.

"I'm desperate," Jacob admitted. "This was needlessly brutal. Hollick is doing this because it's fun for him. If I can't find Taylor within the next couple hours, I don't think I'll see him alive again."

"I put a tracking dot on Tulden when he was— Never mind...he must have found it already," Murph said. "The signal just died."

"Let's pull back to the forward base and wait to see if Tulden comes through before we make any other moves," Jacob said. What remained of Team Obsidian, dejected and with wounds you could see, and those you couldn't, trudged back to their holdout.

"It was a hand for a hand...see." Elton Hollick wiggled the fingers of his prosthetic hand in front of Taylor Levin's remaining eye. The Marine Corporal let out a ragged breath but said nothing.

"Not a big irony fan, huh? That's okay. This will soon be over. Once I can get that data core from your dipshit teammates, I'll be on my way. It really is a shame they moved it like that, huh? You withstood a level of torture I've never had to inflict on someone...and it was for nothing. When you finally gave up the location, it wasn't even there anymore. How's that make you feel?"

"Just end it," Taylor rasped. "I'm no use to you anymore."

"Just murder you? In cold blood? That's a little barbaric, don't you think?" Hollick thoroughly enjoyed himself. Torturing Levin had thrilled him in a way that caused a part of his mind to recoil in horror. Now that he was free to do what he wanted, even if it was ostensibly in service to Margaret Jansen, he was beginning to understand those hidden urges he'd always carried. He now realized that, deep down, he'd always been a sadist.

He looked over at the ruined mess that had once been a strong, faithful Marine, and it gave him a dark thrill to have broken him in both body and spirit. When he was an NIS agent, he'd had to repress these feelings as even a quasi-terrorist group like One World would likely frown upon his methods, but he had to admit they got results. He just had to be careful to keep a tight lid on it and not get sloppy.

When he'd grabbed Taylor Levin, he'd thought it would be a quick interrogation. How could some dumb grunt hold out against a trained NIS agent that had specialized in information extraction? But the kid had proven to be a tough nut to crack, and in doing so, had sealed his own fate. Once things started to get ugly—really ugly—it had quickly devolved from an interrogation into a mindless orgy of brutality. When, finally, the Marine could take no more, it had taken all of Hollick's self-control to stop. By the time he'd snuck back into the hangar and managed to get aboard their ship via an external maintenance hatch, the core had already been moved. Apparently, Brown wasn't as foolish as he'd hoped.

Now, Hollick was stuck. He had no idea where the rest of Obsidian was, where the core was, where Tulden was, and now, he would likely have a body to dispose of since, without medical attention soon, Corporal Levin wasn't long for this world. As he pondered his options, one of his *clean* com units chimed with an incoming message.

"Convenient," he muttered, reading through the message from the ConFed spook. Tulden wanted to meet in person to discuss how to salvage the operation now that Obsidian had gone underground. Hollick narrowed his eyes at that, not sure he believed everything he was reading. After considering all available actions, he decided on the most direct and sent Tulden a response. He'd need to be careful. The ConFed agent was disciplined, smart, and he knew the area better than Hollick did.

"I'm afraid our time has come to an end, Corporal," Hollick said, slipping two com units into his pocket and collecting the other things he'd need. "If your friends get here in time, you'll survive...though I wouldn't plan on entering any beauty pageants. Nothing personal, sport. This is a tough business. Who knows...one day, I'll probably find myself strapped to a chair just like you when I meet my end."

"We can only hope," Taylor said. "The LT is going to kill you.

You've seen what he can do, how fast he is. You'll try to take him down, and he'll tear your head off your neck." It was the most Taylor had said since the real torment had begun, and the comment shook Hollick more than he would have liked to admit.

"We'll see," he said, quickly leaving the room.

17

"He should be back by now."

"He's two minutes overdue, Murph," Jacob said.

"The two hours was a maximum estimate," Murph said. "It shouldn't be taking this long. We're in the middle of a three-headed counterintelligence operation involving us, ConFed Intelligence, and One World. I think we need to consider the possibilities that Tulden sold us out and we're at risk by staying here in a location he knows."

"Sergeant Murphy's reasoning is sound," 707 rumbled. Jacob looked to the battlesynth, but the stoic machine offered no further commentary.

"So, we go back to the ship?" Jacob asked.

"That's my suggestion," Murph said. "Abandon everything here that isn't sensitive and haul ass back to the ship. Tulden will be able to figure out where we are, and we'll be in a place neither can easily attack us at. The hangars are all closely guarded by station security."

"Fine," Jacob said. "Pack it up and let's move. Leave anything that can be left."

All of the gear issued to Scout Fleet was either sourced through contracts by alien suppliers or designed and built so as to not be traceable back to Earth. All of the medical, com gear, and even some of the weapons could all be left without fear of someone finding it and knowing a Terran team was operating out of the room. Jacob had paid for the space with forged credentials and untraceable credit chits.

After the team had quickly broken down the gear and organized themselves for movement, Jacob waved them towards the door. The two battlesynths left first, taking point. They'd only made it through two intersections when 707 stopped short, raising an alloy fist to stop them all. Jacob moved past MG and 784 to see what the holdup was.

"Your ConFed agent is up ahead," 707 said. "He is slumped against the wall and appears to be bleeding quite badly."

"Shit," Jacob muttered, peering around the corner. Tulden was on the ground, obviously hurt badly, but still looked alive. "You think it's a trap set by Hollick?"

"This would not be a good area for an ambush. We have multiple paths of escape, and he cannot engage us except from extreme ranges ahead and behind us. I am detecting no traces of explosives or electronic emissions consistent with a detonator."

"Got it," Jacob said, walking around the battlesynth and approaching the agent. "Tulden? You dead?"

"Nearly," Tulden said quietly. "Just taking a little break before meeting you in your remote base."

"I can save you the trouble. What happened?"

"Elton Hollick was able to surprise me," Tulden said. "I relied too much on my tech that would alert me to a primed weapon in my vicinity, and he came at me with an edged weapon. He found out I had failed to retrieve the core and was...displeased."

"He's not a pleasant person," Jacob said, taking in the severity of Tulden's myriad wounds. Some were deep, others looked to have been inflicted only to cause pain. The thought of Taylor being in the hands of a person who could do this turned Jacob's stomach.

"I don't have much time," Tulden said. "Reach into the pocket on the inside of my left pant leg...down near the foot. There's a data card that has the location of the fleet you're looking for. I would ask that you consider destroying the data core now that I have failed my mission."

"What's on that thing, anyway?"

"Raw intel," Tulden said. "In the wrong hands, it could destabilize the entire region. There are other threats outside of this upstart rebellion that would want it."

"Did you find where Taylor was being— Well...shit," Jacob said as Tulden's eyes closed, and he slumped over. Dead. Cringing a bit, Jacob reached up the dead agent's pant leg, rooting around until he found the pocket with the data card in it.

"Let's go!" he called to his team. "To the ship, double time."

They ran all the way back to the ship, rushing through startled throngs of aliens and ignoring angry shouts as they moved through the market areas and into the hangar staging spaces. When they got to the *Boneshaker*, they found what they'd most dreaded.

"That motherfucker!" MG choked out.

What was left of Corporal Taylor Levin laid in a pool of congealing blood near the starboard slip-drive nacelle. The body had been dumped in one of the two blind areas the ship's external imagers didn't cover. Jacob approached the body, his mind numb and unthinking as he looked down on his friend. A man who had trusted him to lead. A man who he had failed utterly.

Taylor's face was frozen in a rictus of pure agony and the damage that had been inflicted on him was beyond Jacob's ability to comprehend. This was not the act of an operative extracting information. This was purely sadistic and done for pleasure.

He was vaguely aware of Mettler trying to console MG and Murph staring at the body with the same dead detachment he felt himself. Without being consciously aware of it, his weapon slipped from his fingers, and he sank to the deck. When Commander Mosler had been killed, it had hurt, but Mosler had died through no fault of Jacob's. He'd been murdered by a traitor who had been placed on the crew well before Jacob showed up. Taylor, however, had been killed in as gruesome a way as he could imagine because he didn't know what the fuck he was doing. He was a kid out here playing space cowboy and pretending he had the answers, and his hubris and ignorance had just caught up with him, only he wasn't the one who paid the price. Any sane person would have insisted on being relieved and told Captain Webb Obsidian had to be recalled until proper, *qualified* leadership was found.

"Lieutenant, there will be time to mourn your comrade," 707 said gently. "But we should leave this place immediately. Hollick will have certainly alerted station security to the deaths and will have implicated your team."

"You're right." Jacob's voice was a hoarse whisper. "Let's get him out of here."

He turned and saw Sully standing there. The pilot had retrieved one of the stasis bags used for remains that Scout Fleet teams carried with them. When Jacob looked up, he saw tears standing in the taller man's eyes.

"Thank you," he said, accepting the bag. The four remaining Marines of Scout Team Obsidian knelt and prepared Taylor's remains for transport back home. When the bag was sealed and purged with a stabilizing agent that would stave off decomposition, the four of them remained kneeling for a moment. MG and Mettler held hands, their free hands resting on Taylor's chest.

"LT?" Jacob turned to MG, ready to fend off an angry, accusatory barrage.

"Yes?"

"Please, tell me we're going to finish this," MG said. "Tell me we're not turning tail and running back home. You know that piece of shit is on his way to the *Talon* right now. We can finish our mission and nail that son of a bitch." Jacob blinked. He hadn't been expecting that, but the more he thought about it, he realized he should have. His men were pros.

"I won't order you to go on with a mission that should have been scrubbed already. This is really what everyone else wants?"

"Yes, sir!"

"Okay then...let's do it," Jacob said. "Sully, prep us for departure, please. 707, I assume you'll be following in your ship?"

"701 is coming here, and our ship has been sent home on autopilot," 707 said. "We will ride with you in the cargo bay of this vessel. Our ship was a specialized transport that is very high speed, but of little use in a fight. I will inform Captain Webb of our intention to assist you."

Before Jacob could answer, the Battlesynth stomped up the ramp and helped himself to the ship's com room. It had been interesting seeing the hulking machine maneuver into a space that was cramped for an average sized human. His team quickly finished prepping the ship, including a quick and dirty sweep for any bombs or trackers with the help of 784 and his extensive sensor suite. By the time the last of the cargo was cinched down in the hold, and all his people were accounted for, the engines thrummed with power, and Sully had already called for departure clearance.

With the last known location of the fleet now in his possession, Jacob felt like he could see the end of this Godforsaken mission. All he'd have to do now is get positive identification of the *Eagle's Talon*, and then call in the Naval strike force that was waiting to either retrieve or scuttle the stolen cruiser.

Easy.

"Sir, 707 has made contact."

"Give me the broad strokes," Webb said, waving his aide in and closing the hatch behind him.

"The three battlesynths that went to offer Obsidian assistance have decided to remain with Lieutenant Brown for the time being...at least until he completes the mission," Bennet said. "I pressed it for—"

"*He,* Lieutenant...don't call one of them an *it*. Apparently, they take the same type of offense to it that we would."

"Odd." Bennet frowned. "Why would a constructed, asexual being care about gender at all?"

"No idea." Webb shrugged. "I just know they do. It may have something to do with how they were created, or maybe it's a conscious choice in order to relate to biologic species better. It should be easy for you to keep straight since all of the members of Lot 700 are male."

"Fascinating," Bennet said. "Anyway, I pressed *him* for more information regarding Obsidian's actions and intentions, but he refused to provide anything."

"Not surprising. They don't really adhere to our command structure or authority. Those three left because Brown was in danger specifically, not because they give two shits about helping us get our ship back. Battlesynths in general, and Lot 700 in particular, feel like they owe Jason Burke a great debt, so protecting his son is high on their priority list."

"Could you imagine if Burke fully understood that he could command the loyalty of all remaining battlesynths in the quadrant?" Bennet asked. "He could overthrow the government of any planet he liked and name himself emperor for life." Webb gave an involuntary shudder at that.

"Let's hope he never fully realizes it," he said. "I like Burke well enough, but I'm not sure he has the temperament to rule. Try to contact Obsidian and get a status update from them and, in the meantime, I'll have Admiral Sisk move his taskforce towards Colton Hub."

Once Bennet left the office, Webb sent a message to Commander Duncan, asking him to change their course. The *Kentucky* currently loafed towards the planet Olympus, but now he wanted to be nearer the action since it looked like Obsidian would be giving them targeting coordinates soon. He also wanted to make sure Admiral Sisk knew that Captain Edgars might try to enlist his new comrades to keep from being captured, so the human taskforce would need to proceed with caution.

He was carefully crafting his message to Admiral Sisk when a new message alert came in. Since he was a lowly captain, he wasn't really giving orders to an admiral. Taskforce Bravo had been put at his disposal by Fleet Ops to specifically hunt down and recover the *Talon*, but he wanted to make sure his message sounded like a polite request. It was the sort of political niceties that had to be observed within the flag ranks of any military. Once he'd finished that, he checked on the alert and saw that it was from Lieutenant Brown.

It was a full status report from Obsidian, detailing everything since the last time they'd been in contact. As he read it, his mouth hung open in shock. Brown had lost one of his teammates, had been wrangling with ConFed Intelligence on a place like Colton Hub, and had been forced to counter the moves of Elton Hollick. This was the type of mission that would have pushed even his best team leaders to the brink, but the kid seemed to just be pushing ahead. His last paragraph said he thought it would have been best to scrub the mission given his string of failures, but his men asked to press on and to not let Corporal Levin's death have been for nothing.

Webb stopped reading and wiped his eyes. He hadn't known Taylor Levin very well, but he was familiar with the young man's record, as he was with all his Scout Fleet operators. It was sometimes easy to forget there was a real price to be paid when he sent these men and women out into the wild, asking them to risk their lives for information vital to Earth's interests. That the tattered remnants of Scout Team Obsidian were pressing on despite their losses was a testament to the type of people willing to take those risks.

As he read Brown's clinical description of what Elton Hollick had done to Corporal Levin, his rage built. This One World faction bullshit had gone on long enough. Margaret Jansen needed to be stopped, and if Earth wouldn't act decisively to put an end to the threat she represented, he would need to. But first, he needed to find her. There were some resources he could bring to bear, but using outside contractors for this sort of thing was risky. He'd need to be careful to keep his own involvement hidden.

All that would have to wait for the moment, however, as he had more pressing things to deal with. If he could get Jacob Brown and his remaining team back alive and deal with Captain Edgars, he would consider this a costly but ultimately successful operation. He doubted Navy brass would see it that way, however, and he was dead certain this would be his last stint in a leadership role. With most of Scout Fleet being wiped out likely due to leaks within his own organization he seemed helpless to stop, he would have a hard time arguing he was an effective leader who should keep his post.

Such was the nature of the job...but it still sucked.

18

"I wish there was something to look at...maybe just a planet or moon nearby to orient myself. These deep space locations are creepy."

"What's the difference between dying of explosive decompression closer to a planet as opposed to out here?" Murph asked.

"I just said it was creepy, I wasn't looking to start a fucking debate, college boy," MG shot back.

"Shut the hell up back there!" Jacob barked over his shoulder.

"If I survive this, maybe I can get a posting in Space Mobility Command," Sully muttered. "Just fly cargo back and forth."

"You'd miss us too much," MG said. The pilot turned around and fixed such an evil glare on the Marine that Jacob thought things might turn violent.

"Passive sensors are picking up drive signatures from dozens of ships," Jacob said. "It looks like they're forming up to mobilize."

"They probably know their location has been compromised," Sully said. "They'll mesh-out in small groups and form up again in another location to stay ahead of the ConFed. The computer is starting to populate known ship-type signatures. I see the *Defiant*, the rest of the Cridal strike force...and there's the *Eagle's Talon*."

"I see her," Jacob said, his heart pounding. They'd done it. The ship was right there, and now all they had to do was call it in. "Murph."

"On it," Murph said, slipping off the flightdeck and into the com room to call in the cavalry. While everyone babbled excitedly about actually having found the missing fleet, Jacob discreetly punched in a set of search parameters, narrowing down what he searched for in the vast cluster of ships before him. He didn't have an exact engine signature, and the ship he looked for tended to be modified so often that it would have been useless so, instead, he looked for just the generic classifications: gunship-class, medium-range.

When the search came back negative for anything even close to what he had been looking for he felt a surge of relief. His father didn't appear to be flying with a criminal, rogue element being hunted by a ConFed battle fleet...and that relief he felt surprised him. His anger and resentment towards the man remained steady and strong, but he'd been forced to acknowledge that the caricature he'd painted of Jason Burke wasn't quite accurate. From what he'd been told recently from people who knew him, Burke's situation was much more complicated than it appeared.

"Uh oh," Sully said, snapping Jacob's attention back. "The *Talon* has turned and is coming right at us, accelerating hard."

"Get us out of here! Come about and—" Jacob's sentence was cut off from a series of muffled explosions that shook the shuttle. Alarms blared, and emergency pressure hatches slammed shut all over the ship. Sully fought with the controls, but it seemed clear that whatever had happened had completely disabled them.

"Can we kill those alarms?" MG shouted. A moment later, main power flickered and failed, plunging the flightdeck into darkness and silence.

"That quiet enough for you?" Sully asked. They all floated in their restraints as artificial gravity failed.

"Murph! Please tell me you got that message out!" Jacob yelled, his voice painfully loud without the ambient noise of the ship.

"Wish I could," Murph said, floating back onto the flightdeck. "It was still establishing a connection when the power died."

"Is Mettler okay?"

"He's on the other side of the pressure hatch, can't talk to him."

"Where the hell is the emergency power?"

They all sat in silence for some time, nobody wanting to say aloud that if the *Boneshaker*'s emergency power system was dead, so would they be in short order. It would just be a race to see what killed them first, the lack of oxygen or the cold of space leeching the heat from the cabin. Already, Jacob could feel the temperature dropping. Most small ships weren't well thermally insulated, the limited space being used up by the more critical radiation shielding. At least, it seemed more critical until you lost power.

A metal-on-metal grinding along the outer hull was the first indicator they weren't about to freeze or suffocate to death. The *bangs* and *screeches* that reverberated through the interior confused the hell out of them until spotlights hit the ship, blinding them. The sounds they'd been hearing were a clumsy boom operator trying to grapple onto the stricken shuttle to be pulled inside a yawning hangar bay. Jacob shielded his eyes and looked out at what ship was retrieving them.

"Shit," he said, breath fogging in the stale air. "It's the *Talon*. I guess they made us right when we meshed-in."

"Be careful! There are humans in there, goddamnit!" Captain Edgars bellowed as he walked across his hangar deck towards the absolute junk heap of a ship his crew had pulled aboard.

The older generation Eshquarian combat shuttle had certainly seen better days. There were missing outer hull plates, spots that were riddled with corrosion and ravaged by metal-eating parasites. The grappling boom operator tried to gently right the shuttle, but the angle wasn't optimal, and the ship slipped from the mechanical grip and slammed onto the deck with a deafening *boom* that almost took Edgars off his feet.

"As promised, Captain...one shuttle containing a United Earth Navy Scout Fleet crew, as well as the encrypted data core that you wanted."

"All I see is one dilapidated hunk of shit, Hollick, so don't go celebrating too quickly. I'm still going to have you tossed out an airlock if this isn't what you said it is."

"Of course, Captain," Hollick said, smiling so widely it looked painful.

"All right...let's get them out of there!" Edgars shouted. "Ground team, tac team...you're up!"

Two separate crews of spacers rushed forward and swarmed over the shuttle. The first was a group of technicians who would work to open the ship, the second was a tactical response team, armed to the teeth, who would cover all the hatches in case the occupants made a poor decision.

The tech crew pulled over a low-current power umbilical and hooked it into the ship, giving them enough power to do things like operate the hatches, get air recirculating, and turn the lights on. It wouldn't give them enough juice to do something like energize weapons or try to restart their powerplant. As soon as power was applied, the marker lights on the horizontal stabilizers blinked, and the whine of hydraulic accumulators filled the space.

"Sir, this is patched into their intercom through the maintenance port," a technician said, handing Edgars a headset. The captain didn't bother putting it on. He just held the mic near his mouth since he had no intentions of a two-way negotiation with the people aboard the shuttle.

"Attention occupants of the hunk of garbage sitting on my hangar deck...this is Captain Edgars. We know who you are, and I can guess why you're here. Drop the ramp to your cargo bay and get down on your knees, hands on top of your heads, and wait for my Marines to secure the ship and you. Nobody needs to die here today. You're just doing your job and, if you're smart about this, I'll be sending you back to Terranovus where you can keep doing it. Do something stupid, and I'll kill each and every one of you. You have two minutes to comply."

"Captain I was under the impression that—"

"I never agreed to hand them over to you," Edgars said, turning on Hollick. "Keep it up and you might not be leaving here yourself." Hollick shut his mouth, but his eyes blazed with anger.

It was barely thirty seconds later when there were some sharp *clangs* from the rear ramp, and then it slowly dropped to the deck. When the tac team rushed aboard, they found five people crouched down with their hands on their heads. Three people stayed to secure them while the others continued on into the ship. A few minutes later, the five occupants were led out and brought over to Edgars.

"The ship is clear, Captain," the sergeant leading the detail said. "Bio-scanners confirm these were the only people aboard the ship, along with the body of one of their own. None of them were armed."

"You're sure the other is really dead?" Edgars asked.

"He's dead, Captain," the young Marine lieutenant said. "He was tortured to death and hacked up by the piece of shit standing next to you." Edgars looked at his own sergeant, who just nodded grimly.

"I thank you for making the smart decision and coming out without a fight, Lieutenant..." he prompted.

"Brown, sir."

"Brown. Losing a man in action is a terrible thing. You just made sure you didn't needlessly lose more. I will keep my word, and your people will be released back to Earth, but I need one more token of goodwill from you, and I need it quickly. The data core?"

"It's secured under a deck plate in my quarters, sir," Brown said.

"And how do I know there's not a bomb under there instead?"

"Have your Marines take me with them when they check. If I rigged up a bomb, it will take me out, as well." Edgars looked at him for a moment before nodding to his sergeant.

"Go get it."

It was only a few moments later when the sergeant jogged back up and handed the core to Edgars.

"It was right where he said it was, sir. No funny stuff, either."

"Take this to Lieutenant Commander Peterson in Flight Ops," Edgars said, handing the core to a junior officer behind him. "Tell him it needs to be flown out to a corvette-class ship flying near the Eshquarian formation called the *Devil's Fortune*. It's the only corvette in the fleet, so he can't miss it. I need this done ASAP before we redeploy."

"Aye-aye, sir!"

"So, why did you just hand over the core without any bargaining, Lieutenant?" Edgars asked.

"The data core wasn't my mission, Captain," Brown said. "I don't even know what's on it. If you've given your word as an officer that my men will be released, then I see no need to bother with pointless bargaining. Even if I had played games, your people would have eventually found it."

"An admirably pragmatic assessment of your situation, Lieutenant," Edgars said. "We'll talk more later, but right now, we're just a bit pressed for time. I would say my brig doesn't offer much in the way of comfort, but I think it'll probably be an improvement over your ship. I didn't realize Scout Fleet's budget had taken such a hit lately."

"Do more with less, sir...that's our motto."

"Make our guests comfortable, Sergeant."

"Aye, sir."

19

"So now, we're captives aboard a rogue ship, flying with a rebel fleet the ConFed wants wiped out," MG said, staring at the ceiling. "Great plan, LT."

"What do you think took out our main power?" Murph asked, ignoring MG.

"Sully?" Jacob asked.

"It's *possible* there was someone sitting back in our sensor blind spot," the pilot said. He was lying on his back on one of the racks, staring at the ceiling. They'd been tossed into one large holding cell as opposed to being separated, so Jacob assumed they were being monitored by the *Talon*'s crew, hoping to catch some intel about what the Fleet had planned for them.

"Possible but unlikely," Jacob said. "Our subluminal engines were at zero output, so the washout would have been negligible."

"Yep," Sully agreed. "Which means your good buddy, Hollick, planted a device on the ship that our security sweeps missed. Since the main reactor shut itself down in emergency mode, I'm guessing he put charges on the main bus lines."

"That would explain why 784 missed it, too," Murph said. "We were focusing on devices powerful enough to take out the ship, not just disable it."

"We were in a rush," Jacob said. "Nobody's fault there. Did anybody notice there didn't seem to be a lot of people aboard?"

"Maybe they cleared the corridors while we were being moved," Mettler said.

"I don't think so," Jacob argued. "There's a certain feel to a fully crewed ship that this one doesn't have."

"Maybe they—" The hatch to the outer security station clanging open interrupted the conversation and two Marines walked in.

"Lieutenant Brown...the captain would like to see you."

"I'm at the captain's disposal," Jacob said, walking up and turning around so he could place his arms behind him through the slot. It only took the Marine a second to put the restraints on him. They were the plastic kind Jacob knew for a fact he could overcome should he need to. It still tore up his wrists, but he was just strong enough to snap the loops that held the cuffs together if he twisted hard enough.

The Marines unlocked the cell, one waving Jacob through while the other watched the rest of his team. They were polite and not overly aggressive, not even bothering to place their hands on their sidearms while performing the task.

"We appreciate the cooperation, gentlemen," one of them said. "Sit tight, and you'll be heading home in no time."

Jacob walked in between his two escorts in silence, looking around the ship as he went. They didn't bother with any of the clichés like telling him to keep his head straight or to hurry up. After two lift rides and some more walking, he was deposited in front of the captain's office, searched again, and then gently guided through the door. Inside, Captain Edgars sat at his desk. He only glanced up before waving Jacob into one of the chairs and motioned for the Marines to remove his restraints before dismissing them.

"I can handle him from here. Just wait outside the door."

"Yes, sir."

So, Lieutenant Brown...is your crew comfortable?" Edgars asked once they were alone.

"Quite, sir. You were right about the brig being more comfortable than the ship we were on," Jacob said.

"I find it interesting you're choosing to still honor customs and courtesies, all things considered." Edgars steepled his fingers under his chin and leaned back in the chair. Jacob knew he could get across the desk, even in the restraints, and kill the man before the Marines could get back through the hatch. It wouldn't gain him anything, but it was an interesting thought exercise.

"I see no point in being adversarial, Captain," he said. "My team was sent to locate your ship, nothing more. To my knowledge, you haven't been formally charged with a crime, much less prosecuted and stripped of rank."

"And you know that if you antagonize me, your odds of getting your men home safely go down," Edgars said. "You're clever. But then again, all Scout Fleet officers are."

"I don't suppose you'd care to tell me how my ship was disabled, would you, sir?"

"You can thank Elton Hollick for that. He rigged your ship with a couple different little toys he guaranteed were undetectable. When you arrived in this area, he was able to disable your main and emergency power systems. Drink?"

"No, thank you," Jacob said. "I have to ask, sir...are you working with Hollick in an official capacity?"

"Am I part of Margaret Jansen's little club to overthrow Earth?" Edgars snorted as he filled two glasses anyway and set one in front of Jacob. "This is from a test batch a captain in our fleet is making on a planet called S'Tora, although I think this was actually made on Earth."

"A captain in this fleet is making Earth whiskey on another planet?" Jacob asked, smelling the drink and taking a small sip.

"Enterprising man, apparently," Edgars said. "He's brought some whiskey making experts from Earth to set up his own distilling operation on an alien planet out near the Delphine Expanse. My point to this story is that there's no way for One World to reach its goals. Humanity has already moved beyond all that and is colonizing the quadrant."

"A tyrant in charge of Earth is still something to be concerned about, sir."

"But she can't win, Lieutenant. She doesn't have the resources."

"Can I surmise Hollick flew out here, approached you with the knowledge that we were coming and that we had the core?" Jacob asked.

"That's pretty much how it went, yes."

"And how did he know where to find you, sir?"

"I assume he found out when he tortured your teammate," Edgars said. "Is there a point to this?"

"Sir, we didn't know where you were. Hollick had the location the whole time and tried to barter with an agent from ConFed Intelligence," Jacob said. The pieces all started to fall into place in his head. "He promised the agent the location of your fleet if he got us and the data core. After that, he would kill us and deliver the core to you."

"That's not much of a plan. What would be the point in killing a Scout Fleet team and needlessly pissing off Earth?"

"It's personal," Jacob said. "I'm the reason he has that clunky prosthetic. When he approached you, did he want to trade you something? Something you knew or have in exchange for that data core?" Edgars put his drink down, now looking concerned.

"What he asked me for wasn't something I would ever give him… not even if it meant my own death," the captain said, suddenly deadly serious. "Not that it would matter. The thing he wants doesn't stay in one place very long, and it's not really a thing that's able to be stolen."

"Cryptic," Jacob said. "I'll just assume it's far above my paygrade."

"Safe assumption, Lieutenant," Edgars said. "I was involved in the design of the Victory-class ships so I had access to some…specialized…engineering resources on Earth. Hollick is asking for that in return for the core."

"So, you never intended to honor the agreement?" Jacob asked.

"I don't honor agreements with traitors," Edgars said. "And before you point out the obvious hypocrisy of the statement, my involvement in this rebellion is not treason. My crew and I are upholding our oaths to defend Earth. We are not in this for personal gain, money, or power. We fully intend to die in this fight, but it's the right thing to do."

"What's on that data core, sir?"

"It's something that will turn the tide. The ConFed has let us be for now because it knows it can crush us at will. They need to pursue those backing us with resources and logistics first, and *then* their mighty fleet will swoop in and wipe us all out." Edgars took a long pull on his drink. "But they have some critical vulnerabilities that, if hit first, could weaken them beyond their ability to recover."

"Why not take that to the NIS or the Navy, sir? Let them make a case to Earth that it's in our best interest to—"

"To *what*? Earth will never agree to any sort of preemptive strike because the politicians are too scared of offending Seeladas Dalton. The Cridal Cooperative is collapsing in on itself, and Earth is still hiding behind them, thinking they can protect them when the truth is, the Cooperative can't even protect itself." Edgars composed himself, and then stood up.

"Perhaps Earth does need to stay out of this, though. Once the ConFed falls, there are some beta wolves who will try to vie for supremacy. Our little three-world empire would be hard pressed to take them on."

"Why tell me all this, sir?"

"I'm hoping that when I send you back to Terranovus, you'll be able to explain to your superiors why I'm doing this," Edgars said. "Perhaps they'll even simply write the *Talon* off as lost and let me do my job." The captain pressed a button on his desk, and the two Marines walked back in, signaling an end to the conversation.

"One last thing, Captain," Jacob said as he stood. "You need to ask yourself how Hollick had the location of your ship. I think you know the obvious answer to that. They're everywhere, sir...and they're not as harmless as you think."

"Have a good evening, Lieutenant," Edgars said, his voice flat.

Jacob was in a bit of a mental fog as he walked back to the holding cell with his Marine escort. Edgars wasn't what he had expected. He'd almost assumed he'd be facing some sort of deranged zealot, laughing maniacally while he put everyone in danger because he was some sort of combat junkie.

But Edgars wasn't any of that. He was a measured, thoughtful, focused commander who still had enough compassion to make sure his team was well taken care of. Although he seemed aware of the One World threat, he seemed to be heavily downplaying it. It was almost certain the faction had at least one mole aboard the *Talon* that fed intel back to Jansen, but if they always had the location, why go through all the needless ruse with the data core?

"The chow cart will be down in a couple hours to take care of you guys," the Marine NCO said as he closed the cell door and motioned for Jacob's hands so he could take off the restraints.

"Steak and lobster tonight?" MG asked.

"You know it," the guard laughed. "I'll be sure to send the chef down to ask how you like it cooked and if you'd like a nice red wine to go with it."

"You know what, you're a solid guy for a fleet puke," MG said.

While Jacob Brown was escorted back to one of the *Talon*'s detention areas, Captain Edgars sat in his office, the constant stress headache he carried beginning to move to the forefront again.

"Fuck!" he hissed, knocking his empty glass off the desk with a savage swipe. The heavy cut crystal hit the bulkhead and landed on the carpet of his office without even chipping.

How could he have been so stupid as to miss the obvious?

Looking at it in hindsight, there was no way that Hollick could have gotten the location from Brown's crew. If the Scout Fleet team had the location in the first place, they'd have never gone to Colton Hub, they'd have just come straight there. The only way Hollick would have had that information was because Edgars had a damn

One World sympathizer somewhere on his crew. He was already reduced to a less-than-optimum crew compliment thanks to a third of his people opting to transfer off and head back home rather than stay with the rebellion. As such, many were performing multiple functions with a lot of overlap, so trying to track down who had been leaking the intel to Jansen's band of idiots and sociopaths would be damn near impossible. For all he knew, there were multiple traitors aboard.

"Have Hollick brought up from his cell," he said into the intercom, not bothering to listen for a reply. He picked his glass up and set it where the steward would find it before pulling a sidearm from a wall safe and sitting back at his desk. Hollick was a highly trained, dangerous operative who knew most of their security protocols. For this conversation, there wouldn't be any bespoke whiskey or friendly banter. He'd have two Marines standing behind the bastard at all times.

"The...guest...you requested, Captain."

"Bring him in," Edgars said. "You two come in, as well."

"Captain Edgars." Hollick walked in wearing a wide smile. "You wished to see me."

"Just some things to clear up before I release you," Edgars said.

"With your end of the bargain upheld, I hope," Hollick said. Edgars just stared at him for a long moment.

"What you and Jansen want...it doesn't exist," he finally said. "You think the Ark is simply a device that was given to us that we talk to, but that original computer is long gone. The Ark isn't something that can be controlled or manipulated or stolen. It's intelligent, has a will of its own, and it has a mandate. It knows about your little losers club, and it sees you as an enemy of humanity as a whole."

"Then you will help us talk to it," Hollick said. "Assuming I even believe this story, of course."

"Are you daft, boy? The Ark won't likely speak to me once it finds out I stole a Naval vessel and linked up with this rogue fleet. Even if it would, it's not like we can just fly to Earth and waltz up to it."

"You're lying!" Hollick said, his nostrils flaring. "I know you were given a specialized AI interface with advanced engineering knowledge...knowledge about weapons and starship drives that can bridge space instantaneously. We want that device!"

"I just told you...it's gone," Edgars said slowly. "The original interface was built into a run-of-the-mill laptop. One of the first projects the Ark Team did was build a suitable system for it to live on, and once it transferred over, it grew and evolved. It's no longer a thing that can be possessed."

"I got you the data core you wanted. You owe me!" The Marines were now edging in closer as Hollick's slick, in-control façade slipped.

"Look...I really don't give a shit about you and Jansen's effort to take over Earth," Edgars said. "If our rebellion fails, the ConFed will roll over them in short order, anyway, but not before they flatten your Ull allies and all your secret bases. I agreed to tell you where the Ark was, but all I can tell you is where it was the last time I saw it, which was nearly ten years ago."

"Where was it?" Hollick said, now seeming back in control of himself.

"At the Groom Lake Starport," Edgars said. "The original Ark was studied at the old test base facility, which is now a museum and tourist attraction. You can book a tour there from Las Vegas."

"You think you're clever, do you?" Hollick said quietly. "It was foolish to play games with us, Captain."

"I'm doing what I have to do, just like you people think you are," Edgars said.

"When will I be released?"

"We're in the middle of a series of slip-space flights to elude any possible trackers. You'll be given your clearance to leave soon. Until then, you'll remain in your cell."

"Of course." Hollick rose slowly, keeping his hands where the Marines could see them. "I'm sure you'll be as glad to be rid of me as I will be to leave. Warships are not my favorite place to be."

"Good evening, Mr. Hollick." Edgars nodded to his Marines to escort him out. Once they were gone, he punched the intercom button to call the bridge.

"Yes, sir?"

"Tell Chief Willis that I want Elton Hollick's cell under guard at all times. They're not to just use the automated monitoring system."

"Yes, sir. What about the Marines in that other cell?"

"They're fine," Edgars said. "Just have them remotely monitored, but don't waste the manpower on having someone babysit them."

"I'll handle it, Captain."

Edgars sat back, eyeing the bottle on the sideboard for a long moment before caving and pouring another generous drink. It really was good stuff. He made a note to ask the man who brought it to him if he could get in on the ground floor of his little operation. If they all survived this rebellion, he stood to become a very wealthy man once the whiskey went on sale throughout the quadrant.

20

"We just dropped out of slip-space again," Sully said.

"That's what, the third time?" Murph asked.

"Yeah. They must be trying to lose a tail, or Captain Edgars is just incredibly paranoid. So, you met him...what do you think of him?"

"Me?" Jacob asked.

"Yes, you. Did anybody else go up and have drinks with him?" Sully rolled his eyes.

"He's a believer," Jacob said. "He knows that what he's doing poses a threat to Earth, but he genuinely thinks it's a secondary concern when compared to letting the ConFed remain in power in the quadrant."

"What was on that data core we were carrying?" Mettler asked.

"I guess some sort of strategic intel about ConFed vulnerabilities that this outfit can use." Jacob shrugged. "He wasn't about to outline his entire evil plan for me just because I asked."

They all fell silent, waiting for when Sully told them the ship had meshed-out again. The pilot seemed to have a preternatural sense about what ships were doing just by the vibrations through the deck. They were so focused on trying to detect the same thing that when the overhead speaker hissed and popped, they all jumped.

"Lieutenant Brown, are you and your men well?"

"About damn time," Jacob grumbled. "Where have you been?"

"It took us some time to exit the ship without being spotted," 707 said. "784 has created a secure channel to your detention cell. We will monitor it at all times, so if you need to speak to us, just speak aloud. He has also disabled active monitoring that would alert the bridge that something was amiss."

"Outstanding. So...what's your plan?"

"There are various options available to us," 707 said evasively. "Can I assume you would rather the crew of this ship was not harmed or killed?"

"Yeah, let's go ahead and assume that." Jacob rolled his eyes.

"Then we will need some more time to prepare."

"Do that and get back to me," Jacob said. "Try not to get caught."

"There are not very many crewmembers aboard. Accessing the required systems will not be difficult."

"I was wondering when they were going to pop back up," MG said. "It was driving me nuts not being able to talk since they were probably listening."

"We just jumped back into slip-space," Sully yawned.

Elton Hollick paced his cell like a caged animal. Edgars' words had dug into his brain like a worm, driving him into a manic state only made worse by being confined. The idea that the Ark might be something permanently out of their reach was an idea he just couldn't accept. Without it, One World simply had no chance of overpowering Earth's new military. In a frighteningly short time, humanity had fielded a navy that far surpassed the Ull's in terms of sophistication and raw firepower. It also didn't help Jansen only had the help of a small fraction of the Ull fleet while the entirety of the United Earth Navy stood against them.

The Ark would have allowed them to fit advanced systems onto their existing ships and use the technology as a bartering tool to bring other allies into the fold. Without it, they might not even be able to keep the Ull involved. Their alien benefactors grew impatient with Jansen's delays and empty promises. In fact, the relationship had soured to the point that Hollick was cultivating his own back-channel deals with them that would allow him to assume power of One World if the time came that it was necessary to depose Jansen.

He had no particular desire to be a leader. What he wanted was to be the power behind the throne, so to speak. To be the irreplaceable, anonymous, unspeakably wealthy, and powerful voice that advised the leader who was both the figurehead and target of the new regime. He'd studied all of history's powerful second in commands and knew what mistakes not to make, and putting himself at the head of One World before Earth was fully subdued would be a drastic mistake. But all he could do was to try and make sure Jansen held onto power long enough to execute her plan...a plan that required the Ark from Earth.

"What do you want?" one of the guards sitting in the antechamber asked. Hollick stopped pacing and perked his ears up.

"I was sent down to question the prisoner," another voice said.

"Why would they send you of all people to— *Ungh!*"

"We don't have much time," the newcomer said, walking up and using the Marine's security keycard to open the cell. "I knocked him out, but he'll be back up in ten minutes or so."

"You're one of our sleepers?" Hollick asked.

"Obviously," the woman said. "I can get you off this ship, but after that, you're on your own. There's a secondary hangar deck down below—"

"Below magazine one, just aft of the forward batteries," Hollick finished. "I'm familiar with this class of ship. The captain's launch is in that hangar. I assume it's prepped for flight?"

"Always is. Fully fueled and provisioned. We'll be dropping back out of slip-space soon. When we do, someone on the bridge is going to open the hangar doors and disable the departure alert."

"What about him." Hollick gestured to the Marine.

"He'll wake up and not remember the last few hours of his life," she said, showing him the device in her hand. It looked like a variant of something NIS used to knock people out so they'd wake up and not remember how it happened.

"Your bridge compatriot?"

"My partner." She waved him out of the cell and dragged the Marine in, closing the door. Hollick relieved him of his sidearm as he went by. "He's handling everything at the command level. We were both recruited at the academy by a One World operative."

"Let's go," Hollick said. He looked down the corridor before running to the lifts that would take him to the lower decks. He was leaving empty handed, but he was leaving to fight another day.

"Will you need anything from your ship?" she asked.

"No," he said. "I keep it sanitized. Anything important is hidden and encrypted to the point that, by the time someone could crack it, the data would be obsolete."

"Good," she said. "Better to not risk the main hangar deck."

As he moved quickly through the ship, he thought about making a detour to kill Jacob Brown but decided he couldn't risk it. The Scout Fleet team was also probably under guard, and it'd be too much noise while he was still so far away from the lower hangar. If Brown made his way back to the fleet, he had no doubt he'd get another chance to take the little shit out.

21

"Mesh-in complete, coordinates verified."

"Good, good," Edgars said absently. "Configure the *Talon* for normal operations. Begin sweeping the region with active sensors. I want to know what—"

"Sir! We have an unauthorized launch!"

Edgars leapt from his seat, rushing to the station that handled shipboard security, fully expecting to see that Brown's team had escaped and were flying their ship out. What he saw instead was his own captain's launch smoothly pulling out of the *Talon*'s forward hangar and racing away.

"Why didn't the alarm sound?! Fire on that ship!" he barked.

"Targeting system is...resetting, sir," his tactical officer said. "I don't understand what's going on."

"You don't?" Edgars snarled. "We have a traitor in our midst! Find out who—"

"It was him!" a com operator shouted, pointing at a startled ensign manning the auxiliary systems station. It was the station that controlled things like hatch alarms. "I just saw that he was into the exo-hatch panel!"

The two Marines standing sentry on the bridge didn't hesitate. They rushed the ensign as he frantically punched in commands at his station, tackling him to the ground and restraining him. Edgars walked over and looked at the terminal while the Marines searched the young officer, finding an illegal sidearm and what looked like an improvised explosive. The terminal screen showed he'd been into systems he had no need to access to perform his job.

Edgars backtracked the commands and saw the ensign had, indeed, been into the exo-hatch panel, as well as the internal security surveillance system panel. He'd managed to disable all of the automated monitoring of the brig, decks ten through twelve, and the forward hangar. The operating system aboard the Victory-class ships allowed for most of the terminals to be reconfigured per task by allowing the operator to load different *panels*, but each had to be opened by someone cleared to use it.

"How did you get into these," Edgars asked the ensign, who just glared back at him. "Who gave you the clearance codes to bypass the security lockouts?"

"I'm not telling you shit!" the ensign spat. The scrawny kid said it with enough venom and force that even the Marines holding him were startled. Edgars recognized what he was seeing: a zealot.

"One World trash," Edgars grunted. "How do these assholes keep recruiting people?"

"Sir?"

"Just chain him and gag him over there," Edgars pointed to a spot on the deck near the hatch. "And lock the ship down. Security Protocol Alpha-One. Find out who stole my launch!"

"Sir, you'd better take a look at this." Edgars walked over to check the screen on another terminal. It was one of his holding cells, but instead of a prisoner, it held one of his own Marines. The man was definitely alive and screaming at the top of his lungs.

"Which cell is this? Is it the one with the Scout Fleet team in it?"

"No, sir. They're still in their cell. This is the other guy who arrived before them."

"Send someone down to get the Marine out of the cell and find out what happened to him. Assume he's also a part of it, so make sure you disarm him," Edgars said. "Ship Ops!"

"Yes, sir?"

"Get the Sergeant at Arms up here, as well as Major Hernandez. I'm going to need her entire team on alert."

"Aye, sir."

Captain Edgars trudged back to his seat and sat down with a grunt. Damn. This had all gone to shit spectacularly fast. Maybe Lieutenant Brown had been right and One World represented much more of a threat than he'd given them credit for. They'd been able to breed a level of fanaticism into their recruits that was alarming. If that ensign had managed to set off his IED, he'd have killed many and likely disabled the ship to the point the rest wouldn't be much better off.

As he looked around his bridge, he wondered how many others on his trusted crew were traitors. He admittedly saw that as a bit of a hypocritical observation given that, technically, they were all traitors in the eyes of Earth's government right now. He knew he had to at least have two moles, operating in tandem, to have been able to spring Hollick and hamstring the *Talon* just long enough to let him escape. He would need to have his security team go through all the internal camera footage on that deck and find out who had gone down to the brig and overpowered one of his Marines.

"Have we recovered from his little sabotage effort?" he asked.

"Yes, sir. He had put multiple systems into a maintenance test cycle to keep us from firing on the ship, but we're back up and running," his ship ops officer reported. "We're performing a full debug sweep now to make sure he didn't manage to install any malicious software while he was at it."

"Good thinking. Keep me advised," Edgars said. "I'm going to go down and speak with our other unwelcome guests."

"Damnit!"

Elton Hollick had raged about the cabin of the small ship for the better part of two hours, and he was no closer to calming down now than when he started. The op was completely blown, and he knew it. There was simply no way he was going to be able to get the information they needed from Edgars now. He'd punched in the address he needed into the slip-com node terminal that was on the bridge, but he hadn't initiated a channel request yet. He was too spun up to think clearly, and he'd need his wits about him for what was to come.

How had this happened?

A couple years ago he'd been a double agent, cool, calm, and collected as he played both sides of the conflict. Even after having to fake his death so the NIS wouldn't do something rash like try to send a rescue for him, he'd managed to carve out an impressive niche for himself within Margaret Jansen's One World faction. He even managed to skim off an impressive amount of funds and had developed connections in the quadrant he'd intended to use as his exit plan in case Jansen's plans fell apart.

Then, on a fairly routine operation, the whole thing went to shit. Some dumbass engineer they'd recruited had panicked and killed Ezra Mosler, the commander of Scout Team Obsidian. Mosler was a respected, legendary figure within the intelligence community, so Hollick had known there would be some blowback from the ill-advised action. What he hadn't counted on was some nobody second lieutenant tracking him across the damn galaxy like a bloodhound. Jacob Brown was like a lit stick of dynamite, and that dynamite was being carried around by a very drunk monkey. You watched the whole thing with a certain fascinated horror, forgetting the dynamite was lit until it went off and screwed everything up.

Since Brown had wrecked his plans to obtain the Zadra Intel Network, instead, securing it for Earth, it seemed like nothing had gone right for Hollick. From fighting with substandard prosthetics to having simple drops go bad, nothing was going to plan. It was inconceivable that one kid could be that consistently lucky. He'd even managed to somehow stumble onto the data core the rebel fleet was having smuggled out of Saabror space, swooping in and snatching it away from him and using it to execute a similar plan to Hollick's own. After losing the data core at Pinnacle, Hollick had been forced to pursue the Scout Fleet team halfway across the quadrant and adjust his plans on the fly. Since he'd sent his personal tac team back to their base, he'd had to get creative, including trying to double-cross a ConFed Intelligence agent who was playing the same game he was. That had backfired spectacularly, and he'd been forced to deal with the over-confident agent in a fairly gruesome way.

"I guess this isn't going to get any more pleasant the longer I wait." He sat in the seat and composed himself before hitting the flashing green icon. The channel request was accepted almost immediately.

"Where the hell have you been?" Jansen's voice crackled through the speakers.

"I've been a guest aboard the *Eagle's Talon*," he said. "This was a bust. Edgars claims there's no practical way to get the thing we're after."

"And you just took him at face value?"

"Of course not, but I do think he was being honest as far as what he said. The Ark may still be sitting somewhere on Earth, but they've told him that it is no longer a portable item."

"Where are you now?" Jansen asked.

"I stole a ship from the *Talon* and escaped," Hollick said. "Two of our deep-cover sleepers were able to break me out of confinement and put me on it. I believe Edgars intended to hand me over to the Scout Fleet team so I could be transferred back to Terranovus."

"So...you lost the data core, didn't convince Edgars to give us what we needed, and managed to expose two of our moles. This has been a very costly mission with nothing to show for it, Elton." Jansen's voice was calm, and her face showed no strain or tension, but Hollick knew it was an illusion. If she'd been on the bridge with him that moment, he had no doubt she'd have killed him.

"These are the things that happen in the espionage game,

Margaret," Hollick said, rolling his eyes. "I know you used to be little more than a project manager, so let me explain it to you. Not all ops are concluded successfully. In fact, if you can win half the time, you're doing pretty damn good."

"And since losing Weef Zadra, you haven't even won half your battles, Elton," she said. "I assume you have a plan to turn your fortunes around?"

"Of course," Hollick lied. He actually had no idea how he was going to rectify all the trouble that had befallen him of late. "But first, I need to ditch this ship. It's almost certainly got a tracker I won't be able to find or shut off."

"Just pick a spot, and I'll send someone to retrieve you."

"No thanks. I'll not just be sitting around waiting for one of your kill teams to fly out and pop me."

"You are the most paranoid person I've ever met," Jansen chided him.

"Which is why I'm alive," Hollick said. "Don't worry. I'll be in touch once I have my situation straightened out."

"Just a quick question before you go, dear. If you're in that ship, can I assume you just left your own ship on the *Talon*?"

"It's sanitized," Hollick said. "Nothing is stored on the local cores, and I don't keep physical copies of anything. About all they'll find is my dirty laundry."

"Very well," Jansen said. "Get yourself put together, and then get back here ASAP. We have a lot of work to do, and I don't have time for you to hide out in the woods because you think I'm going to do something to you."

After Jansen terminated the channel, Hollick just stared off into space. He didn't trust her to not send someone after him no matter what she said about there being work to do. It was simply in her nature to eliminate problems decisively and, he had to admit, his failures had become a problem. Now that Edgars knew what he was after, he might warn Earth. If the United Earth Council knew what One World was pursuing the thing that was allowing them to field such powerful starships in a shockingly short amount of time, they would clamp a lid on it so tight it would be all but unobtainable. The whole idea had been to gain access to it through subterfuge since main force was out of the question.

"Now, to find safe harbor and a place where I can ditch this ship before Edgars gets around to looking for it," he said. He knew it made him sound a little off, but he often talked to himself out of habit. In his line of work, he would be isolated and alone for months on end, and the need to hear a human voice, even his own, made him sometimes have entire conversations with himself.

After determining a destination, Hollick punched in the course correction and went back to the galley. A man like Edgars would almost certainly have some quality booze aboard his private launch, and after the day he'd had, Hollick felt like he deserved it.

22

"I'm assuming you can track the ship?"

"Of course. We know exactly where it is and where it's likely going, but we don't have the resources to do anything about it."

Jacob had been sitting in an interrogation room in the ship's security section for the last five hours, and the metal chair caused his ass to go completely numb, and he was getting leg cramps. Edgars and his second officer were taking turns questioning him, each asking the same questions in different ways to try and trip him up.

"Call it in to Fleet Ops," Jacob said. "Or NIS. I'm sure those guys wouldn't mind taking a crack at one of their more infamous traitors."

"So, you're still denying you're working with him?" Edgars asked. "I just find it oddly convenient that you, a NAVSOC scout team, just happened to have been posing as smugglers bringing that data core all the way from the Concordian region of space."

"It wasn't coincidence, it was design," Jacob sighed. "We needed a way to get out here so we could scout the fleet and pick out the *Talon*. After that, we were just supposed to call it in. I assume Hollick had much the same plan, but we swiped the data core out from under his nose. Believe me, I'd like to kill him more than you, and if you'd put him in the same cell with me and my team, we'd have torn him apart with our bare hands."

"Likely story."

"You ever hear of an officer named Ezra Mosler?"

"I've heard of him," Edgars confirmed. "He'd been in since the beginning, and the fleet still isn't a very big place."

"Hollick was largely responsible for his murder," Jacob said. "He also killed one of my Marines on this mission. Tortured him to death on Colton Hub. If I get the chance, I'm taking him out."

"So, what are you suggesting? That I just let you go so you can go track him down?"

"That's a viable option," Jacob said. But our ship is—"

"Repaired," Edgars interrupted. "I had my people go through it. They replaced the bus junctions Hollick rigged to blow when my security people were going through it, looking for any nasty hidden surprises." Jacob just blinked in surprise at that.

"I promised I'd turn you loose," Edgars said. "I'm not giving you one of my few slip-space capable shuttles when I do it."

"So, cut us loose now, and we'll go after your launch," Jacob pressed. "Once we leave, you'll just move, anyway, so when I call it in—like I'll have to do—the taskforce won't find anything when they get here."

"Until I'm certain there's not an angle here that I'm missing, you'll remain in our brig." Edgars stood up and slipped his service jacket back on. He made a motion to the camera in the corner, and two Marines immediately came in. "Take Lieutenant Brown back to his cell. Let him rest and get something to eat, and then we'll start this all again tomorrow."

"You're wasting time, sir," Jacob warned. "Hollick might be a bit nuts, but he's not stupid. He's going to ditch your ship as quickly as he can."

"I'll see you tomorrow, Lieutenant."

The walk back to the brig was excruciating as the pins and needles started to work along Jacob's numbed legs. He was frustrated by the fact Edgars, now spooked and paranoid, was dragging his feet. The captain seemed to be crippled by indecision, and by fear now that he'd seen for himself that his ship had been infiltrated by One World.

"Still nothing?" Murph asked.

"He's not going to let us go," Jacob said. "He'd dragging this out, convinced we're part of the plot. He did let it slip that he fixed our ship."

"Trap," MG said.

"What?" Jacob asked.

"It's a trap." MG swung his legs off the rack and sat up. "He just lets it slip that our ship is flight-capable, and then sits back to wait if we'll manage to pull the same trick as Hollick. Then he catches some more traitors on his crew and has all the excuse he needs at that point to airlock us."

"That makes sense, LT," Mettler said. "He had to give you some motivation to want to escape."

"So, do we think the ship isn't fixed? Or that it has a bunch of detachment Marines sitting in it waiting for us to make an appearance?" Jacob asked.

"I'd say it's fifty-fifty if they bothered replacing the blown bus junctions," Murph said. "But he definitely let that information slip for a reason."

"Well, we can't just wait here forever," Jacob said, raising his voice. "You have me, 707?"

"I hear you just fine, Lieutenant," the battlesynth's voice came through the speaker.

"Where are you guys?"

"We are currently hidden in a spare parts locker on engineering deck twelve-bravo. Do we have an execute order?"

"You do," Jacob said. "We need to get out of here, so do whatever it is you're going to do, but remember the restrictions I placed on the op."

"I have not forgotten. Standby, this will take some time to make certain it is done correctly."

The team sat around the cell, tense as they waited for...something. Jacob didn't count on the fact their communications with the battlesynth trio were truly secure, so he made sure they never openly talked about specifics of the plan. If the *Talon*'s technical team had figured out how to listen in on their conversations, too much chatter would lead Edgars' Marines right to where the battlesynths planned to hit, and there would be a fight that would certainly result in human casualties.

It was a few hours later, after their midday meal had been delivered, when Jacob noticed his people yawning and looking bleary-eyed. He could feel a certain fatigue coming on himself, but it looked like everyone else slipped into a trance. A quick look at his fingernails confirmed his suspicions. The darker-than-normal color indicated he was hypoxic. The battlesynths must have decided that reducing the oxygen content in the air and disabling everyone was the quickest way to secure the ship. Before sleep took him, Jacob wondered how they managed to work around the failsafes.

"Oxygen concentration drop was quicker than I would have preferred, but effective," 784 said.

"I detect no alarms," 701 said.

"The system was not difficult to fool," 784 said. "We are holding steady at thirteen percent oxygen concentration. Some people will still be conscious, but any lower and I risk permanently injuring them. Some could even perish if I lower it too close to ten percent."

"This is acceptable," 707 said. "Those that are still awake will be in no shape to pose any threat to us. Lock out this panel, and we will go free Obsidian and make our escape."

The battlesynths had infiltrated Engineering-3, the cavernous bay on the starboard side of the ship that housed the primary environmental systems. One of the spacers there had been easily persuaded to help them tamper with the main system and had even shown them how to make sure the secondary systems didn't kick online when the atmospheric composition deviated from norms. 707 had been disgusted at how readily the human had agreed to help them disable his own ship, but he had to remind himself that not everyone who served aboard a warship was a warrior. A lowly, unarmed technician couldn't be expected to fight a hopeless battle after the battlesynths had made a point of promising they weren't going to kill anyone.

On the way out of the engineering spaces, 701 grabbed five respirator sets, and they started up towards the brig. 707 was in the lead when they rounded the first turn and was hit full in the chest with a plasma blast. It was the low-power charge typically used when aboard a ship, so all it did was scorch his armor, but it knocked him back and put him in full view of the three Marines wearing respirators and advancing on them.

"Get on the ground! Now, I won't tell you again!"

A sharp *pop/whine* could be heard over the background noise of the ship, and 707's eyes glowed a brilliant red. His integrated arm cannons deployed, and his powerplant ramped up. In full combat mode, the battlesynth was capable of engaging a whole platoon of similarly equipped troops. The only thing saving the Marines was his promise to Lieutenant Brown and his natural aversion to needless killing.

707 raised both arms and let loose with a short volley from his cannons, which had been set to one of the stunner modes. The high-energy blasts hit the body armor of the Marines, the current arcing across their bodies and overloading their nervous systems. One managed to squeeze off one more shot before he fell, blasting two of the lights out overhead. The other two battlesynths, also now in combat mode, came around the corner.

"I am impressed," 701 said. "Some of them had the presence of mind to properly equip themselves and correctly assume they were under attack."

"It does not make our job easier, however," 707 said. "We must hurry."

Jacob's vision slowly cleared, and he became aware that the air was very dry and metallic. When he awoke further, he could tell that someone had slipped a rebreather mask over his head and that he was sucking in a higher concentration of oxygen than normal. The glowing red eyes of a battlesynth in full combat mode peering down at him chased the rest of the cobwebs away.

"I guess I don't need to ask how you planned to disable the crew," Jacob said.

"It was not completely successful," 707 said. "Some were able to find respirators, and others are more tolerant to the lower oxygen content of the air and are awake. This was the lowest we could risk setting the system to. It is also on a timer. In ninety-two minutes, the system will reset to normal."

"More than we should need," Jacob said. "I want everyone heading down to the main hangar bay. Sully, do a quick check and see if our ship is able to fly. 784 and Murph will ransack Hollick's ship and look for anything we can use. 707 and I are going to the bridge to get the tracking information we need to run down the launch Hollick stole. 701, you can take anyone remaining that you need and see if you can disable the slip-drive on this ship. Go ahead and make it something they won't be able to fix without help. We'll still need to call in the taskforce to come collect her and complete this mission."

The human members of the team jerked unsteadily towards the barred door that had been ripped from the frame and left hanging on a single ruined hinge. 784 stood in the corridor and issued the weapons he'd collected from the downed Marines to the three different teams as they came out. Jacob looked his people over one more time, and then ran towards the lifts that would take them up to the command decks.

"You plan to pursue Elton Hollick, despite your orders being simply to locate the *Eagle's Talon*?" 707 asked when they were in the lift car.

"You disagree with that?"

"Not necessarily. However, if you hope to have a long and

successful career within the Navy, it might not be advisable to execute an unsanctioned mission."

"I'm not too worried about my career longevity at this point," Jacob said.

"Perhaps, but I can assure you many of your men do care about that," 707 said. "Would you make the choice for them and damage their military careers as well?"

"Let's talk about this once we have things more secured, huh?"

"As you wish," 707 said, waiting until the lift doors slid open on the command deck. The lights in the corridor were completely extinguished.

"Uh oh," Jacob murmured, checking the safety on his weapon, and preparing to step out. A large, alloy hand clamped down on his shoulder and pulled him back.

"Allow me." 707 ducked and rolled out of the lift car so quickly that Jacob could barely track his movements. Apparently, the people waiting in ambush had the same trouble. There were some shouts of alarm, a few sporadic shots, and then the harsh bark of the battlesynth's cannons. Jacob could tell that all of the shots were coming at them from the direction of the bridge, so he ducked down low and turned right so he could cover the opposite direction and prevent them from boxing 707 in with crossfire.

As he did, he could see two Marines in rebreather masks making their way forward. The flash from the weapons behind him reflected off their masks and allowed him to take aim in the dark. He opened up with the weapon set to its lowest power setting, enough to splash against their body armor and singe them a bit, but not enough to maim or kill. This was likely the first real action these detachment Marines had ever seen, and live fire coming their way caused them to hesitate for just a moment, enough for Jacob to rush them and close the gap.

He caught the first one flat-footed and slammed an open palm into the side of his head. The Marine stumbled and dropped without getting back up. The second one, now with his head back in the game, grabbed the hose to Jacob's rebreather and ripped it out. He could immediately begin to feel the effects and was barely able to get his arms up to block the punch the Marine aimed for his head. Not having much time, Jacob gave up on minimizing damage and launched himself at the Marine, pinning his weapon between them and sending them both crashing to the deck. When the Marine tried to bring his weapon around again, Jacob grabbed it and ripped it away, the web sling snapping in two.

"Fucking traitor!" the Marine spat at him. Jacob responded by driving the butt of the carbine into the man's forehead, just hard enough to knock him out. Once he knew his opponent was out cold, he rolled off and removed his mask, reattaching the hose, and then slipping it back over his head. The rush of cool, concentrated oxygen cleared his mind almost instantly.

"I see you have finally finished," 707 said. "While you were playing, I neutralized seven opponents."

"Was...was that *humor?*" Jacob asked. "From you?"

"The bridge hatch is closed and locked, but I believe I can get it open with minimal effort."

"Do it," Jacob said, hefting his weapon. "We're running out of time."

707 ripped an access panel off the bulkhead near the hatch, and then punched through the back of the nook that had contained a first aid kit and two rebreathers. There was a horrible tearing sound as the battlesynth rent the metal of the bulkhead with his powerful arms. Once he had the hole to his liking, he reached into it all the way to his shoulder. Jacob couldn't see what he was doing, but he saw sparks flashing through the gap and heard the whine of what was probably a laser.

It took 707 less than a minute to cut and rip something else loose inside the bulkhead before he emerged. Nodding to Jacob, he gripped the hatch while the human raised his weapon. "Go!" Jacob barked. 707 pulled, and the hatch gave way with a couple metallic *snaps* and slid back into the recess. Before it was fully open, Jacob rushed onto the bridge, blinking in the harsh light, and swept his weapon around the area.

"As you can see, Lieutenant, we aren't offering any resistance," Captain Edgars said. He stood with two others near the front of the bridge, their hands on top of their heads. They were the only ones wearing rebreathers. The rest of the bridge crew was strewn about on the floor where they had passed out.

"And we aren't wanting to hurt anyone, sir," Jacob said, "but I still have a mission and, unfortunately, we both can't get what we want this time."

"So it would seem," Edgars said, looking at the battlesynth. "And it would appear I was severely outgunned from the start. Do the soldiers of Khepri now fight with Earth?"

"I am here for a personal reason," 707 answered. "I am not a representative for the Kheprian government."

"I need the tracking info on the launch, Captain Edgars," Jacob said. Edgars lifted his chin defiantly.

"And my crew needs breathable air, Lieutenant."

"Done. Give me the tracking codes for the beacon, and I'll have the air turned back on," Jacob said. Edgars still hesitated. "Sir, I'm giving you my word as an officer and as someone who doesn't want to see anyone needlessly hurt." The captain nodded to one of his officers wearing a respirator.

"Give him what he wants, Commander," he said. "And what of us, Lieutenant? I'm just supposed to wait around for a recovery team to show up? You realize that once my crew is able to stand again, we're going to overwhelm you and simply fly away."

"Thanks," Jacob said, pushing the lieutenant commander away from the display that showed the tracking codes and beacon address for the launch Hollick stole. He subvocalized the command to take a visual snapshot of the data with his neural implant. "I've already thought of that, Captain. I guess I can go ahead and tell you...the air was already set to come back on in another fifteen minutes or so. We couldn't risk keeping the oh-two content of the air so low for too long, so we built in a timer. As I said, I'm not wanting to get anyone hurt."

"Lieutenant, the hangar team reports that both ships are ready to fly," 707 said. Jacob just raised an eyebrow in surprise.

"So, you really did fix our ship? I thought you were just bluffing to see if we'd try to escape."

"I was at first," Edgars admitted. "I ordered it fixed afterward when it was clear you had no connection to Hollick. I had intended to render your team unconscious in your cell, load you up on your ship, and set you adrift. When you woke up, we'd be long gone, and you wouldn't even have a mesh-out vector to track, and we wouldn't have to risk you having some trap to spring if we took you in awake."

"Sensible," Jacob agreed. Now that he had two working ships, a new plan was beginning to form in his mind. "But, ultimately—" he trailed off as something flew onto the bridge through the hatch. "What the hell?" The concussion grenade went off a second later, sending every biological being to the floor in agony. Edgars and his people had been closest to the blast, and Jacob thought he saw the short lieutenant commander that had given him the data go flying into the forward screen.

707, not even phased by the concussive blast, strode over to the hatchway and opened fire. Stunner blasts poured down the corridor as Jacob struggled back to his feet, his ears ringing and his body refusing to work. By the time he was up, the battlesynth pulled the armored hatch back across the opening and welded it closed from the inside.

"The opposing force is too great for you to make it through unscathed," he said. "We will have to find another way off the bridge." Jacob looked over at Edgars and saw his chest rise and fall. He took a nasty tumble, but he was alive.

"Fucking idiots just fragged their own captain," he said. "Didn't even take a quick peek to see where we were standing. Okay...we need out of here." He walked over to one of the three active com terminals and worked through the menus until he found what he wanted.

"Sully, you there? This is Brown up on the bridge."

"Lieutenant? Yeah, I read you. We're all on the ship and ready to—"

"Tell 701, Mettler, and MG to get over to Hollick's ship," he said, then turned to 707. "Your guy can fly one of these ships, right?"

"Of course."

"Okay, Sully...tell 701 I want him to fly Hollick's ship out and take up position just out of weapons range of the *Talon*. They're going to wait here until the taskforce shows up."

"And what are we going to be doing?" Sully asked.

"I'll let you know when you get up here," Jacob said. "There's an airlock up near the bridge the inspection tender would normally dock to. Come up and get us there."

"On my way."

"That airlock is one deck down," 707 pointed out.

"There's a little secret in the captain's ready room I found out about when I was going through this ship's drawings during mission prep," Jacob said. "Come on."

He couldn't hear the Marines on the other side of the hatch trying to get in over the ringing in his ears, but he knew they were out there, and it added a sense of urgency to what he was doing. After closing and locking the hatch to the small office, he went over to the corner and dug at the carpet until the corner came up, and he could pull it back, revealing the bare deck...and a hatch.

"What is its purpose?"

"Naval R&D has picked up on the top brass's paranoia," Jacob said. He pulled up the handle and turned, releasing the locks. "They see One World traitors around every tree, so when the new classes of ships came out, they were worried about a possible mutiny by sympathizers. This office has a blast-proof hatch, and then this lets the captain escape one level down into a corridor that has multiple exit-only hatches.

"Fascinating," 707 said. "You should go first in case I do not easily fit."

"I'll pull the ladder off so you can just jump down." Jacob was already halfway through the hatch. 707 followed, managing to slip through the opening and close the hatch at the same time. Once he'd landed, he used a cutting laser to tack weld the hatch in three places. "This way."

Jacob led him aft, towards a hatch he knew came out near the airlock, the obvious intent being for the captain to use it to escape if need be. Once they emerged into another corridor, this one with the lights still up and only two crew members sleeping soundly on the deck, it was only a matter of minutes until they were at the airlock, just in time to see Sully gently guiding the *Boneshaker* up for hard-dock.

"I'd say we have completely worn out our welcome here," Jacob said, smiling. "Let's hit it."

For some reason, he felt elated. He'd actually completed the mission. It had cost him dearly, and he would feel that pain soon enough but, for now, it was enough to know the *Eagle's Talon* would soon be back in Terran hands, and before the ConFed had found the rebel fleet's new hiding spot.

23

"We just received an authenticated go-signal from Obsidian, sir!"

"Get us there as fast as she'll fly, Captain," Webb said, emotions flooding his body. Obsidian had actually done it. They'd managed to track down a needle in a galactic haystack and did it in time for them to fix the problem.

"Helm, bring us onto new course," Commander Duncan said. "Maximum slip-velocity."

"Coming about, max slip, aye!"

"The task force will get there nearly a full day before we will, sir," Bennet said from his side.

"That's fine. They'll have work to do securing the ship. Did the message include what's around the *Talon* and the ship's status?"

"Sir, Obsidian reports that the *Talon* is sitting in interstellar space, unaccompanied, and that her slip-drive has been disabled," the com officer reported.

"Disabled?" Webb asked suspiciously. "Ensign, request a full status report from Obsidian."

"Aye, sir."

"What's wrong?" Bennet asked.

"I think our intrepid scout team did a lot more than simply spot the ship and call it in. That's why they've taken so long. Brown boarded her and disabled the drive...either that or he sent those damn battlesynths to do it for him."

"Obsidian reports they were taken captive by Captain Edgars and managed to escape confinement after the *Talon* had already departed the area. They successfully disabled the ship's slip-drive, and then left on their own ship. They're now shadowing the *Talon* out of weapons range." The ensign paraphrased from what looked like a two-page report that had popped up on her terminal.

"Send that to my com unit, ensign," Webb said. "I'll be back in my office."

"Yes, sir."

Webb sat down at his desk, transferred the file over to his terminal with a flick of his wrist, and began reading the detailed report Brown had submitted. The more he read, the more fantastical it seemed. Obsidian had been overmatched when Hollick had been playing them and walked right into an obvious trap, but what Hollick nor Edgars could possibly know was that Brown was coming equipped with three combat-tested battlesynths. From what Webb read, much of the mission's success was due to their intervention. The trick with the environmental system was a particularly nice touch.

"Damn," he said, sitting back and rubbing at his eyes. There was nothing he couldn't do if he somehow convinced all the battlesynths to operate within his command. The thought of that made him smile, then frown as something occurred to him. 707 had asked to accompany him because of some vital matter he needed to discuss, but he'd never actually brought it up. The big machine had just loitered around for a few days until it got a positive bearing on where Brown was and then—*poof!*—they were gone.

They'd played him. Brown had been out of circulation for some time, stashed away until Webb could guarantee his safety and get his team rebuilt, and the battlesynths of Lot 700 didn't like not knowing where he was. As soon as they knew where he was, and that he was in danger, they vanished. He could only laugh at the absurdity of it. Lot 700 represented an unimaginably powerful small-unit fighting force any military would love to get its hands on, but they'd decided sitting on a remote planet and watching over a single human is a better use of their time.

You couldn't make that up, and he needed to be careful who might realize it around his sphere. If certain people in NIS or Fleet Ops realized they could make the battlesynths jump and dance to their tune simply by putting Brown in danger, there was no telling what they'd do to that poor kid.

He stood and checked the wall clocks, calculating how long until they reached the *Talon*. With just under five hours, he had just enough time to grab something to eat and some rack time before the real fun began. The heavy cruiser may have been unable to escape, but it could still shoot.

"This is a huge pain in the ass, LT!"

"Shut up and push!"

The two ships Obsidian had escaped the *Talon* in were now slowly spinning in space some distance away from the cruiser. They were joined together by a flexible cofferdam so the two crews could get their work done. Jacob had put them far enough out that the *Talon* couldn't shoot her guns at them, but a missile strike was still a possibility. He just had to hope that Edgars wasn't that sort of a sore loser. The Terran task force was on its way and would be there shortly, hopefully well before any reinforcements the *Talon* crew might try to call up.

Leaving the ship armed and able to communicate hadn't been optimal, but trying to disable everything in the short amount of time they had was simply impossible. Now, with the ships spinning slowly to keep the tunnel stretched and straight, the crews were busy passing down equipment from Hollick's ship to the shuttle.

When his crew had searched the ship, they'd found nothing. Even the local memory cores had been wiped. It wasn't until the third pass that they'd found something interesting: a com unit that had fallen down off a shelf and had been wedged in the narrow gap between the rack and the bulkhead. One World had decent encryption routines, but their com people couldn't have imagined an expert like 784 would have been trying to access the unit. The battlesynth didn't even bother turning the device on. Instead, like a surgeon, he'd disassembled it and downloaded the data it contained directly off the memory core, bypassing all of the encryption and hardware traps they'd installed if someone tried to slice into it.

The device had been a treasure trove of information once they'd managed to read the data. It had com addresses, encryption codes, locations, names…anywhere Hollick had been and why he'd been there was documented on the device. Jacob guessed he had lost it, had faith that his protective measures would be enough to keep his secrets, and cloned a new com unit afterwards.

There were also some remote data storage sites Jacob was very intrigued with, but in order to access them, he would have to transmit the passcodes from an approved slip-com node, hence why his crew struggled to move the bulky avionics box from Hollick's ship over to the *Boneshaker*. He would have 784 work on tying the device into their systems and downloading the data on the remote sites during the flight out.

"You know the NIS has entire departments available that specialize in this," Murph said.

"You mean the same NIS with all the leaks that NAVSOC apparently has?" Jacob scoffed. "Besides, there's no time. Hollick will get himself someplace safe, hunker down, and then deauthorize all of the nodes on his old ship. The only reason he probably hasn't done so already is because he thinks nobody knows about his data caches."

"Fair enough," Murph said, and then slid in closer to Jacob. "So, why are just you, me, and the tin men going?"

"Because you're an NIS agent, I'm an officer, Sully is an officer... the punishment for this will be a little different than it would be on the enlisted guys," Jacob said. "They might drum us out of the service, but those guys will be sitting in Red Cliff."

Red Cliff was the nickname given to the military internment center on Terranovus. It was a remote base in the middle of the desert, ringed by towering walls of red rock. Escape was impossible, the climate was oppressive, and the suicide rate at the prison was high for those with sentences longer than five years.

"I don't want to lose my job!" Murph protested.

"Then stay here," Jacob said. "But I'm going, and Sully is already onboard with this. If I can nail Hollick, and that's the last thing I do in the Navy, I'll consider it worth it."

"When the hell did you become such an idealist?" Murph hissed. "They put officers in Red Cliff, too, you know."

"Yeah...but not for simply going *slightly* outside the scope of my orders to chase down a target of opportunity that's listed as highest priority for both the NIS and the UEN," Jacob said. "You in or out, Murph?"

"You bastards!" Murph ground out. "If I go with you, I'm in deep shit. If I *don't* go with you, my superiors will think I'm a coward without initiative, and my career is sunk."

"Clock is ticking, my friend," Jacob said. "If you're coming, be on the shuttle in the next twenty minutes."

Murph walked away, muttering to himself. Jacob looked around the interior of Hollick's ship. He stood in a beautifully appointed galley, complete with state-of-the-art food synthesizers, comfortable seats, and an entertainment system that took up an entire bulkhead. It seemed to be a converted VIP craft more than it was a military ship.

"Well, well, well...wasn't that interesting," Mettler said, coming around the corner.

"What was interesting, Sergeant?" Jacob asked.

"That conversation you and *Agent* Murphy were having."

"Mettler, there are very few types of people in this galaxy I can't stand...thieves, people who don't wash their hands after using the head, and eavesdroppers. You're two of the three, and that's only because I don't think I've ever caught you stealing yet."

"You guys can't cut me and MG out of this, LT," Mettler said. "Please, sir...Commander Mosler and Taylor were like family to us, and they're both gone because of this piece of shit." Jacob opened his mouth to deny the request outright but stopped.

"Damnit, Mettler!" he swore. "You want to go to jail for this shit?"

"If I have to."

"Then go get the other dumbass, and we'll talk about this," Jacob said. "No promises since one of these ships has to stay here regardless until the taskforce arrives."

"I'll go get MG."

The UES *Kentucky* meshed-in a mere forty-five minutes after the taskforce did to the unremarkable region of space the *Talon* floated in. Once active sensors were up, Webb could see Edgars wasn't bothering trying to flee on his subluminal engines, and his weapons were powered down. Both good signs the negotiations might not involve blasting one of their own ships with Admiral Sisk's destroyers.

The taskforce had quickly deployed around the disabled cruiser, making sure any avenues of escape were covered while also staying just out of range of the *Talon*'s big guns. Webb also saw there was a small civilian courier ship of unknown origin and assumed it must be Brown's crew.

"Status?"

"The flagship has told us Captain Edgars is waiting to speak with whoever is in charge. Admiral Sisk is apparently unclear who that is," the *Kentucky*'s second officer said.

"Message the flagship and tell Admiral Sisk he is in command here, and that I'm just an observer," Webb said. "Also relay that we would take it as a professional courtesy if we were allowed to listen in."

"Sending message, sir."

A few minutes later, they received a channel tie-in request, and the *Kentucky* was able to see and hear what was happening between Sisk and Edgars.

"This is Admiral Sisk, commanding officer of Taskforce Bravo, 3rd Fleet," Sisk announced with a flourish. Webb suppressed the urge to roll his eyes. The admiral knew this was a moment that would be reviewed by the top brass, and he was hamming it up for the archives. "Observing these negotiations is Captain Webb, commanding officer of NAVSOC."

"This is Captain Edgars of the UEN vessel, *Eagle's Talon*," Edgars said. Webb frowned at his appearance. The captain had red eyes from burst blood vessels and bruising all over his face. Did Brown really need to rough him up that much? "As far as I am concerned, there will be no negotiating. I surrender the *Talon* and am prepared to be taken into custody. I would ask that my loyal crew not be punished for my actions."

"That will be for someone else to decide, Captain," Sisk said. "While I am grateful you appear to be willing to see reason here, why have you surrendered so easily? If you'll forgive me saying, your reputation indicated you wouldn't."

"I stand by my actions," Edgars said. "I feel I did what was in the best interest of Earth, and the galactic community as a whole. But I would never put myself or my crew in the position of firing on fellow humans. Your Scout Fleet operators quite thoroughly disabled my ship, so I am at your mercy. I am ordering my entire crew assembled in the main hangar bay."

"Well...that was anticlimactic," Webb said. "Continue to monitor the situation. Someone patch me through to Obsidian since I'm assuming they're on the small ship sitting astern of the *Talon*." When the channel resolved itself, he stared at two of Obsidian's enlisted Marines and one battlesynth.

"Captain Webb, sir," one of them said in greeting. "I'm Sergeant Jeff Mettler. I've been ordered to—"

"Where is your commanding officer, Sergeant?" Webb interrupted.

"As per the report we're forwarding to you now, sir, Lieutenant Brown and Lieutenant Sullivan are not aboard, nor is Sergeant Murphy."

"I didn't ask you where they were not, Sergeant," Webb said. He could feel his face getting red, and the people around him took a step back.

"They have left in pursuit of the fugitive, Elton Hollick, sir," Mettler said. "They have a lead on where he was escaping to and felt this was a high priority."

"I see," Webb said, his voice soft and calm. "So, you're a kill team now, is that it?"

"I wouldn't presume to know if our designator has been changed, Captain. I'm simply—"

"Shut your mouth, Sergeant," Webb said wearily.

"Yes, sir."

Webb felt his tension headache come roaring to the front of his skull. The UEAS had entire commands propped up to handle these sorts of direct-action missions, and one of his goddamn forward observers had just gone flying out on his own little vendetta. He had no doubt Brown would succeed this time. Since he only saw one of the battlesynths, Webb assumed the other two had left with Brown, which meant there was so much sheer firepower being brought to bear that even someone as slippery as Hollick had little chance. The problem was that Brown was bringing a neutron bomb to a knife fight, and the attention caught by his unsanctioned operation would blow back on NAVSOC and the Navy in general. Most planets didn't take kindly to strangers landing on the surface and trying to blow each other up.

"Let me guess…you don't have any way to reach them, do you?"

"Were you talking to me, sir?" Mettler asked. Webb lost it.

"Weapons! Target that ship with the forward cannons and standby to fire!"

"Wait, wait!" Mettler said, waving his hands. "I only have the slip-com node addresses for the ship we'd been using this whole time. LT didn't leave us any special way to get in touch with him."

"Shall I fire, sir?" the weapons officer asked. Webb thought about it for a moment.

"Not yet," he said. "But be ready to if I say. Sergeant, I'm killing this channel right now, and the next time I contact you, I hope for your sake you've become appreciably smarter."

"I'll definitely work on it, sir."

Webb slashed his hand across his throat to indicate he wanted the channel terminated. He looked over as another pane opened up on the main display and saw that Captain Edgars transmitted a video feed of his crew mustering in the hangar bay as he'd promised. The sensors showed he'd reduced his power output down to levels that would make it impossible for him to fire on the small flotilla of shuttles and transports Sisk had deployed to the cruiser.

No matter what the military judicial system would do to Edgars, the men and women aboard the *Talon* were still Naval spacers and officers who deserved to be treated with a certain level of respect. Some overzealous Marine bashing in the head of a technician not boarding the transports quickly enough could really spark off an ugly scene.

"Do we have any way to track that shuttle Lieutenant Brown stole?" he asked his aide.

"No, sir," Bennet said. "We never had access to the ship and were never able to install a tracker."

"Perfect," Webb sighed. "Not that I expect him to accept the channel request, but I suppose I need to make some effort to contact him."

"Looks like there will be more than just the *Talon* crew facing a court martial," Bennet said.

"Maybe," Webb said. "In Brown's case, it could either be a court marital or a medal of commendation depending on how he executes his self-appointed mission. It's known we give Scout Fleet teams a long leash, and if he pulls this off quietly and actually kills or bags Hollick, it'll just be seen as a hard-charging young officer getting the job done."

"Your opinion, sir?"

"I agree with both points," Webb said. "This will be a real test for him. He'll need to know when he's been outsmarted or overmatched and call an abort before letting those battlesynths raze a city to the ground."

Bennet didn't say anything more as Webb took a moment longer to watch Admiral Sisk's people reclaim the *Eagle's Talon* for Earth.

24

"Tracker is still pinging strong from the surface."

"Which means he's either already swapped ships and is long gone, or he's set up a trap for whoever comes looking for the ship," Jacob said. "Where's it at?"

"It's at a large commercial starport in the southern hemisphere," Murph replied. "Fine tracking puts it in a landing complex that mostly services high-speed courier ships."

The planet they orbited was called Noelin-2, although it was the only technically habitable planet in the Noelin System. Noelin Prime was a barren rocky world without its own atmosphere and a population of close to sixty million beings living in subterranean habitats and a smattering of domes. The only thing remarkable about the system was that it was close to where the *Talon* had been parked. Given the speed advantage the captain's launch had on the *Boneshaker*—which had caused its fair share of trouble on the way there—Hollick should have had two full days already to either set them up or make his escape.

"The ship is almost certainly under surveillance, and likely to be rigged to maim or kill," 707 said. "It is ill-advised to approach it directly."

"Agreed," Jacob said. "But by eliminating the obvious strategy of scouring the launch for clues, we don't really have much of a plan to find a single human on a whole planet."

"What do you want to do?" Sully asked.

"Let's just get down there," Jacob said. "We'll come up with a plan as we go."

"Seems to work as well as when we actually do have a plan." Sully shrugged, calling for clearance to deorbit and rigging the ship for atmospheric entry.

After a bumpy ride, the shuttle touched down on her landing gear two landing complexes over from where the captain's launch sat. Large starports like the one they were at were built with scalability in mind, so they all started with a central main hub, and then spread from there like spokes on a wheel. New landing pad complexes would be built with all the requisite servicing needs for the ships it intended to cater to. These were usually funded by private corporations that had some business interest on a planet and wanted to have dedicated landing space without the hassle of actually owning property on an alien planet.

The ramp had no sooner dropped down when two locals sauntered up, jabbering to each other in the native dialect. Jacob left Sully to negotiate fuel and consumables for the ship and walked back up to meet with the others. Murph looked skeptical as he looked out over the sprawling ramp. The battlesynths were as unreadable as ever.

"I will need to be in the main terminal building in order to access the records of Hollick's landing," 784 said.

"You can do that?" Jacob asked.

"I would not have said so if I could not."

"Maybe you could have mentioned that before we landed and stood around wondering what to do?" Murph asked. 784's head swung over, and he regarded the NIS agent with cold, indifferent eyes without responding. "Or...I could just keep my opinions to myself."

"What will the landing records show us?" Jacob wondered aloud. "What I mean is, would it be worth the risk? The ship is registered to the Cridal Cooperative and is legal to land damn near anyplace, so he wouldn't have used any unique trick to put her down."

"If he left the starport, he would have had to pass through immigration control," 784 said. "He did not have time to retrieve the falsified credentials from his own ship, so he would need to let them scan his neural implant."

"Do we think that the officials here can be bribed?" Jacob asked.

"All beings can be bribed," 707 rumbled. "It is just a matter of price. Bring lots of currency, and we will get the information we seek."

"You coming with us or staying here?" Jacob asked Murph. "It seems like every time we leave Sully with the ship alone, someone sneaks aboard and steals shit or knocks him out."

"I'll go with you," Murph said. "Even if Hollick got aboard and tossed Sully out, this pile of garbage wouldn't get him very far."

The foursome grabbed the things they would need, made sure Sully was okay, and headed off to the ramp that would take them under the landing pads to the underground maglev trains that moved people and cargo around the starport.

The first train to stop had only a few beings, most ignoring them, but a few stopped their conversations to gawk at the battlesynths. The speedy maglev whisked them away and deposited them underneath the main terminal, some twenty kilometers away from their ship, in just over half an hour thanks to all the stops it made. By the time they left, they were pressed into a throng of beings heading for the immigration lanes.

Murph, being trained in this sort of thing and also not nearly as memorable or intimidating as 784, approached one of the officials that roamed among the crowd, answering questions to speed the process along. Jacob couldn't hear what they were saying, but the official seemed scandalized, then angry, and then finally shocked when Murph discreetly pressed a loaded credit chit into their hand. A moment later, the official looked up to the other three and discreetly waved them forward.

"Follow me." The being's voice had an odd contralto quality to it that Jacob, for some reason, found hysterical. He had to keep covering his mouth as he laughed whenever the official would talk. By the time they reached their destination, the official seemed to have caught on that Jacob was laughing at its voice and wasn't amused.

"Through here," was all it said, waving them through a door marked as being for official use in only five different languages.

"Could you *please* be a bit more professional?" Murph hissed after the door closed behind them.

"I couldn't help it," Jacob protested, looking around the open office area they were in. "Well, at least this doesn't look like a trap."

"We're in the landing area security office," Murph said. "Someone should be along shortly to help us."

"That alien didn't seem too pleased about the bribe at first."

"That was my screw up," Murph said. "I'm rusty at this. I offered way too much to start out with, and she thought I was with internal security and setting her up. She was insulted until I explained I was just some dumb rube from beyond the Orion Arm."

"What will this office provide us?" Jacob asked.

"For the right amount, I'll provide you with access to our landing and takeoff logs while I look the other way," a voice said from the back of the room. "If you need anything further, it will be more." Jacob looked over the alien approaching them. He was a different species than the last official had been, and one Jacob hadn't interacted with before.

"I appreciate the direct approach here," he said.

"This is a business," the alien said. "As long as we don't let anyone access official government records, they don't mind if we make a few credits here and there letting people access the information directly. I take it you're looking for a specific shipment or vessel?"

It all clicked in Jacob's mind. They were selling information on specific incoming cargo so enterprising pirates could figure out who carried what and jack the loads. If they were cool with that, it was highly unlikely they'd care about two humans trying to hunt down another human.

"We're actually looking for another being, one like us." Jacob waved his hand to indicate him and Murph. "He, ah...has something that used to belong to us. Perhaps there was a misunderstanding and, in any case, we'd like it back."

"Of course," the alien said, almost laughing. "And the ship your...friend...would have arrived on?"

"It's the VIP launch sitting on pad eighty-one of the Sinda complex," Murph said. "He's the only passenger." The alien went over to one of the terminals and navigated through the menus until, after only a few short minutes, he had a decently clear picture of Elton Hollick exiting the ship on the display.

"This is him, I presume?"

"It is," Jacob said. "How much more will it cost to track him?"

"The best I can do is tell you where he exited the starport from," the alien said. "And that will cost you ten thousand."

"Ten thousand *credits?*" Jacob choked on the amount. It wasn't that he didn't have it, there was a principle involved. "You've already screwed up and told me he isn't here at the starport anymore. I'll give you five to point me in the right direction."

"Eight and a half."

"Six and a half," Jacob said. "I'll go as high as seven, but my friend here gets to punch you in the chest." The alien glanced at 707 in alarm.

"Six and three quarter?"

"Done."

The information was already queued up so the alien entered a few commands to display it, and then stepped well back. Murph and 784 inspected the screen, then looked at Jacob and nodded. Jacob tossed the alien his payment, and then held up a five thousand credit chit.

"This could be yours if you have a way for us to get out of here without bothering the poor, overworked people in customs," he said. The alien looked at it greedily.

"They really do have too much work as it is, and you seem like upstanding, fine beings," he said. "I'm sure you won't be any trouble. This way."

They were led out of the office and through a series of service tunnels that had doors interspersed along the way. Eventually, they came to the door their tour guide wanted, and he unlocked it by waving his hand in front of a scanner. When it popped open, Jacob could see they were about to exit into the terminal just behind the security checkpoint. All they'd have to do is walk out the exit and hope nobody noticed where they came out of.

"A pleasure doing business with you." Jacob handed over the chit.

"Of course," the alien said.

"Let's hurry up and get out of here," Murph said. "We stick out a bit, and I don't trust him not to call security if for no other reason than to force us to bribe *them* also. This planet looks decent enough, but it's as crooked as I've ever seen."

They made it outside without any trouble, walking down the wide footpath and into a crowded marketplace, where they tried their best to blend in. Jacob checked his com unit to make sure he was able to reach Sully, and then found a quiet spot for them to pull out of the rush of beings and talk.

"So, what did you find out?"

"Hollick left the starport much the same way we did, but he had to visit a currency exchange to withdraw chits to pay his benefactors," 784 said. "After that, he was escorted out of the terminal through a worker's entrance and last seen heading towards a part of the city that is known for high crime and narcotics trade."

"A place for someone like him to disappear," Jacob said. "He didn't have any hard cash on him, so he'd had to have at least one account linked to his neural implant or a hand chip and used that to pay off the officials. Does that help us?"

"Not really," Murph said. "Just knowing he has secret accounts doesn't help us find him here. Most operatives at his level have at least a few they can draw from, and they're well-shielded."

"He has to have either contacts or know of someplace safe he can hide out if he picked that area to flee to," Jacob said. "He's a bad hombre, but he gets jumped by a local narco-gang, and they'll swarm him under."

"The danger that exists for him also exists for us," 707 said. "I would prefer to not fight our way through a civilian area."

"Murph?" Jacob asked. "I'm a little out of my depth here."

"How much cash did you grab when you left the ship?" Murph asked.

"Seventy-five thousand in various denominations, all ConFed credit chits," Jacob said. "A little less now after bribing the customs guys."

"What the hell, LT? Were you planning on buying a house here and retiring?" Murph said.

"I don't know how much shit costs out here," Jacob protested. "You just said grab enough for bribes!"

"Yeah, for a couple lowly immigration officials, not the damn governor!"

"Is this a necessary conversation to have right now?" 707 asked. "You are drawing attention to us."

"Fine, fine," Murph said. "I think I know a way we can maybe find him and get safe passage through that area."

"You plan to purchase protection from one of the gangs," 707 said.

"It's a straight-forward approach, but it works," Murph said.

"Making certain you choose the right gang to hire presents some risks, but they are easily mitigated," 707 agreed. "How would you like to proceed?"

"One of the most prevalent drugs in this sector is called Oci-Eight, or just Eight," Murph said. "It's a neural enhancement drug that works across a broad spectrum of species and is used medically to increase nerve stimulation, though not sure why you'd want to do that since I'm not a doctor. The street gangs took the basic formula for that pharmaceutical and distilled it down to create Eight. We don't have time to work up the ladder by grabbing a user to find a dealer to find a distributor and so on...we need to grab someone higher up."

"Is there a plan somewhere in this boring-ass lecture?" Jacob asked.

"Eight has to be kept cool or it begins to break down quickly. Dealers have figured out all kinds of ways to hide it, but the bottom line is, that if someone is carrying a large quantity of the stuff, there will be a large thermal signature from the method they use to keep it chilled," Murph said. "We can scan the local Nexus for warnings of which areas to stay away from, then go there and grab us a distributor and make an offer."

"This sounds dangerous as shit with a *lot* that could go wrong," Jacob said. "If it goes south and we're forced to defend ourselves, we'll be employing military-grade weapons against local yokels on a planet where that sort of thing doesn't really fly."

"It's your call, LT," Murph said. "This is my best shot to get Hollick before he disappears again. It's a plan he won't likely employ himself due to lack of funds and his own incredible arrogance, so we'd have a slight advantage, but that window is closing fast."

Jacob weighed the risks of going through the plan as opposed to letting Hollick run free. The man had done incalculable damage to the UEAS, not to mention the personal carnage he had wreaked in Jacob's life, but now they were talking about involving the local population, and there were strict regulations governing that sort of thing. Grubby drug pushers though they may be, Earth had adopted an absolutist policy when it came to putting the populations of other planets at risk with their covert operations. He'd been lectured and reprimanded about them multiple times after he'd set off a powerful bomb in an industrial district as a diversion on his first mission.

In theory, he agreed with the controls Earth had imposed on Scout Fleet operators, making sure they weren't out in the wild ripping and tearing and generally causing a groundswell of hatred for humans. Practically, though, Elton Hollick and those he employed had been doing just that for some time now. Alien worlds didn't give a flying crap about human internal politics, and whatever Hollick did reflected on them all as a species.

"Let's do it," he said finally. "We need to nail this bastard before he has a chance to come at us again. What do we need?"

"Ground transportation that will hide the battlesynths and a throw-away device that can connect to the local Nexus," Murph said. "I don't want to leave any trace that we were here if I can help it."

"I'm on it," Jacob said, standing and heading towards the market center with 707 in tow.

25

Sully sat alone on the flightdeck of the *Boneshaker*, sipping coffee from a mug and watching the ships come and go while monitoring the coms and watching the computer chew through the data they'd stolen from Hollick. What was in the machine represented the last of the Rocky Mountain Coffee the team had swiped from a disused NIS safe house. It had been grown and roasted on an alien planet, but damned if he could tell the difference.

"Oh, yeah...that's good shit," he said appreciatively. A *beep* from the console let him know the computer had completed the first pass of the data and had results for him to review. Many of the names were codenames, but there were slip-com node addresses attached to them that the computer had automatically tried to cross-reference with those it had in its own database. It was a longshot...but there had been a couple matches. The first name that popped up made Sully forget he held a mug, and it slipped from his hand, dumping scalding hot coffee down the front of his pants.

"Shit! Son of a bitch!" he screamed, wiping at his groin in vain and willing the pain to stop. As the liquid cooled and the pain subsided, he leaned back in the seat, sighing in relief.

He stared at the ceiling for a moment, not wanting to look at the screen again. When he forced himself to do so, the name was still there: Lieutenant Walton Bennet, UEN. The personal aide to Captain Marcus Webb and a man privy to most secrets at the top of Naval Special Operations Command had been in contact with Elton Hollick on many occasions. Sully was no code slicer, but he knew enough to begin to dig down and try to correlate the known address with any messaging services and see if there might be a smoking gun sitting out there somewhere before he went accusing someone of being a traitor. As he worked, he saw how Hollick and One World would have managed to wipe out most of the active Scout Fleet units with such precise, perfectly-timed strikes. Bennet would have had access to the teams' locations and status, able to pass them on in real-time.

He'd been skeptical of Brown's almost unhinged paranoia when he'd agreed to fly them out here without clearing it with NAVSOC, but now it seemed like the young lieutenant might have been under-selling the danger the whole time. Sully liked to believe the people he served beside held the same values of integrity and honor he did, so seeing proof someone at the top had been selling them out the entire time turned his stomach. If Bennet had been the one to get Team Diamond wiped out, it would be a race to see who could get to him first, Sully or Webb.

After two more cups of coffee and another forty-five minutes, the computer had chugged through the data available. It gave Sully a list of blind-drop messaging services he would hand over and not try to access himself as well as another group of people that were in Hollick's circle he routinely talked to. Some of the names he recognized within the special operations community. Others, he had no idea who they were other than they were on Terranovus. Over sixteen people in total who appeared to be working with Earth's enemies, and that was likely just the beginning. It was quite depressing, actually.

He slipped his headset on and keyed up the com he had tied into the local net and punched in the access code he wanted.

"Go for Brown," Lieutenant Brown answered almost immediately.

"It's Sully. The computer just got done crosschecking some of that data, and it looks like you were right...Hollick has been talking to someone at the very top of the chain of command. It's pretty easy to see how he's stayed a step ahead of us."

"Who was it?" Brown's voice was...fearful?

"Bennet. Webb's aide," Sully said.

"Thank God!" Brown's explosive exhale was annoyingly loud in the headset.

"What?"

"The way you were building it up, I thought you were going to say it was Webb himself," Jacob said. "We'll figure out a way to tell the captain without his shit weasel aide intercepting the message and— Hhuh? Oh, you can do that? Why didn't you say that earlier?!"

"LT?" Sully asked.

"It turns out the battlesynths have a way to get messages to each other," Brown said. "707 said he'd try to let 701 know. They should still be in short-haul com range so Mettler can tell Webb personally."

"I see. Should I—"

"I'm being told to keep that information classified. Apparently, not too many people are trusted with the fact these guys have some sort of covert communication network."

"Got it," Sully said. "So, I should just sit on this?"

"Bundle it up and get it ready to transmit, but just sit on it for now."

"Copy. Sully out."

"So, that asshole, Bennet, was one of the leaks this whole time?" Murph asked. "I never trusted him, even after he covered for Webb during that coup that one admiral tried to pull off a year or so ago."

"The one who tried to assume command of NAVSOC? Didn't they send her back to Earth?" Jacob asked.

"That's the one," Murph said. "So...how does your long-range com network do its thing? Do each of you have a—"

"It would be best if you forgot what you heard about that," 707 said, his tone making it clear the conversation was over.

"You got it, Tin Man," Murph snorted, leaning back. Jacob gave him a warning glare before turning around in his seat.

Jacob had managed to hire a vehicle that could be piloted manually or be tied into the city traffic management system. It was also large enough to accommodate two battlesynths in the cargo area without the humans being smashed against the windows. Now, they were on their way to the second location Murph's search algorithm indicated would have narco-gang activity after the first one had been a bust. They'd sat around in the area for two hours, and all they saw were low-level pushers and a couple of deliveries from runners, nothing on a scale like they needed. The good news was that the battlesynths were able to detect the minute thermal fluctuations with enough accuracy to pick out targets.

"Holy shit, man...Hollick is probably already dead if he came down through this area." Jacob watched out the window as the vehicle rolled past aliens that gave them open, challenging glares, and a few even pelted their ride with whatever they had handy to throw.

"I'll bet he had something set up already," Murph said. "Probably not this planet in particular, since that would be too coincidental to believe, but maybe a standing agreement with one of the smuggling outfits that runs drugs on the planet. He contacts them, they put him in touch with people down here who can hide him, and then he waits it out until the smugglers have a load leaving and have room for him aboard."

"Damn. This guy is slick," Jacob said. "I don't think he's going to have his guard down enough for us to get close without him seeing us a mile away."

"We have the advantage right now, but you are right not to underestimate your quarry," 784 said. The vehicle rolled through an area that seemed to be kept much cleaner than those they'd just passed. The buildings were free of graffiti, and there were even children running around on the walkways.

"I believe we have just passed what we are looking for," 707 said. "Stop the vehicle up ahead."

"The alley?" Murph asked.

"Affirmative."

Jacob commanded the vehicle to stop at the next legal parking spot and waited. The alley worked to their advantage, but it also made it more likely they'd be killed quickly if these thugs decided a shoot-strangers-first policy was best. Everything hinged on the fact Murph thought he could get close enough to give his sales pitch before they decided to kill the off-worlders and be done with it.

"Let's do it," he said. They all piled out of the vehicle and moved towards their assigned places. Jacob and Murph made a direct line to the alley, the two battlesynths tried to remain as inconspicuous as they were able while getting in position.

When Jacob rounded the corner to move down into the gap between the low buildings, he saw that there were three vehicles similar to the one he'd rented and a group of locals standing around talking. On the surface, it didn't look like anything nefarious was going on. The aliens were well-dressed and laughing, the vehicles were clean and modern, and as far as anyone could tell, it was just a group of couriers delivering packages to the street-side businesses. But if 707 said he'd spotted something, then Jacob had to trust he knew what he was talking about.

"Greetings!" Murph said loudly, not wanting to get too close and surprise them. When they stopped talking and looked at the pair of humans, Jacob got a completely different vibe from the group. These were dangerous people.

"You two lost?"

"We were looking for you, actually. We have a business proposition," Murph said.

"You don't know what business we're in," the one that emerged as the leader said. "So, how could you possibly be propositioning us?"

"I assume you're in the business of being able to find things in your own territory," Murph said. "Like, maybe we pay you a lot of money, and you tell us where someone we're looking for might be hanging out. You're not in that sort of business? You don't like easy money?"

"Kill this off-worlder scum," one of them said. "He reeks of military. We don't need this type roaming around down here."

"You military?" the leader asked. "Maybe law enforcement the capital hired to clean up down here?"

"I'm a person willing to pay to find my...friend," Murph said. "Other than that, we don't need to know each other."

"*My* friend thinks I should just kill you. Why wouldn't I just do that, and then take any money you have on you? That easy enough for you?"

"It would be easy, but unwise," Murph said. He pulled three, one-thousand credit chits from his pocket and tossed them over, one at a time. The alien caught them all in turn, squeezing the onyx wafers so they would display the value loaded onto them.

"This is all you have?"

"That's just to let you know we're serious," Jacob said. "Consider that payment for your time so far. Imagine how much we'd give you for the information we need."

"Here's the problem," the leader said, pocketing the chits. "We see this type of thing down here all the time. You're probably a couple ex-military types hired to track down someone who ripped your boss off. We tell you where he is, but he probably isn't wanting to die peacefully, so all of you end up turning my home into a warzone. Am I close?"

"Close enough that it doesn't matter who we really are," Jacob said. "We just want our guy, and we want to make sure nobody down here gets hurt. We'll take him without any collateral damage."

"How can you do that? You can't even guarantee you'll walk out of this area with your lives and money still in your possession."

"Oh, I think we'll manage just fine," Jacob said, crossing his arms in front of him.

"What—" the leader's words were drowned out as two battlesynths roared into the alley. They'd leapt from the rooftops where they'd been waiting for the signal and fired their repulsors just before hitting the ground, but they still hit with enough force to crack the street. Both stood and moved over to flank the two humans, their eyes glowing red and arm cannons deployed.

"Meet my *other* friends who ensure the fight is short and one-sided," Jacob said. There was some frantic whispering among the group in their native dialect, with fearful glances tossed the strangers' way. Battlesynths were rare, but everyone knew what they were. The stories about what they could do were wildly exaggerated in news media and entertainment, but that only served to make having two of them standing there all the more frightening. Their presence just took Jacob and Murph from being a couple ex-military flunkies to being heavy hitters who demanded a degree of respect.

"What kind of money are you offering?" the leader asked, his entire demeanor shifting to one of almost subservience.

"You find the guy we want and give us good intel that lets us grab him, and I'll give you forty-thousand credits, all untraceable ConFed chits," Jacob said.

"This friend must have really made you angry," the alien said. "What's he look like?"

"Same species as us, skin color similar to mine," Jacob said. Murph was a dark-skinned African-American, and Hollick was a pale skinned Anglo. Even though most species in the galaxy had variations in skin tone depending on where they were from on their own planet, it still seemed to cause confusion when they saw the same trait in *other* species. "I have an image of him on my com unit."

The leader came over and looked at the image on Jacob's device, and then explained how he could transfer the image to them. Once that was done, and a few more credits had changed hands, the gang promised they'd be able to find the general area Hollick was in within a day, an exact location within three.

"You'll need to do better than that," Jacob warned. "This guy is slippery, and he isn't wanting to hang around here very long. I'll be back here the same time tomorrow, and I hope you'll have something for me."

"We can't exactly go looking in buildings that don't belong to us," the leader protested. "These things can take time."

"It's likely he's staying in a place that's owned by one of the smuggling cartels that services this city, if that helps," Murph said. The alien seemed to consider that for a moment.

"It does narrow it down. Come back tomorrow, and we should have something for you."

The Obsidian crew walked out of the alley, not bothering to look behind them or even appear hurried. Once they were back in the vehicle, Jacob waited around long enough to make sure they got a good look at what he was in but didn't wait so long as to make it obvious.

"Well...that part went surprisingly easy," Murph said. "Wanna take bets on how the next part goes?"

"Nope," Jacob said, engaging the auto-drive. "I give it even odds that this plan backfires, or Hollick does an end-around, and Sully gets jumped again just before the asshole steals our ship."

"There is a third option," 707 said. "Hollick might kill the two of you first, and then try to steal your ship."

"Thanks for the vote of confidence," Jacob deadpanned. "Trust me...I'm pretty sure I know what I'm doing."

"Good enough for me," Murph yawned. "Your dumb luck has somehow been working out better than my years of training and NAVSOC's bottomless barrel of resources."

They spent the rest of the evening making the rest of the necessary stops to execute Jacob's somewhat complicated plan to draw Hollick out. The only part that made him nervous was the amount of time and effort they were burning when the chances were good they were already too late and the slippery operative was already safely off-planet. If Jacob had miscalculated, he just prayed he was the only one caught in the blowback and that the rest of his people could cut and run...live to fight another day.

Either way, this would be the final confrontation between him and Elton Hollick. By tomorrow night, one of them would be dead.

26

"Captain Webb, you have an incoming channel request from the battlesynth on the ship sitting off our port flank."

"Thank you, I'll take it in my office," Webb said distractedly. Securing the *Eagle's Talon* had been anything but straightforward now that the regular Navy was involved. When the admiralty found out they'd actually captured the ship with Edgars alive, they sent out five additional ships loaded down with parts, engineering crews, and, of course, a gaggle of flag officers who now wanted to pin their names to the successful operation. They were the same ones who would have been calling for Webb's head on a platter had things gone south. When Webb had first transitioned from being an operational asset to a desk jockey, the reality of politics in the upper ranks had horrified him. Now? Now, he barely noticed it. He wasn't sure he liked what that said about what he'd become.

"Captain Webb," 701 greeted him once the channel encryption had synced up.

"What can I do for you?" Webb asked. "Please tell me this isn't more bad news."

"I am afraid it is more bad news," 701 said. "Lieutenant Brown and Lieutenant Sullivan have made progress tracing Elton Hollick's known associates within your organization. Your aide, Lieutenant Bennet, appears to have been passing information directly to Hollick for the last two years." Webb felt like someone had kicked him square in the balls before he'd even had a chance to tense up.

"You're mistaken."

"We are not. The data is irrefutable. The node address he is using is a relay connection on Terranovus assigned specifically to him. The full trace shows the relay was accessed by his personal com unit on multiple occasions."

"Do you have the data?" Webb asked.

"It will be forthcoming," 701 said. "I am simply giving you warning to have a care what information your aide is privy to. What you do with that warning is up to you. The full data package will be sent as soon as Lieutenant Sullivan has finished compiling it."

"How about you ask my people to come back here and give it to me personally," Webb said.

"They are not receiving communications, only transmitting," 701 said. "Lieutenant Brown fears the leaks within NAVSOC are so numerous that he cannot risk exposing himself through normal channels."

"He's probably not wrong there, but he's still way, *way* off the reservation with this," Webb said. "You talk to them, you warn all the Naval personnel that I probably can't protect them from the consequences of this...but I understand why they're doing it."

"Do you not see the nobility in what they do?" 701 asked.

"I just said I understand, didn't I?" Webb snapped. "The problem is that when people just start doing whatever the hell they want like this, order and discipline breaks down. It's not their place to make up their own missions and fly halfway around the quadrant like they're some sort of vigilante hit squad. Brown may think he's being noble and high-minded with this sacrificial move, but what he's doing is wrong. He's damaging NAVSOC and the Navy with this selfish move."

"He is much like his father in that regard."

"And I'd been hoping this whole time he wasn't like his old man," Webb said.

"You have given me some things to ponder, Captain," 701 said.

"Yeah? Well, have fun with that." Webb stabbed at the button to kill the channel. With all the shit flying around in his orbit right now, the last thing he needed was for some enigmatic, self-aware killing machine to want to have an existential conversation about the morality of disobeying orders. And now, they'd dropped yet another bomb in his lap. How the hell could Bennet be the traitor? That was utterly impossible…wasn't it?

"Bennet, get in here," he practically shouted at the intercom.

"Sir?" Bennet asked, not fully entering the office. The young officer looked exhausted like the rest of them. Webb stared at him hard for a few seconds, trying to detect something he had missed this whole time with his most trusted subordinate. "Sir, is everything okay?"

"I need you to take the next shuttle over to the *Talon*," he said finally. "I want you to be my eyes and ears over there. With all the Fleet brass around, I want to make sure we're documenting everything carefully so NAVSOC doesn't get screwed when they start submitting their reports."

"You want me to go over there…just to watch?" Bennet frowned.

"Is that a problem?"

"Of course not, sir, but it just seems like there might be someone more suited to the task," Bennet said.

"And I told you I want you to do it. I need someone who will give it to me straight," Webb said. "You're dismissed, Lieutenant. The next shuttle…be on it."

"Aye-aye, sir," Bennet said stiffly.

He wasn't sure he believed that Bennet was one of the leaks he'd been fighting. Hollick was very good at misdirection and hiding his real actions, so Bennet's name and access codes could have been used as a ruse by someone else on Taurus Station. In the meantime, however, he could stash Bennet where he wouldn't have access to anything critical coming out of Webb's office and still be performing a useful task at the same time. If it came out that he wasn't the mole, then Webb would not have accused one of the people he most depended on of being a traitor.

"I really hope that's the worst thing I have to deal with today," he groaned, digging around in his desk for the headache meds the infirmary had given him.

"It's time. I'll be right out here."

"Thanks," Jacob said. "If he kills me, make sure you return the favor."

"You got it."

Jacob climbed out of the vehicle and walked back towards the alley they'd been in the previous day. The streets and walkways were almost deserted, and there was a quiet, tense feeling about the place, as if everyone knew something unusual was happening. He hoped that was just because the gang they'd picked to help them had that much influence on their turf. That had been the indicator Murph was going by when he picked them, at least. The area was much cleaner and more orderly than others in this district, and that indicated this gang had such a strong presence that the rest of the petty criminals, like vandals and pickpockets, steered far clear.

Only one of the vehicles he'd seen yesterday was parked at the end of the alley today, and the leader he'd tossed the credits to was the only person in sight. He walked down at a leisurely pace, trying to convey a sense of calm and confidence he certainly didn't feel. The alien he walked towards leaned against his vehicle, not fidgeting or looking around, but the guy was the leader of a street gang and probably didn't spook easy.

"You have what I want?"

"You're alone?" the leader asked. "You're either very stupid or wildly overconfident."

"Maybe I just trust you'll do the right thing in your own best interests," Jacob said.

"So...stupid. Got it."

"I asked a question."

"Let me ask you one instead...did you really think this was going to work? Did you *actually* think you could just walk into an area you know nothing about, flash a few credits, and we'd fall all over ourselves trying to obey your commands?"

"I assumed you were a smart businessman," Jacob said. "I figured even a lowlife, gutter trash narco-pusher like you would be able to see the easy credits in what I was asking. I also didn't think you'd want to piss off someone who had two battlesynths with him."

"Yeah? Well I don't see them here now," the alien said. "We've been tracking you since you came back into our area today, so we know you didn't bring them with you. What happened? You run out of money to pay for their services?"

"I'm hearing a lot of pointless chatter from someone who is, to be honest, beneath my notice," Jacob sighed dramatically. "Either give me what I want and collect your fee, or I'll be on my way to talk to one of your competitors...hopefully someone smarter this time."

"Always with that mouth," a new voice from behind him said. "You just never shut up, do you, Brown?"

"Hollick," Jacob ground out. "Nice to see you."

"Lose the weapons, asshole. Oh, and don't worry about Agent Murphy. My good friend Pucva here has his people watching to make sure he doesn't interrupt us," Hollick said. Jacob tossed his weapons on the ground, moving slowly and deliberately. From the sound of his voice, Hollick was about five meters back, too far to try and grab him before getting blasted.

"So, you guys are good buddies already, huh?" Jacob asked the leader, whose name was apparently Pucva.

"Like I told you...you can't just walk in someplace and act like you know everything. You're so ignorant you even mentioned the truth in passing, and it never dawned on you what that meant," Pucva said. "Yeah...your guy is in tight with the cartel that runs our product and is under their protection. If we handed him over to you, they would send in a hundred enforcers to kill us, our families, and anyone who might remember our names, and then just start over from scratch."

"He doesn't need your life story, Pucva," Hollick said. "In fact, you can go ahead and get lost. I can handle this twerp."

"Gladly." The alien turned to leave.

"Pucva," Jacob said, stopping him. When the alien turned back, he lobbed the two credit chits he'd palmed out of his pocket to him. "No hard feelings." Pucva picked up the ten thousand ConFed credits Jacob had tossed and just stared at him, dumbfounded.

"Touching," Hollick said. "Collect the money and get the hell out of here. I won't tell you again."

"Good luck," Pucva said to Jacob before hopping into his vehicle and disappearing.

"Turn around," Hollick ordered. Jacob spun slowly and saw that Hollick held a nasty looking plasma sidearm. The blaster was big enough to leave a sizable hole through him at full power without any protective armor on. "Just you and me now."

"It's just you, me, and that huge ass pistol you're holding," Jacob laughed. "Don't try and act like this is anything but an execution. But since you haven't killed me yet, I'm assuming you want to know something."

"What could I possibly want to know from some pissant jarhead first lieutenant?" Hollick asked. "I'll get the real information I want later out of Murphy. No, no, no...I want you to stand there for a bit and let the fear build. You don't know what I'm going to do, and the uncertainty is beginning to eat at you. Will I torture you first? Maybe blast your hand off like you did me? Or will you luck out and I'll just pop you in the head? It's the not knowing that's the fun part."

"You're a sick fuck, Hollick," Jacob said. "I'm going to enjoy killing you." At this, Hollick laughed uproariously.

"You're nothing if not fun, I'll give you that," he said. "Before you depart this mortal realm, maybe you'd like to hear about how Taylor Levin died...all the little details from when he tried to hold out as long as he could before betraying you."

The words seared into Jacob's brain like a branding iron. He saw red, tasted blood, and heard nothing but a roaring in his ears as his high-power adrenal response—a gift from his father—prepped his body for combat. An animal snarl escaped his lips and even Hollick looked startled, taking a step back and raising his pistol. Just when it looked like he might shoot, a blaster bolt came from a trash pile to the right and blew the gun from his hands.

Hollick howled in pain and looked around wildly, spinning to his left just in time to see a battlesynth stand and shake off the remnants of the trash it'd been hiding under. Knowing he was now vastly outgunned, the spy turned to flee, but a second battlesynth stepped out of a doorway, blocking his retreat. Their glowing red eyes were brilliant points of scarlet in the darkening alley. Hollick spun around again, desperate for an exit.

"*Now* it's just you and me," Jacob snarled and stalked towards his prey.

"You think you can take me, kid?" Hollick laughed, but it sounded high-pitched and forced. "I've had more hand to hand training than your entire team put together."

He was right. Hollick had been one of NIS's premier field agents, trained in multiple forms of combat from the best instructors Earth could find including those from the Galvetic Legions. He was in peak shape, an experienced fighter, and backed into a corner. This was a dangerous person someone like Jacob should be afraid of.

But he wasn't. What Hollick didn't know was that Jacob had been given a terrible gift at birth, genetic mutations passed on from his father that made him faster and stronger than any human currently on Earth. Fueling all of that strength was an inferno of hatred and rage for a man who had taken two people he truly cared about and killed them with no more thought than he'd have given to stepping on a bug.

Hollick stepped into Jacob and feinted with his left before swinging up hard with his prosthetic right, trying to catch him off guard with the hard, synthetic fist. Normally, the move would have let him pull his right arm back quickly enough to block, but he was about to learn a painful lesson. Jacob moved back just enough to let the strike miss, and then, so fast that Hollick barely saw him move, delivered a crushing left-hand blow to his exposed body. Ribs cracked, and the hit carried enough force that Hollick left his feet, flying a few meters before landing flat on the pavement.

As Jacob stomped towards him, Hollick now looked at him with genuine fear. The agent climbed to his feet, crying out as his crushed ribs ground against each other and his insides. When the Marine was close enough, he tried to step inside his guard and use the strength of his prosthetic hand to go for a pressure point, but again Jacob was too fast. He grabbed the synthetic limb and, with a quick yank, tore it off and tossed it away. When Hollick tried to counter with his remaining hand, Jacob slapped it away and slammed his fist into the agent's gut as hard as he could, lifting him off the ground again and feeling something tear under the skin.

"I might have just shot you if all you were was a traitor and a spy," Jacob said calmly while Hollick wheezed and vomited bright red blood onto the ground. He tried to crawl away, a futile action of a man going into survival mode. "But you killed my friends." He reached down and grabbed Hollick by the throat and lifted him off the ground with one arm.

"You killed them...*because it was fucking fun for you!!*"

He launched Hollick into the furthest building with an overhead throw that sounded like it shattered Hollick's shoulder where it impacted. When Jacob turned to move towards him again, Hollick stared at him, but no longer seemed to actually see him. It didn't matter...he would still feel it.

An armored hand grabbed Jacob's shoulder and squeezed hard.

"You do not honor your fallen comrades by becoming like him," 707 said quietly. "You are a warrior, not a murderer, Jacob."

The words crashed down on him like a waterfall. Cold and forceful, they washed his emotions away until all that was left was the dull ache of missing his friends and the shame of letting them down. He looked at the pitiful sight that had once been a man he'd had nightmares about. Ezra Mosler would be disgusted at seeing his young protégé torturing the man just for some sense of petty revenge.

He looked down the alley and saw the small sidearm he'd discarded earlier and walked over to retrieve it. The pistol felt like it weighed a ton as he walked back over to where Hollick lay, moaning and trying to grasp at his shattered shoulder.

"Hollick...look at me," Jacob said, waiting until the agent looked up. There was still a spark of defiance and rage there. Good. There was no satisfaction in executing a terrified animal. "I could arrest you and let them take you to Earth to stand trial, but you don't deserve that. *This* is what you deserve. A death nobody will remember in a stinking back alley on some planet nobody has ever heard of."

"Do it," Hollick said, almost sounding relieved. Jacob squeezed the trigger.

It was over.

"Please check on Murph," Jacob said.

"784 is already there," 707 said. "He has messaged and said Murphy is unharmed, and the gang has dispersed. They are coming back towards us now."

It only took Murph and 784 a few minutes to make it from the vehicle to the alley. Jacob briefly wondered why they hadn't just brought the vehicle with them.

"You okay?" Murph asked, grabbing Jacob by the shoulders and looking him over. He'd never been happy with the plan when Jacob had outlined how he wanted to take advantage of the fact the street gang would almost certainly doublecross them. It had been a risky play with Obsidian having such limited resources available, but in the end he'd agreed it was their best shot at drawing Hollick out.

"I'm good. He's not." Jacob turned away from his grisly handiwork.

"Fitting death for the man," Murph said, looking down at the body. "What the hell? Did you run him over with a truck first?"

"We will need to dispose of his body before the authorities find it," 784 said.

"Let's wrap it in some of that sheeting, and then toss it in the rental," Jacob said. "We'll see if we can sneak him back onto the starport, and then put him in the hold of the captain's launch."

"Really?" Murph asked.

"The Navy is going to have to send someone to come get it, anyway," Jacob said. "Or we can take it with us and toss it out in orbit."

"Let's do it that way," Murph said. "It's one thing to report we eliminated a threat...it's another to have to explain dead bodies to investigators."

27

"He's in the airlock, propped up against the outer hatch. When we hit five hundred klicks of altitude, we'll cycle the lock, and he'll become a beautiful streak of light in the night sky."

"We find anything else useful on him?" Jacob asked.

"Not really...and thanks for saving that duty for me," Sully griped. "I'm a pilot, not a coroner."

"You once told me you grew up on a farm and didn't mind being around dead things," Murph said.

"That wasn't me volunteering to go rooting around through a dead guy's pockets," Sully shot back. "Anyway, he had another com unit that 784 is working on right now. If it has anything other than—"

"Obsidian, you will want to see this," a voice boomed from the galley.

"Maybe he found something." Sully shrugged.

"What've you got?" Jacob asked once they'd all squeezed into the galley.

"We were able to access one of Hollick's remote data storage sites,"

784 said. "It was a combination of the access codes locked in his com unit and a biometric scan of his retina."

"It's a good thing we pulled all the biometric data off him before he started to rot," Murph said.

"Gross...but good point," Jacob said. "What did we find on this storage site?"

"At first, it did not appear to be anything of value, but when the correct decryption routines were applied, I discovered Hollick had compromised the One World communications network, allowing himself access to things he shouldn't have been privy to," 784 said.

"Sneaky bastard installed backdoors into their network," Murph laughed. "I guess that's one downside to being an organization built completely from traitors. You can't trust anybody."

"Indeed," 784 said.

"So, what sort of stuff can we dig into?" Jacob asked.

"With a more powerful computer and better com suite, there would be significant intelligence to be gleaned."

"Such as?"

"The location of Margaret Jansen, for example." 784 said it so matter-of-factly the import of it didn't sink in for a few moments.

"Ho-lee shit!" Murph drawled.

"This is it," Jacob breathed. "We can wipe out One World by taking out Jansen."

"It would probably be better to capture her alive, but decidedly more difficult," 707 said.

"Who do we even give this to?" Jacob asked. "I don't want to sound like I wear a tinfoil hat, but there doesn't seem to be any place within the UEAS chain of command that isn't compromised by One World sympathizers."

"And if Jansen is alerted her system has been infiltrated, she'll just shut it down and reset," Murph said. "But it's not like we can just go after her ourselves."

"Let's not throw that away too quickly," Jacob said. "Why *couldn't* we go after her? A smaller team with precise knowledge would have better than even odds of surprising her."

"What the hell? Are you serious?" Murph spluttered. "No. Not only no, but fuck no. We're already in trouble for this little field trip, but if we go that far off the reservation, we'll be hung out to dry."

"If you go after Margaret Jansen without the approval of your command...we will remain and assist you," 707 said. Jacob looked at Murph and raised his eyebrows.

"You're not helping things here!" Murph said to the battlesynth. "We can't just go rogue! We're not a—"

"Damnit, Murph...if we turn this information over to NAVSOC, Jansen will be alerted to it within days," Jacob cut him off. "This is real. We're at war, even if our side doesn't acknowledge it. One World has infiltrated every level of government, and they've just wiped out two thirds of the active Scout Fleet units we have. Yeah, we'll have to break the letter of the law here, but we're doing it for the right reasons."

"That's dangerous thinking, Lieutenant," Sully spoke up. "That same excuse has been used by lots of people to do some pretty horrible shit throughout history. You're *sure* we're on the right side of this?"

"I absolutely am," Jacob said. "I'm not proposing we assassinate someone without being ordered to. But just a quick strike to grab her and drag her back to Terranovus? That would be worth looking into."

"Don't tell me you're going along with this, too?" Murph demanded. Sully just shrugged and smiled.

"I came along for the ride this far," he said. "The way I see it, if we succeeded in grabbing Jansen, it might even clear away our sins for flying out here and popping Hollick."

"So, how would we even do it?" Murph asked. "We sure as hell aren't pulling off a mission like that with *this* pile of garbage. Hollick's ship would be too easily recognized by Jansen's people and the captain's launch over on the other pad isn't a tactical vessel."

"I know of a ship that we can...borrow," 707 said vaguely. "It would be a vessel quite up to the task."

"You're just not going to stop, are you?" Murph glared at the machine.

"How about this," Jacob said, raising his hands in a placating gesture. "We go check out this other ship, we dig through the data 784 has found, and see if there's a workable mission plan to be made from it, and *then* we decide if we do it or just come back and turn ourselves in." Murph seemed to deflate a bit as it was clear he was outnumbered badly.

"What about the others?" he asked. "MG and Mettler will want in on this if we do it."

"I have an idea how to kill two birds with one stone on that front," Jacob said.

Marcus Webb read through the report four times before he even bothered to open the accompanying data. It had been sent to him by Brown and Murphy, relayed to him through the ship the rest of Obsidian still sat on as the fleet prepped the *Talon* for departure. It showed him that, without a doubt, Bennet had sold them out to One World. All the timestamps lined up and Obsidian had somehow managed to dig through Hollick's personal com services and cross-match all of the times Bennet had reported things to him that had directly led to NAVSOC personnel being targeted in the field. He archived the data and shut the terminal before leaning back and squeezing his head with his palms.

Defeated.

He just felt completely and utterly defeated. Having his inner circle breached like this and to not have had even a tickle of suspicion put him in a dark place. At every turn, it seemed that Jansen and her crew had outsmarted them, digging in a little deeper with each operation while the United Earth Council and UEAS Central Command refused to even acknowledge it was happening at all. Director

Welford had admitted to him that the NIS was also infested with sympathizers that he couldn't seem to root out, and when they did find one, they never made any headway figuring out *why* people were willing to commit treason for One World. It just never made any damn sense.

At least now, he knew where there was one of One World's top moles and how to get his hands on the rat bastard. He tried to figure out what was the best way to handle it, and possibly who was the best person to handle it since right now he'd be just as likely to blow Bennet's head off as try and talk with him. Webb knew he would have to arrest his aide de camp just so they could begin the interrogation process and see what they could uncover. That meant that the wheels of military justice would chug into action. Formal charges would have to be filed, Bennet would get access to legal counsel, and access to him would be completely restricted. It also meant that word would get around that the head of NAVSOC couldn't even notice that his own close, trusted aide worked against him.

There was also a more practical problem. From what Edgars had told him, One World had infiltrated quite a few ship crews, and if he arrested Bennet and threw him in the brig on the *Kentucky*, would he have a damn mutiny on his hands? He needed someone he could trust, someone able to watch his back. He had someone in mind, but it might be difficult to convince him to help out. Swallowing his pride, he keyed up the com terminal in the office and accessed one of the external short-range radios for a ship-to-ship channel.

"Sergeant Mettler," he said when the channel resolved. "I assume 701 is still there with you?"

"Yes, sir," Mettler said, climbing out of the seat. The camera angled up automatically to frame the next closest face, this one the burnished gray alloy of a battlesynth's facial armor.

"701, I have a favor to ask of you," Webb said. "I know your people have said they don't want to get involved with internal human politics, but I hope you'll see this as a special exception."

"I am listening," 701 said. Webb laid it all out for him and explained what he wanted. The whole time, the battlesynth stood impassive and motionless, just staring into the camera.

"The long and short of what I need is someone incorruptible here on the *Kentucky* in case any One World sleepers activate and try anything cute when I take Bennet into custody," Webb finished.

"Lieutenant Bennet is on the *Eagle's Talon* right now?" 701 asked.

"Yes."

"I should go there first and assist in his apprehension."

"Not necessary. I'm having him come back here on the regularly scheduled shuttle, and then you can be there with me when he comes through the airlock," Webb said. "I'll have the corridors cleared, and we'll get him into confinement before anybody really even knows what's happening."

"An acceptable plan," 701 said. "I will be coming in through the portside, aft engineering airlock. Please ensure the outer hatch is open."

"That ship can't dock to an engineering airlock," Webb said. "They're meant for EVA and— Oh. Got it." 701 terminated the channel, and Webb got up to head down to engineering to meet his guest. He always forgot for some reason that battlesynths could operate in space, even being able to navigate through the void over incredible distances. It was part of what they were built to do. One thing that was a little odd was how quickly 701 had agreed to help him. It made him suspicious, but he didn't want to openly question him right after asking for a favor.

He waved to the bridge crew as he stormed out of his office, hurrying down the central corridor to get to the lifts. The *Kentucky* wasn't that large of a ship, so it only took him five minutes to get to the port engineering bay, but by the time he got to the maintenance airlock, there was already a battlesynth outside the hatch, calmly waiting for him to open it up. Webb swiped his ID and punched in the command code that would allow him to cycle the lock. His credentials would also automatically keep that activity off the ship's log unless he put it there manually.

"Let's go ahead and—"

"Bridge to Captain Webb," his com unit chirped aloud. It would only do that if the bridge crew were trying to reach him in an emergency.

"Go for Webb."

"Sir, that ship that has been shadowing us just came about and is accelerating away at full burn. It's...surprisingly quick, sir."

"Can you catch it?" Webb asked, glaring at 701.

"Negative, sir. If we had started after it right when it took off, there may have been a chance to disable it, but we were taken by surprise. We can try to— Never mind...it just meshed-out. I apologize, sir."

"Not your fault. Log it and let Commander Duncan know what happened. Webb out." He put his com unit back in his pocket and turned to his guest. "I suppose now I know why you so readily came when I asked."

"Yes," 701 said simply. "Mettler and Marcos needed a diversion to allow them to escape out of range. I volunteered. I will still honor our agreement to assist you here, however."

"How noble," Webb said through gritted teeth. "I don't suppose you can tell me where two enlisted Marines—neither of whom are qualified to pilot a ship, by the way—are heading in such a hurry?"

"They are going to meet with the rest of their team, Captain," 701 said, his calm demeanor only further infuriating Webb. "The ship is equipped with a sophisticated AI piloting system. Apparently, Elton Hollick was not much of a pilot either."

"You told me *why* they left, not *where* they were going."

"It would be unwise to discuss this in such an open area. I will disclose to you what I know, but I would advise we wait until we are in a secure location."

"Follow me," Webb said. He led the battlesynth past mildly surprised crewmembers and back into his office just off the bridge. While he no longer felt completely safe, even on his own ship, he was reasonably certain the office hadn't been bugged.

"Obsidian has managed to discover much of Hollick's secrets after his death," 701 said as soon as the anti-eavesdropping systems came on. "Hollick had built in several access points to One World's communications network that allowed him access to information Margaret Jansen would have not wanted him to have."

"Yeah I can understand why she wouldn't trust him," Webb said. "What'd they find out?"

"Much. Most importantly, they found that Hollick had a way to track Jansen's location in real-time. They are going to attempt to apprehend her and bring her back to Terranovus before she finds out Hollick has been killed and her system may be compromised," 701 said. "Lieutenant Brown stressed he would have much preferred to turn the information in, but after discovering who one of the moles inside NAVSOC was, he felt that if he handed in Hollick's data cache, someone would almost certainly tip off Jansen."

"He's going to apprehend her? Why not just hit her with an orbital strike once he has a location?"

"He said that it wasn't their place to be judge and jury. Obsidian will try one time to take her by surprise and arrest her. If they fail or feel like the risk is simply too high, they will return to Taurus Station and surrender themselves for disciplinary action."

"What a bunch of fucking heroes," Webb sneered. "Brown of all people knows how dangerous of a precedent he's setting with these stunts." He leaned back and took a deep, cleansing breath. "But...I understand where he's coming from. It at least sounds like he's being smart about it. Just one quick hit, and if they miss, run like hell. Are your two compatriots staying on with them?"

"707 and 784 have volunteered to remain with Obsidian for the duration of this mission."

"I do feel a lot better with those two watching their backs," Webb sighed. "I can't fault his logic, but I also can't condone his actions. He knows there are ways to contact me directly that would be secure, but he doesn't want to do that because he knows I'll order him home. Instead, he'll just pretend I don't exist while he executes his own agenda. If Command finds out about this, Obsidian will be listed as a rogue element and cut off. They'll be arrested as traitors the moment they try to come back in."

"They understand the risks. Lieutenant Brown thinks the chance of success is worth the potential consequences. I have brought more data for you to look through once you have calmed down. After you see it, it will become clear just how badly you have underestimated your opponent and how that mistake has brought you to the brink of disaster."

"Ouch," Webb said. "I'm willing to let this play out...*briefly*. If they start making too much noise, or they completely shit the bed out there, I'll have no choice but to disavow them and let the Navy send the wolves after them. There's no doubt the brass would order me to deploy a kill team for them."

"Then I am obligated to inform you that 707 and 784 will do whatever is necessary to protect the son of Jason Burke...even from his own people."

The thought of that chilled Webb's blood. He also understood there was an implied threat in the comment.

"Your help notwithstanding, I think you need to consider your stance very carefully," Webb said. "We have granted you political asylum on one of our planets. Some might consider it...ungrateful... that you're threatening the safety of our military personnel as they execute their duty."

"Our commitment to the Burke family remains firm," 701 said. "If circumstances put us at odds with being welcome on your planet, we will leave peacefully and willingly."

"I just don't understand this debt you think you owe Burke." Webb shook his head. "He didn't start out intending to be a liberator, even if that was the end result. Just send him a thank you card and maybe a nice bottle of whiskey and move on with your lives."

"That is not our way."

"Apparently not," Webb sighed. "Well, you can relax...for now. I'm in no shape to mount a mission to try and intercept Lieutenant Brown so, for the moment, I'm forced to leave him to his own devices. But I think we both know that by far overreaching even the loose orders Scout Fleet teams operate under, he has effectively ended his career in the Navy."

"You could retroactively issue orders for his mission," 701 pointed out. "Claim they were held back for OPSEC reasons due to the myriad leaks in NAVSOC."

"And if I do that to save Brown, I'm telling everyone under my command they really don't have to follow the rules just as long as they really, really believe they're doing the right thing. Come on... you're a soldier. You know that's not how these things work."

"I am just offering potential solutions to your problem," 701 said. "However, you are correct that morale and discipline suffer if open disobedience is tolerated. I do not envy you the choices you will have to make in the coming months, Captain." Webb just grunted and picked up his service coat, slinging it on.

"Between you and me, my career is not likely to survive all of this, anyway, so it'll be the next guy's problem," he said. "Let's go...the shuttle should be docking in ten minutes, and I ordered Bennet to be on it. I sent a couple of my detachment Marines over first, and they'll be the only other ones on the return trip escorting him back."

"Is he really so dangerous?"

"Bennet? Nah. He's an aide for a reason, and it's not because we have too many badasses in combat arms," Webb said. "But desperate, trapped men are unpredictable, and that can make anybody dangerous."

When Lieutenant Bennet stepped off the shuttle and saw Webb's face and a battlesynth there to greet him, and looked at the five Marines behind him, his face took on a wild, panicked look.

"Take him," Webb said. 701 moved so fast it seemed like he teleported across the small antechamber in front of the docking hatch. He spun Bennet around and slapped the restraints on him so quickly the administrative officer didn't even have time to cry out in protest. 701 stepped back and motioned the Marines forward, pointing wordlessly to the left thigh pocket of Bennet's fatigues.

The sergeant in charge of the detail moved up while his men covered the prisoner and rooted around in the pocket, pulling out a device that looked like two cylinders taped together and attached to an older com unit. 701 held his hand out, and the Marine deposited the device into the alloy palm without question. The battlesynth looked the device over carefully before finally pulling off one of the components under the com unit.

"Clear," he said. "This is an improvised binary explosive device. He used a com unit as the trigger so it would require his biometric signature as well as being easy to clear through security scans."

"Got a little arts and crafts hobby on the side, Lieutenant?" Webb asked.

"Sir, I can explain if you—"

"Sergeant!" Webb barked.

"Lieutenant Walton Bennet, you are under arrest for the charge of treason against the United Republic of Earth," the NCO said formally, his voice not betraying the hatred that shown in his eyes. "You are hereby remanded into custody of the Master at Arms of the Terran starship, UES *Kentucky*, to be transferred back to Terranovus for formal arraignment. You have the right to legal counsel. You have the right to silence. Anything you say can and will be used against you regardless of whether your attorney is present. Do you have any questions?"

"Sir! Please, let's just go somewhere and talk about this before it gets out of hand!"

"Oh, we will," Webb promised. "You will be accompanied to your new accommodations by these Marines, and this battlesynth will be there to make sure any other One World traitors aboard my ship don't decide to do something stupid and kill you before you can be questioned."

"Kill me?!"

"You don't think they'll risk trying to free you and escape, do you?" Webb laughed. "You're a loose end now, Walton. If there are any other sleepers aboard the *Kentucky*, they'll start getting very creative to try and silence you. Bearing that in mind, you'll probably want to have a list of names ready for me when I come down to visit you. Sergeant, please take the prisoner to the brig."

"Aye, sir," the Marine said. The detail formed up around Bennet with two in front, two in back, and the sergeant keeping a hand on the prisoner while they walked. 701 ranged ahead of the group, leading the way. The sight was a punch in the gut Webb hadn't expected. Damnit, he had *liked* Bennet. Trusted him, and was doing his best to mentor him as a leader. To have the young officer betray him so completely left Webb's stomach twisted into knots.

Maybe Brown was right. In the last year alone, One World had managed to subvert so many of their own people that any strike he might order against Jansen herself would probably fail before it even left dock, her people making sure they sabotaged the effort the entire way. How were they getting to these people? And Bennet carrying a just-in-case suicide bomb? That was so antithetical to the man's mild nature it made no sense. Would he have actually triggered it?

"I heard there was some excitement down here," a voice said from the hatchway. Webb spun and saw Commander Duncan, the *Kentucky*'s CO, standing there.

"You heard that, huh?" Webb asked, moving his hand down and behind him towards the sidearm he had in a holster at the small of his back.

"Saw it, actually," Duncan said, pointing to the cameras covering the docking hatch. "I made sure I killed the feed to the other stations on the bridge once I realized what was happening. So, your aide is one of Jansen's?"

"The proof is compelling," Webb said, moving his hand away from the weapon. "It appears he's the one feeding them real-time intel that let them hit all the Scout Fleet teams in the field at once."

"This One World shit is getting out of hand, sir," Duncan said. "If they can so completely infiltrate NAVSOC, even with all the screening we do on personnel before they come to Taurus Station, what do you think the rest of the Navy looks like?"

"I think they took special interest in our operation, but I get your point, Commander."

"Do you think we'll ever get to actually hit back at them? The Ull couldn't stand up to the Navy we have now. We don't have to sit and cower behind the Cridal's skirts anymore."

"Not my choice to make," Webb said. "I'm leaving that battlesynth down in the brig to make sure nobody gets any ideas about trying to kill or free Bennet. Go ahead and ask the rest of the fleet if we're clear to withdraw, and then we'll head back home and get him the hell off your ship."

"You think there are others aboard the *Kentucky*, sir?"

"I hope to hell there isn't."

28

"You guys have any trouble finding the place?"

"We didn't have to do shit," Mettler said. "This ship flies itself. The autopilot has a sexy woman's voice and can actually hold a better conversation than MG."

"That's a pretty damn low bar," Murph said.

"LT, I can't work under these conditions," MG said. "I need to be surrounded by professionals, not these lame asses who can't even come up with an original burn."

"If you're all done, we have a couple decisions to make," Jacob said. "First off...this is the last chance any of you will have to back out. If you have any doubts, I'm begging you, get back on the ship and head home. I can't promise they won't drop the hammer on us when we finally come back in. Chances are good I'll end up in jail, the rest of you will probably just get kicked out."

"We're in it to the end, LT," MG said. "It's not just about Commander Mosler and Taylor anymore...these bastards have killed our friends. If I get kicked out after this, it'll have been worth it."

"Yeah, what he said," Mettler chimed in.

"So, what the hell are we doing here, LT?" MG asked.

"I've been made aware of a ship we can...*borrow*," Jacob said evasively. "The person who owns this ship isn't currently using it, but they're also not going to be very happy we took it. Either way...it's here, we need it, so let's just get it and get moving."

"That's hardly an answer," Sully complained.

"It'll be easier if I just show you. Or...we can try to pull this mission off using that." Jacob waved to the hissing and smoking Eshquarian shuttle that had burned up *something* on the bumpy de-orbit. It had landed hard enough to stress the starboard landing strut, and from inside the ship, they could still hear a half-dozen different alarms squealing.

"I would rather immigrate to this planet and live here the rest of my life than ever fly in that thing again," Sully declared.

"We are wasting time," 707 said.

"Let's get Hollick's ship stowed in the hangar I've arranged for, and then we'll be on our way," Jacob said.

"The ship isn't here?" Murph asked.

"It's at a private facility," Jacob said. "And before you ask why we didn't just land there, I'm not certain there aren't some active anti-aircraft measures in place."

"What planet is this again?" MG asked.

"It's called S'Tora," Murph said. "The same place they make that coffee you like."

"Cool."

"Still not talking, huh? That's okay. The NIS will probably get a hold of you first and, under the new Imminent Threat and Security Act, they'll be allowed to put the screws to you before the JAG manages to send your appointed defense team down."

The *Kentucky* flew to Olympus, not Terranovus as previously planned. Once Webb had reported to his superiors how his aide had been the one responsible for allowing Scout Fleet to be decimated,

Command decided it would be best to avoid Taurus Station for the time being. Webb had been down twice to talk to his formerly-trusted righthand man, but Bennet was simply staring at the wall, refusing to acknowledge anybody.

"Suit yourself." Webb stood up and turned to leave.

"You can't beat her."

"Excuse me?" Webb turned. The voice had been so soft he almost hadn't heard it.

"You can't beat her," Bennet repeated. "It's not just the military she's infiltrated. It's our politics, industry, she even has supporters within the Cridal power structure."

"How is that even possible?" Webb asked. "She's been exiled for almost a decade!"

"She had been working on this long before she was stopped by the Cridal the first time," Bennet said. "Much of her network is still in place, and people are still willing to listen to her when she starts promising things. The Cridal don't like the fact that humanity appears to be fractured, and there is a growing movement within the Cooperative that wouldn't mind seeing Jansen take over and put an end to the pointless, wasteful bickering. She's made promises to them...something about a new type of superluminal drive and an engineering resource she calls the Ark. They're very interested in it, and she's made it clear that if she was in charge on Earth, the shipments of weapons would increase unabated."

Webb knew of the Ark, but he wasn't sure exactly what it really even was. He *did* know the drive technology she promised was from the wreckage of a starship Omega Force had shot down over Washington DC many years ago. Nobody admitted to even knowing where all of that had been shuffled off to. There were rumors about what the Americans had done with it, but nothing he'd ever seen proof of.

"Is that why you joined her? Because you think she'll be in charge eventually no matter what?" Webb asked, hoping to keep Bennet talking.

"It seems inevitable." Bennet shrugged. "They came to me after certain accounting indiscretions of mine involving NAVSOC funds and some questionable purchases. In order to keep them from reporting me to OSI or the IG, they asked instead that I do a couple small things for them, like letting them know when you'd left the base. It snowballed from there and, before I knew it, I was in too deep to ever get back out."

So, Bennet had siphoned some funds away from the slush funds NAVSOC used to keep its operations secret and bought himself a few things, but the wrong people found out. Having a file opened on you by the Office of Special Investigations or the Inspector General was a career death sentence, so it wasn't insignificant leverage they'd had over the young officer.

"People died because of you. A lot of people who were friends and colleagues," Webb said. "Why didn't you stop that?"

"It all just seemed so pointless." Bennet leaned against the bulkhead. "They try and kill us, so we go and kill them back. They try and steal assets from us, we go and—"

"You're talking about the actions of two nation states," Webb interrupted, tiring of the flimsy justification Bennet tried to push off on him. "Jansen doesn't even have the full support of the Ull. She is a usurper, a murderer, and a traitor to not only her country, but her planet and species."

"What's the difference?" Bennet shrugged.

"You can pretend to be nihilistic about what you've done, but deep down, you know you got a lot of people killed who trusted you. Many of them have—had—families back on Terranovus I will now have to personally visit and tell their children, wives, and husbands that their Marines and Spacers aren't coming home. *You* did that. You did it because you're weak and a coward of such monumental proportions you'd allow an atrocity like that to happen rather than face the consequences of your own actions. What'd you buy?"

"Excuse me?"

"What'd you buy? With the money you stole from the ops accounts."

"I got a new car for my girlfriend back on Earth," Bennet said. "A few other small things on top of that."

"I hope she appreciated it, at least." Webb sneered. At this, Bennet just let out a sad, defeated laugh.

"She wrote me a letter after I bought it for her...said things weren't working out between us."

"You sold your soul for a car to try and keep a girl on another planet who was probably already done with you the minute your shuttle took off to bring you here," Webb said. "If you had just owned up to that when it happened, you'd have maybe lost some rank and got a slap on the wrist, but that first domino led to this...a pile of orphans, widows, and widowers."

"I think I'm done speaking now." Bennet's face went stony, and he rolled over on the rack, facing away from the bars.

"I'd have almost preferred that you were a zealot and a true believer," Webb said. "That I can at least understand and, on some level, respect. Your reasons? They just sicken me."

Webb left the brig, needing to be away from the traitor before he vomited onto the deck. All the carnage Bennet had caused because he was too scared to own up to doing something stupid. How many others were like him? He imagined that same line of reasoning, that self-preservation at all costs mentality, but applied to powerful politicians and titans of industry. It was no wonder they couldn't seem to dig out all the sympathizers...they were going about it all wrong. These weren't misguided revolutionaries. They were hopeless cowards who would sell out their planet to save their own sorry asses.

29

The ride from the small spaceport—almost small enough to just be considered an airfield, even though it technically launched ships to orbit—was quiet and tense. When they'd reached a security gate after traveling down a coastal road for a few hours, 707 reached out of the vehicle and punched in a sixteen-digit security code so quickly Jacob couldn't make out any of the numbers. The gate rolled aside, but the vehicle refused to move from there.

"We will need to walk the rest of the way," 784 said. "This is a declared exclusion zone for public transportation."

"Interesting," Murph said, sliding out of the vehicle.

They closed the gate, collected their meager belongings, and marched up the road towards an outcropping that jutted into the sky. Once they'd crested the shallow rise, they could see enormous doors set into the side of the mountain and a decent-sized landing pad in front of that. There were a few haphazardly placed utility buildings around the area, and enough debris had been blown onto the pad to make it seem like it hadn't been used in a while. When they reached the doors, 707 again entered an even longer security code string that unlocked a small, man-sized door inset into one of the larger ones.

"This is intense," MG said. "I feel like it's either going to be a surprise party in there, or maybe we're being tricked and they'll knock us out and steal our organs." Murph just rolled his eyes and walked through the door first.

Once they were inside, the interior lights came up automatically, and they got their first glimpse of the ship Jacob intended to *borrow*. It was a menacing, black, sleek ship that dominated the center of the hangar. There was evidence it had recently been worked on, but she looked to be in perfect shape. Sully let out a low whistle and walked around, looking her over.

"Is this an actual gunship?" he asked. "Looks like a Jepsen, but she looks like she's been heavily modified. The main engines are wrong, and the wings look like they were replaced at some point."

"Uh, LT...is that a damn *Camaro* sitting over there?" MG asked, pointing to where a bright red 1968 Camaro convertible sat.

"Who the hell owns this ship, Brown?" Murph asked. "No bullshit." Jacob took a deep breath and let it out while they all gathered around him.

"This ship belongs to my...father," he said, the last word a struggle to get out. "This is a Jepsen Aero DL7 heavy gunship. It is, in fact, the same one you probably remember from the old news videos when Earth was attacked those first two times. She's called the *Phoenix*."

"It's *that* ship?" Mettler asked. "You're going to steal this ship from — Wait, who the hell is your father?"

"His dad's name is Jason Burke," Murph provided, his face showing that all the pieces had fallen into place in his mind. "He's a mercenary of sorts, who was abducted from Earth years ago. My question is, if the *Phoenix* is here, where the hell is Omega Force? I'm not stealing this ship just to have Crusher rip my arms from their sockets."

"Omega Force is currently using another ship," 707 provided. "The *Phoenix* was badly damaged in the battle over Miressa. When I suggested this ship, it was my hope the local crew here had had enough time to repair her. It seems I was correct."

"I've heard of them," MG said. "I don't think they're going to be too happy we stole their ship. How tight are you and your pops?"

"Let's just say it would be best if we get her out of here and off-planet before he finds out what I'm doing," Jacob said, turning to 707. "So, how do we get in? The ramp is raised and locked."

"If my suspicions are correct, your biometric reading should access the ship," 707 said. "It was a measure put in by your father after the first time you met him."

"Why?"

"My assumption is he intended to leave the ship to you should something happen to him."

"How do you know all this?" Murph asked.

"I was a passenger on this ship from Khepri to Terranovus," 784 answered. "While we were grateful for the help, we didn't entirely trust Burke at that time. I accessed the ship's main computer and browsed whatever information on him I could find. It was how we discovered your existence, Jacob Brown."

They continued to talk back and forth about how the battlesynths had so much access to the intelligence they did, but Jacob ignored them and approached the ship. There was a small security panel on the portside main landing gear strut, which had a blinking light to let him know it was active. He placed his palm flat on it and let it read his DNA and a dozen other metrics to determine if he was who he claimed to be and if he was under duress. Now that he'd been reminded, he remembered his dad doing the initial bio scan while he gave the tour of his ship. As a fourteen-year-old kid, he had been so overwhelmed with meeting his father for the first time in his life and talking to actual aliens that the ship herself had seemed rather mundane.

"Hello, Jacob."

"Huh, the ship remembers me, I guess," Jacob muttered.

"Oh, I'm not actually the ship, but I do have control of many of the major systems," the voice said.

"Okay, so who are you?"

"My name is Cas. Before I allow the ship to drop the ramp and let you and your crew aboard, may I ask if you have your father's permission to be taking this vessel?"

"Not exactly," Jacob decided lying would be too complicated. He didn't even know what the hell he was talking to. "But I figure since he wasn't using it at the moment, and I sort of need it, he'd be okay with it."

"I'm sure," Cas said, sounding like it thought the whole idea was hysterical. "But hey...I don't like to butt into family business. If he was dumb enough to add you to the access list, then he deserves to come back home and find his ship missing. Welcome aboard!"

There was a loud clanking from the aft of the ship, and the rear ramp swung down, hitting the hangar floor with a *thud*.

"It worked? Cool," MG said.

"Let's go on up and see what her status is," Jacob said. "Not sure how we are on fuel and consumables. Also, there seems to be some sort of AI active right now that isn't like any I've ever talked to."

"That would be a new addition," 707 said, looking at his partner.

"It says its name is Cas," Jacob said. "Ring any bells?"

"It does not," 784 said.

"Okay then," Jacob said. "After that ultra-helpful answer, I guess we should go ahead and get started."

"Hangar doors are fully open," Jacob said from the copilot seat. It had taken nearly six hours to prep the ship for launch. Cas had helped the entire time familiarizing them with the ship's workings, otherwise it would have been days. Sully had done a double take when he saw the pilot station and the very familiar stick-and-rudder flight control configuration. "You're sure you can fly her?"

"This will actually be easier than just hopping into a ship with an Eshquarian or Aracorian-type helm," the pilot said. "This is all familiar. The fact the regular pilot on this ship is human makes everything a lot more intuitive."

"Ramp is up and locked, pressure hatches are all sealed, and everything is green across the board," Jacob said.

"Rolling back now," Sully said, nudging the taxi joystick aft a bit.

There was a groan as the heavy gunship rolled out of the hangar and into the sunlight. "My engine panel is green, so I guess 784 has everything sorted in engineering. You know how to close the hangar back up?"

"Cas?" Jacob asked.

"I can take care of that," the AI said. Sure enough, the hangar doors rolled closed a moment later.

"We have departure clearance from the local controller all the way to orbit," 707 said from one of the sensor stations along the port side of the bridge.

"Engines up, standby," Sully said and fed power to the grav-drive. The *Phoenix* throbbed and rose slowly from the pad. "Gear up."

"Gear coming up," Jacob said, toggling the control. "Up and locked."

"Here we go." The nose swung out over open water before Sully pushed the throttle forward a bit, and the gunship leapt away from the small peninsula. His eyes widened in shock for a moment, and he experimented some more, nudging the throttle up a bit further. This time, there was a deep rumble, and the ship accelerated rapidly across the water. Sully brought the nose up a bit and smiled tightly to himself, pushing the throttle up to about seventy percent. The *Phoenix* responded immediately, hurtling them across the sea as if shot from a cannon. Even with the artificial gravity up, the pull from the engines pressed them into their seats before the pilot pulled the power back and angled the nose up to catch their orbital vector.

"This thing is insanely overpowered!" he smiled. "Even the Corsair wouldn't be able to keep up with her down in an atmosphere."

The *Phoenix* clawed her way up out of S'Tora's atmosphere and the first wisps of doubt threaded through Jacob's brain. What they were doing was, on its face, insane. He'd just swiped his dad's beloved ship, which was bad enough, but now they were heading back towards the Orion Arm to try and capture a woman who had so far eluded everyone the UEAS had sent after her. Having the two battlesynths with him was some comfort, at least. Not only were they seasoned warriors and savvy operatives, they also seemed to have at least a passing familiarity with the *Phoenix*.

"Navigation?" Sully asked.

"First waypoint is entered and locked," Jacob said. The copilot station was configured for a small Veran named Kage, an alien with four arms and a diminutive stature, and Jacob felt like a clumsy oaf trying to manipulate the controls. "Slip-drive is available, mesh-out point on your display."

"Got it."

The gunship tore across the S'Tora System, a sparsely populated star system near the boundary of what was called the Delphine Expanse. His dad had really picked an out of the way place to call home. The thought of Jason deliberately isolating himself out here, as far away as he could reasonably get from him, sent a pang of sympathy through Jacob. The complicated feelings he had towards his father were something he didn't like to dwell too heavily on, but that was going to be damn near impossible as long as he was aboard this ship. He was even staying in his dad's quarters and wearing his clothes. This mission promised to be quite the head trip in more ways than one.

Five and a half hours after lifting off from the planet, the *Phoenix* meshed-out of system. Her new crew had no idea how they were going to accomplish their mission, no idea of the true capabilities of the ship, and no idea whether they would be welcomed back home as heroes or criminals afterwards. But there was a job that needed doing. It was a shit job, so that naturally meant it would fall to a Marine to get it done.

EPILOGUE

"You actually managed to get him back without him suiciding?"

"Barely. 701 got to him before he could tie his pants to the edge of the rack and attempt to hang himself. You going to be able to handle this?"

"Oh, yes. We have complete legal authority to do the interrogation before he's formally charged," NIS Director Michael Welford said.

"Distasteful, but necessary," Webb sighed. He and Welford spoke over one of Earth's new hyperlink com systems that allowed a full holographic representation to be transmitted in real-time. It was like he and the director sat in the same room together. As far as he knew, it was a technological breakthrough only Earth had achieved.

"And now, your prodigy has decided to go all in, you say? He's going to take on Margaret Jansen and win the war all by himself?" Welford asked.

"Him, his crew of degenerates, and two battlesynths," Webb said. "The situation is less than ideal, to say the least."

"You're not pursuing him to try and stop it?"

"My command is depleted. Commander Toma has informed me

that 3rd Scout Corps has nothing available to try and track him down with. The rest of NAVSOC is in a similar state. If I ask the NIS to do it, I'll have to formally declare Obsidian a rogue element."

"I see your problem," Welford said. "Solutions?"

"I've reached out to the Viper to try and appeal to her humanity. She told me where I could roll that up and shove it," Webb said while Welford laughed. "She and Abiyah are also still actively tracking the rebel fleet Edgars was with. She didn't admit it, but I think she might have actually been hired by Seeladas to kill Admiral Colleran."

"The Viper doesn't really do wet work unless it's personal," Welford disagreed. "As far as I know, she and Colleran got along fine the few times they've met. So, she's out. You already know what I'm going to suggest, right?"

"I've been putting it off. If I call them in on this, I might not have to wait around for Jansen to try and have me killed."

"Risks of the job." Wellford shrugged. "I'll let you know what we find out from Bennet on a back channel, and then hand him back over to you for processing."

"Thanks," Webb said. "And Michael? Only go as hard as is absolutely necessary. He's an idiot and technically a traitor, but I don't like the idea of anyone's frustration being taken out on him."

"We're very good at this," Wellford said. "Don't worry." The channel closed, and Webb could tell he'd offended his friend at the insinuation the NIS teams would torture Bennet for the fun of it. He was hurt and angry beyond belief that Bennet had betrayed them all, but he didn't have it in him to hate the kid even after all the damage he'd caused.

Pushing away thoughts of Bennet and NIS interrogations, Webb steeled himself for what he had to do next. The slip-com address he'd just entered was to a secret relay installation that would automatically connect his channel via another slip-com channel to his intended recipient. It was a common method used by smugglers that made tracing the connections nearly impossible. He held out hope the person he was trying to get a hold of would just ignore the call, and he could instead send a tactfully worded message.

"Webb?" a sleepy voice asked. "What's up, douchebag?"

"Oh, you're up," Webb said, his voice flat. "Great."

"Don't sound too excited to talk to me," Jason Burke said, rubbing the sleep out of his eyes. "It's not like you called and woke me up or anything. Is this important?"

"This could take a few minutes to explain, Jason," Webb said. "Do you have a few minutes, and are you sober?"

"Yes, and mostly."

"You remember how you asked me to keep an eye on Jacob for you? Well, funny story..."

Thank you for reading *Boneshaker*.

If you enjoyed the story, Lieutenant Brown and the guys will be back in:

Vapor Trails

Terran Scout Fleet, Book 3.

Subscribe to my newsletter for the latest updates on new releases, exclusive content, and special offers:

Also connect with me on Facebook and Twitter:

www.facebook.com/Joshua.Dalzelle

@JoshuaDalzelle

Check out my Amazon page to see my other works including the #1 bestselling military science fiction series: *The Black Fleet Saga* along with the international bestselling *Omega Force Series*.

Printed in Great Britain
by Amazon